the seeing

Books by Bill Myers

The Wager
The Face of God
Eli
When the Last Leaf Falls (novella)
Then Comes Marriage (novella with Angela Hunt)
The Dark Side of the Supernatural

Fire of Heaven Trilogy

Blood of Heaven
Threshold
Fire of Heaven

Soul Tracker Series

Soul Tracker
The Presence
The Seeing

Children's Books

McGee and Me (book/video series)
The Incredible Worlds of Wally McDoogle (comedy series)
Imager Chronicles (fantasy series)
Secret Agent Dingledorf (comedy series)
Elijah Project (suspense series)
Blood Hounds Inc. (mystery series)
Baseball for Breakfast (picture book)
Bug Parables (picture book series)

Young Adult Books

Forbidden Doors (supernatural suspense series)
Faith Encounter (devotional)
Get Real (devotional)

BILL MYERS

Bestselling Author of *Soul Tracker*

the seeing

book three

ZONDERVAN®

ZONDERVAN.com/
AUTHORTRACKER
follow your favorite authors

34867985 4/07

ZONDERVAN®

The Seeing
Copyright © 2007 by Bill Myers

This title is also available as a Zondervan audio product.
Visit www.zondervan.com/audiopages for more information.

Requests for information should be addressed to:
Zondervan, *Grand Rapids, Michigan 49530*

Library of Congress Cataloging-in-Publication Data

Myers, Bill, 1953 –
    The seeing / Bill Myers.
       p. cm. — (The Soul tracker series ; bk. 3)
    Includes bibliographical references.
    ISBN-10: 0-310-24237-1
    ISBN-13: 978-0-310-24237-6
    I. Title.
  PS3563.Y36S44 2007
  813'.54 — dc22

                       2006024641

Published in association with the literary agency of Alive Communications, Inc., 7680 Goddard Street, Suite 200, Colorado Springs, CO 80920.

Interior design by Michelle Espinoza

Printed in the United States of America

07 08 09 10 11 • 10 9 8 7 6 5 4 3 2 1

Finally and always for Brenda ...
at the center of my heart

a note from the author

don't feel it's necessary to read either the first book in this series (*Soul Tracker*) or the second (*The Presence*) for this one to work. Our hero's references to the past have more to do with pride than to what has happened. But, just so there's no frustration, here are a couple quick sketches of the past two stories, vague enough so they won't ruin your read if you feel like checking them out.

SOUL TRACKER

Luke's dad is wracked by guilt over the supposed suicide of Luke's older sister. He stumbles on an organization designed to track the soul after it dies. Desperate to know where his daughter is, Dad takes part in an experiment visiting heaven, hell, and everything in between.

THE PRESENCE

Both Dad and Luke become unknowing participants in an experiment allowing people to experience the Presence of God. In the process they see deep into the spirit world as well as into their literal souls. Luke's eyes are damaged and he only catches glimpses of what is happening. Still, when Dad finally releases his protective hold over the boy, Luke winds up leading their group to safety. As they head home they find a piece of the goggles that the head of the experiment had used to observe them. Goggles that, with the unique damage to Luke's eyes, allow him to begin seeing ... Well, that's pretty much where this next one begins.

Thanks for continuing or beginning the journey with me.

Blessings,

Bill

www.billmyers.com

"I have given them the glory that you gave me, that they may be one as we are one: I in them and you in me. May they be brought to complete unity to let the world know that you sent me and have loved them even as you have loved me."

Jesus Christ, a prayer

prologue

the whirlwind appeared from behind the rocks, its magic shimmering and undulating in the moonlight.

Momtakwit froze. His heart pounded against the leather pouch of datura root—the only thing he wore against his naked chest. He knew the pillar of sand and dust was *Kutyai*, an evil spirit. But tonight he needed to save all of his powers to battle an entity far more wicked and treacherous.

He turned to the mountain looming before him. Already he had seen the pictographs drawn in the cave by other shamans of other times ... warnings that he had entered the domain of the mighty *Tahquitz*, hater of all that is human.

Now he must turn back. If he wished to live, he must leave.

But, of course, he could not.

Tahquitz had stolen too many souls, ravaged too many of the village.

As the most powerful shaman in the Dog Clan, Momtakwit must confront him. He alone had been selected to drive the evil being from Coachella Valley and redeem the land. For the sake of his family. For the sake of his tribe.

The whirlwind spent itself into gusts and finally wisps, before it disappeared altogether.

Momtakwit inhaled deeply, then continued his climb. Soon he would arrive at the top of Tahquitz Peak and descend into the evil spirit's home. There he would finally see Smashing Wall.

He had never been there, but legend spoke of how the men of his peace-loving village had once become so possessed by Tahquitz's evil that they gleefully hurled the skulls of their captured prisoners against the wall's flat surface.

He thought again of the prophecy, the word spoken over him after three days fasting in *Spirit House*. Prophecy that clearly stated his bloodline would drive *Tahquitz* from the mountain. And now, as *Tahquitz's* power increased, as men, women, even children throughout the valley practiced more and more of his evil, it was determined this was the time to act.

A gust of desert wind swept up the face of the mountain. He closed his eyes.

Tahquitz was near.

He thought of taking the datura now, of chewing it and allowing its powerful magic to course through his body so that he might be prepared. But *Tahquitz* was crafty. He could easily hesitate until the medicine wore off and leave Momtakwit unable to enter the spirit world to do battle.

No, he would wait.

His people had waited generations for this confrontation.

He could wait a little longer . . .

part one

one

the guy's BO made Luke's eyes water. He had long greasy hair, an eleven o'clock shadow, jeans as brown as they were blue, and a crumpled, stain-riddled Hawaiian shirt.

"This your first time to Agua Rancheria?" He sniffed loudly, wiping his nose.

Luke gave a nod and looked out the bus window, hoping to end the conversation.

No such luck.

"You'll like it. The desert, I mean. Nothing but nothing as far as you can see." He sniffed louder.

Luke stole a glance just in time to see the guy pinching away a drip of hanging mucus with his hand. His *gloved* hand. In the middle of June. Proof that the man was not only homeless but a mental.

"And those stars at night, I tell you—" another sniff—"God must have been having a fine day creating those."

This time Luke didn't respond.

The man didn't notice. "'Course the casino's kinda messing stuff up. All that bright light and razzle-dazzle. But get away from it and the place is beau-*tee*-ful."

As discretely as possible, Luke cupped his hand over his nose and mouth. They'd picked the guy up in Palm Springs about thirty minutes ago. If Luke's geography was any good it meant he'd only have to endure another five or ten minutes of his company before stepping off the bus and getting some fresh air.

In truth, the man was only a minor nuisance—the last in Luke's ongoing campaign to get away from home ... and Dad.

"You're smothering me again!"

"I just don't think being gone all summer is a good idea."

"Six weeks," Luke argued, "it'll only be six weeks."

"That's nearly two months."

"You'll be in New York half that time."

"That's got nothing to do with it."

"You're always saying I should get a job, save for college."

"It's too far away."

"It's two hours. I'm fifteen years old, Dad. Fifteen!"

And so they continued. For the most part it had been a standoff ... until Preacher Man had weighed in. Good ol' Preacher Man ...

"Come on, David," he insisted, while working on a bag of potato chips at the kitchen counter. "Let the boy go."

It was an unusual friendship—a middle-class, white-bread family and an old black street preacher. Then again, considering what they'd been through these last couple years ... his sister's death, his dad's visits to heaven and hell, and later where they literally saw each other's souls and the spirit world ... well, maybe it wasn't so unusual after all.

"You already met Pastor Virgil and his wife." Preacher Man continued munching. "They don't come any better. And they definitely need help gettin' that church of theirs fixed up."

"Yes, but—"

"Probably do the boy good. Get him out in some fresh air, doin' some real work for a change, 'stead of always playin' with that computer."

"What about his eyes?" Dad argued. "He barely remembers to wear his sunglasses around here. What's going to happen if he gets out in the bright desert sun and forgets—"

"I won't forget!"

"You say that now, but—"

"I won't forget."

And so the war continued. It had taken nearly a month to wear him down. Even at that, Luke had to use every weapon known to adolescence—forced cheerfulness, willingness to do household chores (even when unasked), and listening to the man's perpetual naggings and repeatings without so much as an eye roll.

It had nearly killed Luke, but somehow he had succeeded. He had won. Now he was heading out to a desert community for six weeks to help some old pastor fix up some old church ... and to finally enjoy a little independence.

The bus turned off the main road and entered the town. As it did, Casino Rancheria filled Luke's window. It was a monstrous complex of white limestone, giant waterfalls, and fountains complete with roaring rapids and life-sized bronzed replicas of Native Americans in canoes. Portions of ocher-colored pottery protruded from the walls, where mural after mural of desert wildlife had been painted to look like Indian art. And lining the entrance, a dozen Native American heads, twenty feet tall, gazed toward the desert, their faces creased and weathered by the sun.

It seemed everywhere Luke looked he was reminded of Indian culture. And for good reason. According to Pastor Virgil, that was part of the deal when the casino leased the land from a local tribe.

As the bus passed the red-carpeted entrance, Luke noticed a handful of protestors carrying signs and placards reading:

GAMBLING IS A DISEASE,
GOD IS THE CURE

KEEP YOUR MONEY,
AND YOUR SEX, VIOLENCE, DRUGS, CRIME

ILL-GOTTEN GAIN
EQUALS
ILL-GOTTEN PAIN

A tanned blond guy in his early thirties was leading them. He shouted things Luke couldn't quite hear while bored security guards stood nearby. Apparently, none of it really mattered, because despite the demonstrators, hordes of people just kept swarming in and swarming out.

Luke reached into his nylon windbreaker and pulled out what almost passed for the broken half of a pair of night-vision goggles—complete with various wires cut back. Although he had trimmed them, he didn't have the heart to completely remove them.

In truth, he hoped to find a way to make the goggles work like they had for Orbolitz—back when the old guy claimed to use them to see into "higher dimensions." More importantly, he hoped they would earn him the respect he never fully received. Luke had always felt special ... chosen. And, if he ever got the things to work, they would definitely help prove his point.

Imagine how different folks would treat him if they knew he could see into the spirit world. It was one thing for those TV preachers and everybody to be jabbering about that stuff, but if he could actually see it ... well, that would sure get them to sit up and take notice. At the very least he wouldn't be treated like some stupid kid anymore.

He raised the broken goggles to his sunglasses and looked at the familiar smears of light and darkness that, for some reason, only he was able to see. Chances are it was because he'd fried his eyes while climbing that microwave tower, or whatever it was, up in Washington. But it made little difference. The point is, despite Dad's protests, Luke took them wherever he went. And the more he used them, the more he was able to recognize recurring patterns and formations of light.

It wasn't much. But being able to see the faint traces did set him apart ... a little.

This time the smears darted about the casino—particularly in and out of its entrance. He turned and focused on the protestors. Although the smears seemed a bit more flighty and agitated than normal, they acted pretty much the same as they did around any other group. He started to remove the goggles when something caught his eye off to the right of the casino—a jagged peak, flattened on one side, part of the mountain range they'd been following for the last hour.

It had no fleeting smudges of lights around it, and Luke wasn't surprised. The lights usually just hung around people. Instead, what caught his attention was the very top of the peak. It was covered in a shadow. But thicker than shadow. Not as dense as a cloud because he could still see through it. But it was a specific darkness that rippled and quivered. It seemed to pulse ever so slightly ... almost as if it were breathing.

Almost as if it were alive.

m isty! Misty, where are you?"
Pilar slammed the front door to their penthouse suite, the largest at the casino, and stormed across the white carpet toward the hallway and her daughter's bedroom. She was not happy.

"Misty?"

She arrived just as her sixteen-year-old appeared in the doorway. The girl still wore her sleeping sweats and flip-flops. Her hair was unkempt, as thick and black as her mother's.

"Oh, hi, Mom." She sounded too casual. "What brings you home?"

"You were in the Surveillance Room again, weren't you?"

"What do you mean?" She blinked, pushing up the world's ugliest pair of tortoise-shell glasses. "You told me I could never go in there."

"I know what I told you, and you were there, weren't you?"

"What? Why would I—"

Pilar raised the small electronic box she'd been carrying, complete with dangling cable.

"What's that?"

"Security found it attached to the back of their computer."

Misty took it into her hands. "Hm, I wonder what it's for?"

Pilar sighed wearily. "You know how the casino frowns upon you hacking into their surveillance system."

"But, Mom—"

"No 'but Moms.'"

"Why do you always blame me? You're always blaming me for everything!" It was the girl's attempt to go on the offense by playing victim. "It's like you don't even trust me."

Pilar crossed her arms. "Nice try, no sale." She shifted her weight and noticed Misty doing the same, obviously trying to block her from seeing into the room.

"Besides," Misty quipped, "what do you care? It's the white man's casino, and we both know what you think of the—"

"My personal feelings have nothing to do with it. What you're doing is wrong, it's proprietary information, and it makes them nervous. It makes Bianco nervous." She shifted again and Misty mirrored her action. "What are you doing in there?"

"In where?"

"Misty?" Pilar tried to see past her.

Once again Misty blocked her view. "It's just video games and stuff."

"Right, and it's the 'stuff' that's got me worried."

"Why are you always so suspic—" She was interrupted by the howl of a cat. Twirling around, she cried, "Balzac!"

She raced into the room, Pilar right behind.

The place was a Radio Shack gone berserk—electronic consoles, gizmos, and gadgets everywhere you looked, except the floor, which was covered in an equal amount of clothes—some clean, some dirty—but all, Pilar knew, would be dumped into the dirty-clothes hamper.

Then there was the cat box. By the pungent odor, she guessed it hadn't been emptied in a week ... or two.

Stuffed off in the corner was a small twin bed with the mandatory grouping of stuffed animals. But the long table in the center of the room was the obvious focus of activity. A table cluttered with wires, circuit boards, soldering iron, and the innards of a hundred who-knew-whats.

Directly behind it, on another table, a dozen different-sized monitors were stacked on top of each other, all glowing.

"Balzac ... oh, you poor thing!" Misty had scooped the jet-black cat into her arms. "How many times has Mommy told you not to go sniffing around all those mean electrical circuits."

He definitely looked dazed. And for good reason. As Pilar leaned closer she saw he no longer had whiskers. Well, he did, but they were now melted into little corkscrews. That and the smell of burning hair was a sure sign that the cat had used up a few more of his lives.

"Poor baby," the girl soothed, stroking him. "Poor Balzac."

Pilar looked up at the wall of monitors. She moved in closer, not believing what she saw. "Is that what I think it is?"

"I was just—"

"Is that Bianco's office? Did you bug the manager's office?"

"Mom, you know something's going on. I mean, the way he's got everyone running all over the—"

"Did you just bug my boss's office?"

She turned to Misty.

The girl raised her shoulders in a helpless shrug. "Sorry."

Pilar sighed wearily, dropping her head and slowly shaking it.

a wave of hot fresh air struck Luke as he stepped off the bus. But he was grateful for it—especially the "fresh" part.

"Praise God, there he is now!"

He looked over to see Pastor Virgil and his wife—he'd forgotten her name—shuffling down the sidewalk toward him. The spunky old-timer wore a Panama straw hat, dolphin-print shirt, leather sandals, and khaki shorts which showed off far too much of his brown saggy knees.

Fortunately, his wife was dressed a bit more modestly.

"Good to see you, son." The pastor arrived, throwing his arms around him.

Surprised, Luke answered, "Thanks, it's good to—" he gasped at the old-timer's strength—"see you ... too."

They broke apart as Virgil turned to his wife. "Isn't it good to see him, Fiona?"

"Yes, it is." She offered her wrinkled, sun-browned hand and Luke shook it.

"Yes, it is," Virgil repeated, "yes, it is." Then slapping his little belly, he looked about, beaming. "Welcome to Agua Rancheria. What do you think?"

"It's ... nice."

"Nice? It's glorious! Now I don't wanna be spreading rumors, but folks say God Himself has a time-share here." He flashed another grin, laughing at his joke.

By now the driver had opened the luggage compartment under the bus and was pulling out Luke's bags—all four of them.

"Whoa," Virgil exclaimed. "These all yours?"

Luke nodded, somewhat embarrassed. "Yes, sir."

The old guy whistled. "Didn't know we were going to have a fashion devo on our hands."

"Leave the boy alone, Virgil."

Luke tried to explain. "I wasn't exactly sure what to wear, I mean out here in the—"

"It don't matter, son." He reached for the luggage.

"No, here," Luke offered, "let me get that."

But Virgil was already trying to lift the largest bag.

"That's way too heavy, let me—"

"I got it, son, I got it." With great effort, the little man finally lifted the suitcase. "Fiona," he gasped, "wanna give the boy a hand with them others?"

"No, please," Luke protested.

"Nonsense, she's as strong as a—"

"Really." Luke quickly gathered up the other three. "I've got them."

"Suit yourself." Virgil turned and staggered up the sidewalk. "Car's just a little ways—"

He was interrupted by another voice. "We'll catch you later, friend."

Luke turned to see the man in the Hawaiian shirt stepping off the bus, heading in the opposite direction.

"Uh ... right." With hands full, Luke managed a nod.

"One of your Hollyweird buddies?" Virgil teased.

"Uh, no, I just met him on the bus."

Virgil nodded. "Probably homeless. We get our share of 'em this time of year. Usually aren't dangerous—long as you don't get too friendly. We don't bother them, they don't bother us."

The bus gave a belch of black smoke and started pulling away.

Fanning away the fumes, Fiona asked, "So, Luke, how was your trip?"

"Pretty good."

"That's wonderful." Virgil was breathing heavily. "'Cause you're going to need all the strength you got, once we get to working on that church. Twenty hours a day can really tucker a fellow out."

Luke threw a concerned look to him, then to Fiona.

She smiled. "He's just playing with you. He calls it—what do you call it, dear?—oh yes, 'humor.'"

Luke smiled. Though he'd only spent a few hours with them when they'd visited Preacher Man in LA, he remembered all too well how the couple communicated.

She continued, "Don't pay him any mind, Luke. Nobody ever does."

Ignoring her, puffing harder, Virgil asked, "How's your dad? And Billy Ray?"

"Preacher Man's doing great. And Dad, he's, you know, Dad."

Virgil flashed a grin over his shoulder. "Still making you crazy, is he?"

"I didn't know it was that obvious."

"It's hard to get much past these old eyes."

"Right," Fiona drolly replied.

"It's true, I see everything."

"Unless it's the garbage that needs taking out, or all the repairs that never get done."

"Selective vision, woman. These eyes see life from a select perspective."

"Closed and from the recliner."

"Drip, drip, drip ... Drip, drip, drip."

Fiona explained, "That's his way of reciting the Bible to me."

Virgil quoted, " 'A quarrelsome wife is like a constant dripping.' Proverbs 19:13."

Fiona countered, " 'If a man is lazy, ... the house leaks.' Ecclesiastes 10:18."

The old-timer frowned, searching for a response.

Luke had to smile.

They walked by a large billboard with a picture of the casino he had just passed. Written across its front, diagonally, in big red letters, were the words:

DEAL ME OUT!

"What's that about?" Luke asked.

"More of Travis Lawton's handiwork," Virgil replied.

"Who?"

"Our city's newest gift from God—least that's what he thinks. He's found a loophole in a local ordinance. Thinks we can force a vote and drive out the casino."

"Why would he want to do that?"

"Lots of reasons," Fiona answered. "Prostitution, drugs, corruption. Our overall crime rate has gone up 400 percent since the casino moved in."

"Is that what the protestors are about?" Luke asked. "I saw some folks picketing in front of the casino."

Virgil nodded. "Pastor Lawton and his congregation—they're foolish enough to think if they get rid of the casino, they'll get rid of our troubles."

"And you don't think so?"

Virgil shook his head. "The casino is only the symptom. Lawton and his people are fighting shadows. They're totally clueless about the real sickness."

"And that is ..."

"You'll know soon enough," the quirky old man answered as they continued down the street. "You'll know soon enough."

ook at this putz." Peter Bianco sat with his meticulously polished black leather Guccis propped atop a large teak desk. Across the office, a row of surveillance monitors displayed various angles of the casino's front entrance—shots of the demonstration. More importantly, one close-up shot of their leader ... Pastor Travis Lawton. "Does this guy ever sleep?"

"Apparently not." The answer came from Joey Popiski, a balding, middle-aged man with far too much cream filling in the center and wearing way too much Old Spice. He forced a phlegm-filled chuckle. "Not when he's made you the focus of his personal jihad."

Bianco stared at the screen without comment.

Popiski leaned toward the desk, trying to continue the conversation he had begun earlier. "You wouldn't have to start me off as a headliner. I could be somebody's warm-up."

Popiski's claim to fame had been working on *Saturday Night Live* in the eighties as a comedian/impersonator. Now, with waning popularity, he had enough clout to get into Bianco's office, but not enough to be taken seriously.

"I don't even need to have my name on the marquee, at least in the beginning."

Bianco watched the monitors as his gall continued to rise. Finally, swearing under his breath, he sat up in the chair and reached for the intel folder that Security had prepped on Travis Lawton.

"And then in say, six months, once I've established myself, we can talk about better billing and better money."

Across the office, two large men in identically tailored suits—Tweedle Dee and Tweedle Dumb, Bianco called them—continued sweeping the room for electronic bugs.

"And from there, who knows. I mean, if I'm bringing them in, anything goes, right?"

Running his hand over his gray buzz cut, Bianco continued flipping through the folder. Nothing. They had nothing on this pain-in-the-butt preacher. Nothing, except …

He reached for his glasses to take a better look. That's when Tweedle Dee's surveillance wand began buzzing.

"Got something, boss."

He looked up, then rose to his feet and crossed the room.

Tweedle Dee pulled out a small camera, no larger than an M-16 shell, from the side of the farthest monitor.

"That's it?" Bianco asked.

"Yes, sir."

He took it into his hands. It even looked like an M–16 shell. He turned it over until he spotted what had to be the lens. Then leaning into it he shouted, "Not funny, Misty. Not funny at all!"

He turned and headed for the bathroom.

As he entered, the motion sensor lights flickered on, revealing the white marble walls and gold fixtures. He raised the toilet lid and dropped the camera into the bowl with a rewarding *kerplunk*. Reaching for the lever, he flushed it, and watched the camera swirl away—a fitting end to his problem.

He stepped from the bathroom and glanced back at the monitors. If only he could dispose of his other headaches so easily.

As Bianco walked back to his desk, Popiski, not the brightest candle on the cake, started where he left off. "I wouldn't even have to include my agent, not that he does me any good. It could all be under the table until—"

The intercom buzzed and the secretary's throaty voice spoke. "Mr. Bianco, your call has come in."

He moved to the phone. "Good, good, put him through."

" — on a trial basis, that's all, I'm — "

"All right!" He turned to the comedian. "All right, you got the job! On a trial basis! Now go on, get out of here!"

"Thank you, Mr. Bianco, I promise you, you won't — "

He shot a look to Tweedle Dee and Tweedle Dumb. Taking their cue, they moved across the plush carpet, gently gripped Popiski on either arm, and escorted him toward the door.

" — and if there's anything I can ever do to return the — "

"Good-bye!"

At last the fat man was out of his office.

"And shut the doors!"

They softly closed.

Bianco paused a moment, looking at the phone. Then taking a breath to clear his head, he reached for the receiver and turned to the tinted wall of windows. "Senor Velasco." He sat on his desk, suddenly all confidence and good humor. "So good to hear from you."

The voice on the other end was cordial but definitely businesslike. "Good afternoon, Mr. Bianco."

"How are we doing today?"

"They tell me you are incurring some difficulties."

"Difficulties?"

"People in your community. There are some who do not wish for your presence."

Bianco rubbed his forehead. "I'm not sure what you mean."

"Demonstrators. They are trying to make you leave."

"Oh, those." Bianco forced a laugh as he turned back to the monitors. "Just a handful of religious fanatics."

"Fanatics who are opposed to your presence?"

"It's the American way. They're merely exercising their constitutional rights."

"I trust such rights will not interfere with our plans."

"What? No, no, of course not. Believe me, they are a minor nuisance." Once again he stared at the monitor featuring Lawton.

"I sincerely hope you are correct."

"Believe me, in a day or two this will all blow over. By the time you arrive, no one will even remember them." He glanced at the intel folder on his desk and pulled it toward him.

"You see no problem then."

"None whatsoever."

"And should it persist, the problem. You have adequate means to remedy it?"

"Absolutely. You have my word on it."

"Good. The stakes are too high for us to have any distractions. I think you would agree."

"Of course, Senor Velasco, of course." Once again he opened the folder. "I absolutely, one hundred percent, completely agree."

uke rocked in the old porch swing, enjoying the night.

The town with its glaring casino lights was far enough behind the house that it didn't affect his view of the stars. They were so bright it was like looking at a photo taken by one of those space satellites.

And so intense he almost felt he should wear his sunglasses. The desert too. Even without the moon, the desert and mountains glowed in bright, blue-white.

Talk about beautiful ... and peaceful.

Well, everything except the mountain peak. It was hard to explain, but even now he sensed a strangeness about it. So much that he'd gone back to his room and retrieved the broken piece of goggle to find out what he could see. He'd barely pulled it from his pocket and placed the lens against his eye before he heard the screen door groan and Virgil step out.

"Lord have mercy, can that woman cook."

Luke quickly lowered the lens, discretely removing it from view.

"Makes no difference how they sass ya, you find a woman who can cook—" Virgil slapped his belly as he approached—"and you've found yourself a mighty good thing."

Luke nodded. "I bet."

Easing himself down on the swing, Virgil asked, "Still got them goggle things, I see."

Caught, he brought the broken piece into view. "What, this?"

Virgil smiled. "And I'm bettin' they still make your daddy nervous. You called him, let him know you got here okay?"

"Yes, sir."

"So what'd you see?" He motioned to the goggles.

Luke shrugged. "Nothing. I was just about to check out that mountain over there."

"Tahquitz Peak?"

"That's its name?"

"Local Indians have some pretty interesting legends 'bout the place."

"Legends?"

Virgil gave a stretch. "They believe there is an evil spirit living on it—ruling that entire range of mountains, and the Coachella Valley down here."

Luke turned to him.

"*Tahquitz*, they call him. In the old days they said he used to sneak into the villages at night and kidnap their virgins—dragging them into a canyon up there and having his way with them."

"Some legend," Luke mused.

"If that's all it is."

"What do you mean?"

Virgil looked at him, then changed the subject. "I noticed you're still having to wear sunglasses?"

Another shrug. "Yeah."

"Doctors still aren't sure what's wrong?"

"Not yet."

"Kinda makes you mysterious, though, don't it." Chuckling, Virgil added, "Bet the ladies love it."

"I, uh, wouldn't know."

He laughed and slapped Luke on the leg. "You will, son. Mark my words, you will."

After a polite moment, Luke returned to the topic. "You think there's something more than the legend?"

"What's that?"

"The mountain, you said, there was more."

Virgil paused, then answered, "You ever hear of something called spiritual strongholds ... principalities?"

"Princi-what?"

Virgil smiled. "The Bible talks about it." Looking at the mountain, he quietly quoted: "'For our struggle is not against flesh and blood, but against the rulers, against the authorities, against the powers of this dark world and against the spiritual forces of evil in the heavenly realms.' Ephesians 6:12."

"You're talking about the spirit world?" Luke asked.

"That's how I read it."

"Like what Dad and I saw up in Washington—all those angels and demons scattered everywhere."

"Probably. Though I doubt they were really scattered."

"What do you mean?"

"There seems to be specific territories that the spirits rule over. Regions that they influence."

"Influence?"

Virgil looked at him, sizing him up another moment, before continuing, "Ever go some place and feel things you can't explain?"

"Like what?"

"Like lust."

Luke blinked.

"Or maybe some great hunger for power? Or greed? Or maybe just the feeling that something ain't quite right?"

Luke fidgeted, recalling all too well his feelings up in Washington. "Maybe. A little."

Virgil held his look, then continued, "I remember the first time I went to LA. I was practically bowled over by feelings of lust. And Washington, DC—not only did I feel lust, but a real desire for power, so strong it was palpable."

Luke frowned. Until now he'd figured *he* was the only one getting those feelings about places, that it was just his imagination. But ever since Washington State his impressions had been growing stronger. Ever since he'd heard the words *"Be still and know."* The very words that, when he'd practiced them, allowed him to guide Dad and the others to safety.

"Ever wonder why certain areas experience the same problems over and over again? New York with its greed and violence. Jerusalem, the center of all that hatred and war. Even Abu Ghraib with its unspeakable brutalities."

"Wait, what?"

"Remember that prison in Iraq where some of our soldiers were performing all them vile things on folks?"

"Yeah, sort of."

"Doesn't it surprise you that it was at that exact spot, Babylon, where for centuries some of the worst inhumanities ever were performed?"

"You're saying ... these spirits, that they control and rule these areas?"

"Not only rule them, but in some instances, they fight to defend them."

"Defend them? From who?"

"From us."

"Us?"

With a groan the old man rose and walked to the porch steps. "I've tried for over thirty years to take this valley for God. Oh, we've gotten a few converts here and there, but it's always felt like swimming in molasses."

"And you're thinking it's spirits that are stopping you?"

Looking to the mountain, Virgil nodded. "Since the time of the Indians this valley has been a playground for sin and immorality."

"Really?"

Virgil threw him a glance and headed down the steps to the front yard of rock and sand. Luke rose and followed. Only when he arrived did the old man continue.

"Before you were born, this valley, particularly over at Palm Springs, was famous for its promiscuity. This was the place the big Hollywood stars came to gamble, to drink their liquor, to do their drugs, to have their immoral affairs. Later, it became a mecca for college kids on spring break—the same gambling, same alcohol, same drugs, and sex. Then them killings in 1988."

"There were killings there?"

"Some teenagers. 'Fore you were born."

"And now?"

"Now ... the casino."

"Is that why that minister guy's picketing the place?" Luke asked. "He's trying to stop it?"

"And that's why he'll fail ... miserably."

"What do you mean?"

"He's using the arm of the flesh."

"The what?"

"The wrong weapons."

Luke stared, not understanding.

"Come with me tomorrow. You'll see what I mean. He's holding a rally, trying to get all the churches fired up to band together. Come with me and I'll show you how he'll fail."

Luke frowned, not answering.

"So—" Virgil brightened—"tell me what you see with that goggle thing."

"I ..."

"Go ahead. Take a gander."

Luke looked back to the mountain, hesitated, then dug in his pocket. He pulled out the lens and brought it to his eye. As on the bus, he saw the dark, churning shadow. Only in the bright starlight and without the glare of the sun, he could see more detail. He wasn't sure, but it seemed to be rotating ... swirling.

"What do you see?"

"There's like this black cloud."

"And?"

He squinted. Although faint, he saw what looked like tiny tributaries stretching out from the blackness. He'd seen something like them before, in his biology book, like a brain cell or something—its long, hair-thin tendrils reaching out, some all the way down to the valley floor.

"There's these little tentacle things coming down from it."

"Coming down from it, or going up?"

"I can't tell. But they're shooting back and forth all across the ground. Real jerky. Like skinny electrical currents. They're all ov—" Suddenly he gasped. "One's coming at us!"

He pulled the lens away but saw nothing. No current, no tentacle ... until a black shadow appeared over their heads.

It was a bird. A crow or raven. And it was diving straight toward them!

Luke cried out, raising his arm. But the thing was too close and he was too slow.

It struck the top of his head, claws and flapping wings. It tried pecking at his face, his eyes. He yelled, ducking, trying to swat it away, to pull it off. Virgil shouted and slapped at it ... until, finally, the thing flew off, cawing in frustration and anger.

"Are you all right?" Virgil yelled.

"What was that?"

"A crow. A crow that—" Virgil stopped and looked up.

Luke followed his gaze. The thing had circled and was coming in for another attack.

"The house!" Virgil shouted. "Get into the house!"

Luke spun around and ran up the steps, pausing just long enough to turn and help the old man.

The bird swooped under the far end of the porch and came at them.

Luke arrived at the screen door, yanking it open and stepping behind it just in time to block the creature. It hit the wire mesh, flapping and cawing, trying to tear its way through to him.

Luke and Virgil raced inside, stumbling into the front room, slamming the door behind them. The screen rattled and banged as the bird continued its attack, squawking and cawing until it was apparent it could make no more progress.

Finally, it gave up and took off, cawing as it flew away.

"A crow?" Luke cried. "That was a crow?"

Virgil nodded, leaning over, trying to catch his breath.

"How weird was that!"

"Weirder—" Virgil took another gulp of air—"weirder than you think."

"What do you mean?"

"When's the last time ... when's the last time you ever saw a crow flying at night?"

two

"there's a time for prayer, and there's a time for action!"

Pastor Travis Lawton, the young guy Luke had seen picketing the casino, sat at the front of his church early Saturday morning jabbing his finger on the table before him. Luke was no expert at accents, but he could tell the guy was from New England ... probably Boston or Maine, one of those places.

"And right now — "

Suddenly Virgil was on his feet. "Right now, we should be praying harder for this community than we've ever prayed in our lives."

Travis paused, obviously summoning up his patience. "Of course we should, Pastor. I could not agree with you more. But there's a balance and, well, sometimes you get a little ... what I mean to say is that upon certain issues you can sometimes — "

"Go ahead, spit it out. I sometimes what?"

"I have great respect for you, sir." He motioned to the handful of clergy and concerned citizens sitting in the first rows of the sparsely adorned church. "You have been in this community longer than most of us combined. And I am certainly the new kid on the block, but sometimes I fear ..." He paused, searching for diplomacy.

Virgil didn't give him the chance. "What do you fear?"

"I fear that it is possible to become so heavenly minded that we are of no earthly good."

Virgil snorted and shook his head. "Why am I not surprised."

Fiona tried pulling him back down to their pew, but he shook her off.

Another minister—middle-aged, graying, and to Luke's surprise, a woman—turned to him from the front row and spoke. "We are God's mouth, are we not? We are His feet and hands. If we don't step forward and stop them, who will?"

"No one is suggesting we do nothing," a tall thin man to the right argued. "After all, that's why we've come together."

"Who said anything 'bout doin' nothin'?" Virgil argued.

"Gentlemen, please ..."

Luke continued to watch with mild amusement. The young pastor had called the meeting to bring together those opposed to the casino. Something about a referendum or something to get it on some ballot. But it hadn't taken long for the whole thing to turn into a free-for-all. Civil, but definitely a free-for-all. How could so few people have so many opinions? Luke suspected it had as much to do with the LA news crew taping from the back of the church as it did with any differences.

A Catholic priest to his left spoke up. "I think what Pastor Virgil is saying is that it is difficult to legislate morality."

"Would you say the same thing about murder?" the woman minister asked. "Or abortion?"

It was the priest's turn to exercise patience. "I am merely stating that—"

She cut him off. "Aren't we called to be salt and light?"

"But in a manner God decides."

"And how exactly do you propose we know what that manner—"

"Excuse me." The reporter approached from the back. "Excuse me, may I ask a question?"

Travis looked up. "Certainly."

"If you should succeed in closing down the casino, what would you say to the nine hundred employees suddenly finding themselves out of a job? About the hundreds of thousands of dollars the casino is currently bringing to your town?"

"I would say, keep your filthy lucre!" a mother with a fussing baby answered from the third pew.

Others weighed in with their opinions ... simultaneously.

"You're treating the casino people as if they're our enemies," the priest shouted.

"If they're not, who is?" the woman called back.

Virgil remained standing, obviously not done making his point. (Luke wondered if he ever finished making his points.) "All I'm saying ..." He yelled louder, "All I'm saying is you can't stop what's happening by human effort."

"What would you have us do, Pastor?" There was no missing the exasperation creeping into Travis's voice. "March around the walls seven times and expect them to fall?"

"It worked before."

"It worked because God gave them a direct command."

"And God doesn't do that anymore, does he," Virgil scoffed. "He doesn't have prophets who speak to people. That's what you believe, isn't it?"

"Pastor, this is hardly the forum for airing our differ—"

"Signs and wonders, they're not for today, are they?"

"Now is not the—"

"Am I right?"

Wearily, Travis quoted, " 'Where there are prophecies, they will cease; where there are tongues, they will be stilled ... when perfection comes, the imperfect disappears.' "

"And Jesus was the 'perfection.' "

The TV camera moved up the aisle for close-ups.

"Yes, after Jesus came we no longer needed the gifts."

"Tell that to the Apostle Paul—to all those who came after Jesus." Virgil beamed as if scoring a slam dunk. "You know what the real difference is?"

"I'm sure we'll find out."

"The real difference between you and Paul is, he was baptized in the Holy Spirit. He had the *full* gospel which empowered him to—"

Travis's anger finally erupted. "I received the Holy Spirit when I received Jesus Christ as my Lord and Savior!"

"They're two separate events. Read your Bible!"

Again Fiona tugged on Virgil.

"I do read my Bible," Travis snapped. "And I pray ... at least in a language I understand."

"Ah, so it all comes back to that, doesn't it? Tongues. The work of the devil."

"Your words, not mine."

The pretty pregnant lady sitting beside Travis gently touched his arm, but he paid her no heed.

"Gentlemen, gentlemen." The woman minister was on her feet. A fact that both Virgil and Travis appeared to resent—though it was Travis who cut her off.

"Listen, Mrs. Lewis, I really don't think—"

"*Reverend* Lewis."

"Right, *Reverend*." There was no missing the irony in his voice.

"People, please." Now the priest was on his feet. "May I suggest we spend this time getting to know one another, perhaps praying as one body so that we—"

"Pray to whom?" Virgil demanded. "Mary? Your saints?"

The priest's face reddened.

"Gentlemen," the woman minister shouted.

"Just tell me who I'm praying to!" Virgil insisted.

The priest's voice was cool and even. "I guess it would depend on what language you're praying in."

"Oh, that's good, real good."

And so it continued—the discord growing as the camera continuing to catch it for the evening news.

as per her weekly ritual, Pilar breezed into her mother's room at the Cahuilla Nursing Home. With any luck she'd be out of there in twenty minutes.

"Hi, Mom."

The old woman turned from the window, beaming a toothless grin. "Pilar."

Pilar stooped down to the wheelchair for her obligatory kiss. "Here's your peanut brittle." She set the box on the table beside her. "Opened and ready for your pleasure."

"Ah, my peanut brittle." The woman took the box into her tiny shriveled hands. She rummaged around for the perfect piece and popped it into her mouth. "The white man brought the Cahuilla many griefs, but peanut brittle was not one of them."

"Hey, Amma."

The woman peered through her milky eyes. "Misty! Child!"

Following the routine, Misty also stooped down for her kiss. The woman took her hand and patted it. "Why is it I never see you anymore?"

"I was here last month."

She strained to hear. "How's that?"

Misty spoke louder, "Sorry, Amma. The place sorta creeps me out."

The old woman smiled. "Me too." She offered her box. "Peanut brittle?"

"No, I'm good."

Pilar had begun making her rounds. She never got used to the smell of disinfectant and old people, but she had a job to do and she did it—a concept she feared her own child would never grasp.

"The Heritage Festival is tonight," she said, as she replaced last week's carnations on the table with fresh ones. "Wish you could join us."

Not hearing, Amma smacked her lips. "These peanuts, they are different; not the same brand."

"They were out of the other."

The woman didn't respond as Pilar tested the bone-dry dirt of a dying fern by the window. "How you can eat that with no teeth is beyond me."

Still not hearing, Amma reached to the table for a bowl of perfectly smooth peanuts. "These—" she spit two or three into the bowl—"I am not so fond of." She wiped her chin and continued. "But the candy ..." She squinted her face into a smile. "Mmmm ..."

Once again she patted Misty's hand, which she had not released. "So why are you here?"

"Can't a girl visit her own grandma?"

Turning to Pilar, Amma asked, "What did she do this time?"

Pilar had filled a glass from the bathroom and was pouring it into the fern. "She bugged Bianco's office."

Amma grinned. "Hidden microphone?"

"And camera," Misty bragged. "The dude didn't know it for almost forty-eight hours."

"And your punishment is to come see me."

"No, Amma, I love seeing you."

"Bull pucky."

Misty giggled.

Checking the dust on the venetian blinds, Pilar explained, "Her punishment is to stay in my sight until I can trust her not to do something else to the man."

Amma cackled quietly and reached for another piece of candy. "Why must you torment him so?"

Misty shrugged. "Because he's a jerk?"

"And yet, *Mukat*, in His all-knowing wisdom, has chosen the man to be your mother's partner, the key to our people's deliverance."

"Mother ..." Pilar had heard this a thousand times.

"You know the prophecy."

Apparently she'd hear it a thousand and one.

"It clearly states that you two are to form an alliance that will deliver our—"

"Mom, he's a business partner with the tribe, that's all." She popped her head back into the bathroom, checking on toilet paper.

"The prophecies say he is more. My grandfather, the greatest shaman of our clan, saw it all when—"

"Yes, I—"

"—the young dream helper spoke to him in the desert. When she said one of his descendents would join forces with the white man to -"

Pilar finished the phrase, "—deliver our people. Yes, yes, I know." She crossed to the bed. "Believe me, I know."

"And, since I'm starting to slip from my prime, the edict must obviously apply to you."

Pilar sighed loud enough so even her mother could hear.

"Besides, he's not such an awful-looking man. Perhaps a bit older than you'd prefer, but—"

"Mother—"

"I've seen the way he looks at you."

Pilar raked her hand through her hair as she scowled at the wastebasket overflowing with used tissues.

"Besides, Misty—wouldn't you like some brothers and sisters?"

"Misty's right," Pilar insisted. "The man's a jerk."

"Is he?" the old woman asked. "Or is he merely white?" Before Pilar could reply, Amma continued, "I have told you before, you must put aside your hatred of the white man or you will never be free."

"And I have told you, I have no problem being his associate. The Council of Elders offered me the position and I gladly accepted. To think of Peter Bianco as anything more than a business associate is—"

"The prophecy says there is more, that there must be a union."

Pilar threw a helpless look to Misty.

"Don't look at me," the girl quipped. "Prophecy is prophecy."

"Please ..."

"You're always saying I shouldn't ignore our heritage."

Again Pilar raked her hair. "Can we change the subject, please?"

Amma popped another piece of candy into her mouth. "We can change the subject, but we cannot change our destiny."

Pilar shook her head and continued moving about the room doing what had to be done. Amma could believe all the prophecies she liked, but the bottom line was that her daughter, Pilar Blackstone, was no different from the millions of other single moms in the business world—dealing with aging parents, rebellious teens, lecherous bosses, and overextended credit.

Those were the areas where real deliverance was needed.

So everything that pastor guy's doing is like totally useless?"

"I didn't say that."

"I thought you said—"

"I said mostly useless."

Luke frowned and shifted to better utilize the 2.3 inches of leg space in the back of Virgil's ancient VW Beetle. To make matters worse, he shared the seat with some end table the man had recently made from desert sticks and a slice of tree trunk. Fiona was driving. Apparently Virgil's license had been suspended. The details were vague, something about running over the scooter of a meter maid who had just given him a ticket. He claimed it was an accident.

"How can you be so sure?" Luke asked.

"I'm not." Virgil reached into the pocket of his bright turquoise shirt—just as loud as yesterday's, this time featuring swordfish—and pulled out a pocket New Testament. "But this is."

Luke looked to Fiona. But instead of disagreeing with her husband, as was her custom, Fiona glanced to the Bible and quietly nodded.

Virgil flipped the pages, found what he was looking for, and handed it back to Luke. Keeping his finger on a verse, he said, "Here, read this."

Luke took the Bible and read: " 'The weapons we fight with are not the weapons of the world—' "

" 'Not the weapons of the world,' " Virgil interrupted. "You see that word, not?"

Luke continued: " 'On the contrary, they have divine power to demolish strongholds.' " He looked up. "Strongholds. That's what you were talking about last night?"

"You got it." Virgil reached for the Bible.

Luke was about to ask for more information when he noticed the car slowing.

"Why are we stopping?"

"We visit various places throughout the week and pray over them," Fiona explained.

"That's right," Virgil said. "Sometimes ten minutes ... sometimes ten hours."

"Ten hours?" Fiona scoffed. "We've never spent ten hours praying anywhere in our lives."

"Well ... we should."

Suppressing a smile, Luke looked out the window. They'd pulled in front of a long, one-story building of wood and adobe. "Why here?" he asked.

"It's a major hot spot," Virgil answered.

Luke adjusted his sunglasses. He tried reading the word that had been burned into a wide plank over the door. "Kaah-u-illa—" he'd mutilated the name and knew it—"Nursing Home."

"*Cahuilla*," Virgil corrected. "It's the local tribe of Indians in this valley."

Fiona turned off the car. It coughed and sputtered before finally giving up the ghost.

"And you pray here because ..."

"Not here." Virgil slammed his shoulder against his door once, twice, three times before it finally opened. "There." He motioned to the building beside the nursing home. One whose name Luke could more easily read:

PALACE OF PLEASURE
ADULT VIDEOS AND TOYS

"You still got that piece of goggle?" Virgil asked.

"Right here."

"Bring it with."

Luke grabbed the broken goggle and unfolded himself from the car. Dry heat hit his face like an oven. He joined the couple as they moved up the uneven sidewalk toward the building.

"Now I ain't saying you'll see somethin', but go ahead and hold that thing up to your eye."

"Here?"

Virgil nodded as they slowed to a stop. "Yup."

A bit self-consciously, Luke brought the lens to his sunglasses.

"What do you see?"

"Just the usual streaks and stuff."

"Are some darker than others?"

"Yeah, there always are."

"Would have been interestin' to know how much of that darkness was flyin' around Pastor Travis this morning."

"Virgil ...," Fiona reproved.

He gave a shrug. "What about a pattern? You said sometimes you see patterns."

Luke stared harder. Usually, if he looked long enough, he could make out certain repetitions. This was no different. Actually, a little easier. Because, like the casino, there was definitely activity near the building's entrance.

But even more above it.

As with the mountain last night, there was a concentration of darker smears hovering over the center of the roof, with thin, shadowy arms flipping from it, sometimes reaching all the way to the ground. Brighter streaks were also present, but they tended to dart about the outer edges.

With last night's encounter fresh in his mind, the whole thing made Luke more than a little uneasy. "It's kinda like the mountain," he explained. "Everything's sorta spiraling."

"Spiraling?" Virgil asked.

"Yeah, sorta. Mostly the darker arms. Some are spiraling in, others spiraling out. Like a vortex or something, but they're going both ways at the same time."

"All right." Virgil replied. "Now we're going to start praying, maybe do a little singing. So you just—"

"What, here?" Luke nervously lowered the lens.

Virgil grinned then quoted, " 'Whatever you bind on earth will be bound in heaven, and whatever you loose on earth will be loosed in heaven.' "

"Let me guess, more Bible?"

"Of course."

"Don't worry, dear," Fiona assured him, "we'll keep it low-key."

"But—"

"Go ahead." Virgil nodded to the piece of goggle. "Keep watching."

Reluctantly, Luke raised it back to his eyes.

"And tell us if you see any changes."

"Right."

Although Luke wasn't crazy about the open display, he was also curious. He remembered all too well what had happened in the lodge, back up in Washington—the impact Preacher Man and the others had on the spirit world when they began singing and stuff.

Virgil started off, his voice just above a whisper. "Praise you, Jesus. Praise you, Lord, praise you ..."

Fiona joined in. "Holy Lord. Holy ... Holy ... Holy ..."

"Bless you, God. We give you honor and glory ..."

Luke concentrated on the images in the lens. The lights and shadows started to move faster.

"Thank you, Lord, we exalt you, we lift you up ..."

The dark center started to contract, growing denser, more defined. Soon, Luke realized he was looking into some type of hole. A hole that the darker shadows raced into and out of—while the brighter smears of light around the outside also seemed to be increasing, intensifying as they moved in on the shadows.

Ever so softly, in almost a whisper, Fiona began to sing.

> *"All hail the pow'r of Jesus' name!*
> *Let angels prostrate fall."*

Virgil joined in.

Neither one could carry a tune—their thin, reedy voices hitting as many bad notes as good. But it didn't seem to matter. Not to them. And not to the lights and shadows. Because, the more they sang, the more activity they caused.

*"Bring forth the royal diadem
And crown Him Lord of all!"*

The hole continued to solidify, growing more and more vivid. The same was true with the dark swirling arms. Their reach was half of what it had been before, barely stretching beyond the building—but now they were much more concentrated, so real that Luke thought if he had been on the roof, he might have actually felt them. Not that he'd want to. Even at this distance he was feeling a cold chill.

All this as the intensity of the brighter smears also increased, as they continued closing in, forming a type of circle around the darkness—a ring that grew brighter as it pressed in tighter and tighter. Soon it was so bright that even with his sunglasses Luke's eyes began to ache. But he would not turn away. He had to see what—

"Hello, Virgil. Holding church again?"

The singing stopped. Luke lowered the lens to see a good-looking woman with long dark hair. Beside her was a younger girl, about his age, maybe older. So beautiful that for the briefest moment he forgot to breathe.

Virgil answered, "Just the usual battle against the forces of evil."

"Now there's a surprise."

They continued talking but Luke barely noticed. All he saw was the girl ...

"Looks like you have a new convert."

"And always got room for one or two more," Virgil replied. "We're still meetin' at 11:00 every Sunday—9:30 for Sunday school."

He'd never seen anyone like her. Thick, shoulder-length hair, eyes so dark he could barely find their pupils, and those cheekbones. She was like some Greek statue. Or that Pocahontas chick in the Disney cartoon.

She caught him staring and he glanced away, embarrassed to find his mouth hanging open. He heard Fiona

introducing him. He smiled, he nodded, he was pretty sure
he even said something. But when he looked back into
those coal-black eyes, he couldn't remember what.

"How's Amma?" Fiona asked.

"The same," the woman answered.

"Virgil made her a little night table."

"Really, I'm impressed."

The old man shrugged. "It's not that big a thing."

"I'm sure it's not," the woman replied.

"We were taking it to her just as soon as we finished
here," Fiona said. "Would you like to see?"

"Certainly ..."

The grown-ups moved off.

Luke had intended to follow but couldn't seem to find
his feet. Then, suddenly, he was alone ... with her.

"So what you got there?"

"What?"

"In your hand."

"My what?"

"Your hand." She looked at him like he was a mental.
She wasn't far wrong.

"Oh, this." He raised the broken piece of goggle. "It's
just, uh—"

She reached for it and he gave it to her. At that moment
he would have given her anything.

She held it to the light and looked through it. "What is
it? Part of some night-vision scope or something?"

"Sort of."

She lowered it and began a careful examination. "Cell
processor architecture. Pretty complex stuff." She looked
up. "Night vision doesn't need all this."

"They're, uh ..." He cleared his throat. "Actually,
they're experimental."

"Crazy." She sounded even more interested. "Where's
the rest?"

"Broken ... they're, uh ... broken."

"And these wires ... looks like they went to a power pack."

"Honey?"

She looked up, flipping back her thick glossy hair.

"Let's get going."

"Just a sec."

"Now."

"I said, just a—"

"Now."

With a sigh of exasperation, she handed him the piece of goggle and shouted, "Can I drive?"

"You know better than that."

She turned and headed off, completely forgetting Luke. No "Good-bye," no "See you," no "Would you like to have your heart back?" Nothing.

Just her curvy, sleek body floating off to join her mother in their top-of-the-line Land Rover.

As she arrived and climbed inside her mother called, "You two coming to the Heritage Festival?"

"Is that tonight?" Fiona asked.

"Yes, ma'am. Plenty of good food. Crafts. Art. Lots of culture. But don't worry, Virgil, I'm sure there'll be something of interest for you too. If not, you can always cast out a few demons." She closed the door with a chuckle.

"Laugh all you want," Virgil called.

"I usually do." She grinned. "With you, I usually do. Good-bye, Fiona."

"Good-bye, dear."

She fired up the Land Rover and they pulled away ... but not before the girl turned to give Luke a brief wave.

A wave ...

She had turned ... she had raised her hand ... and she had actually waved ...

To him.

He didn't know her name, but she had looked back, she had raised her hand, and she had waved ... to *him*.

bianco reached for the stereo remote, pointed it at the media wall, and cranked up Miles Davis so high it made the young reporter wince.

"Mr. Bianco," the kid complained. "Do we really need that so loud?"

"Trust me," Bianco said as he turned from the windows and crossed back to his desk, "we do."

The reporter, obviously not understanding his precaution, returned to the topic at hand. "Look, Mr. Bianco, as I explained to you—"

"I know, I know." He took his place behind the desk. "You've got your job and the public has the right to know."

"That's correct."

He leaned toward the kid. "Mr. Fortenbra, Michael. I hardly believe what happens out here in the middle of the desert is of interest to anyone. Compared to your LA stories, our petty disagreements are minor blips on the radar."

"Perhaps. But we'll let the public make that decision, if you don't mind. After all, knowledge is power. And if they want that empowerment, they should be entitled to it."

Bianco tried to overlook the lecture. It came with the boy's youth and ambition. Not that there was anything wrong with them—as long as they could be channeled correctly.

He reached for the intel folder on Pastor Travis Lawton and gently pushed it across his desk.

The reporter hesitated, then took it.

Bianco knew it wasn't much, but the kid *was* young and there was that ambition.

He quickly skimmed it, paused, then looked up, scowling. "This was twelve years ago. He was still in college."

Bianco stared at him, saying nothing.

The kid looked back at the file. After a moment, he shook his head. "No, this is mud raking. Totally irrelevant to the story."

"Is it?" Bianco asked. "What about hidden psychological motives behind picketing us? Deep-seated guilt from a sordid past?"

The reporter continued staring at the folder.

"Knowledge is power," Bianco repeated the lecture. "The people have the right to be empowered."

Fortenbra hesitated another moment, then looked up and closed the folder. "I'm sorry." He pushed it back across the desk. "It's just not right. It's not good reporting."

Bianco nodded. "Well, I'm certainly no expert at reporting." He forced a smile. "I promise I won't be a reporter if you promise not to run casinos."

Fortenbra returned the smile. "Sounds like a plan. Whatever the case, you have my word that I'll be fair with the story and let the facts speak for themselves."

"Good, good. I wouldn't want it any other way."

Then, just as the reporter prepared to rise, Bianco reached for another folder on his desk. "There is, however, another piece of information you may be interested in."

He slid it across to him. The kid glanced down, saw the name on the cover, and looked back up, startled. "My wife?"

Bianco motioned him to open it.

He did, quickly scanning the information until he came to a stop and reread a section. When he looked up, the color had drained from his face. "Where did you get this?"

"You didn't know?"

"Of course I knew, but she was just a child. Still a minor. Where did you get this?"

Bianco shrugged. "Knowledge is power. I like to be empowered."

Fortenbra swore softly and shut the folder. "That was so long ago. How did you ... this would destroy her, you know that? If people found out."

"Not only her, but I'm afraid it wouldn't be so healthy for the family, either. What are the girls now, five and seven? Impressionable ages. Not to mention your audience of viewers—impressionable, I mean."

Fortenbra glared at him and swore louder.

It made little difference. The important thing was, Bianco had him. He could see the sweat above the kid's upper lip. With a shrug, he reached for the folder.

But the reporter held on, staring at it. Then, a bit woodenly, he spoke. "And to ensure that doesn't happen, that this information remains confidential ..." He looked up at Bianco. "You want me to mention what Travis Lawton was accused of during his sophomore year at college—even though the girl dropped all charges?"

"No, you're right." Bianco nodded over to Lawton's folder. "That's old news. By itself, it would be of little interest."

"Then, what do you—"

"I want new news, Michael."

The reporter frowned.

Bianco explained, "We've seen his actions in the past. And rumors of other infidelities do, shall we say, *persist*. My question is whether or not he has truly reformed—whether or not he has truly repented."

"And if he has?"

"That would be of little use to me, either. But if he hasn't ... Well, now that would be a story we could both get some mileage out of."

"I don't ... understand."

But he did understand, Bianco could see it in his eyes. So, with a sigh of pretended resignation, he again reached for the folder. "I'm sorry to hear that, Mr. Fortenbra. Not only for you, but for your—"

"Wait, wait."

Bianco stopped as the kid weighed the implications. "Are you saying that we should set him up?"

"Of course not."

"Then—"

"I see it as more of a test. If he passes, well, then he passes—so much the better for him. But if he doesn't ..."

"You're suggesting a trap."

"I'm suggesting nothing, Michael. As I said, I won't run your business if you don't run mine." He watched the wheels continue to turn.

"I'll need some time ... some resources."

"Of course. My resources are at your disposal. But time ..." He leaned back. "Well, I'm afraid we have very little of that."

"How ..." The reporter shifted in his chair. "How soon?"

"The sooner the better."

And then, just as Bianco knew he would, Michael Fortenbra slowly began to nod.

three

The night was both cool and warm. Cool, from a slight desert breeze. Warm, from the pavement radiating heat it had stored up during the day's relentless sun.

Strings of clear, bare lightbulbs hung overhead. What few trees there were glowed with miniature white lights. As far as Luke could tell, the whole town had turned out for the festival. He even caught a glimpse of the homeless guy he'd ridden into town with ... still wearing his gloves. Fortunately, he didn't see Luke.

Unfortunately, Luke was bored out of his skull.

Here he'd been in town for over a day, supposedly helping some guy repair his church, and he hadn't even seen the place. Then there was the company ... not that the old folks weren't great people, but 24/7 of their incessant chattering and bickering was more than he'd signed up for.

And now this Heritage Festival thing.

No offense, but he didn't particularly give a rip about Indian pottery, dream catcher hoops, row after row of turquoise jewelry, and booth after booth of Southwestern art. Seriously, if he saw one more painting of a pink and purple sunrise or sunset over one more range of violet mountains, he'd hurl.

Nor was he particularly thrilled about being introduced to every senior citizen in Agua Rancheria. Wasn't there anyone in town under twenty?

Actually, it wasn't *anyone* he wanted to see. It was a definite *someone*.

And *that's* what kept him going.

His diligence finally paid off when he spotted her with a couple friends over in the bank parking lot at the chili cook-off. But now what was he going to do, just stroll on up and start a conversation?

"Hi, remember me? Wanna see my goggles?"

Not exactly the suave sophistication he hoped for (although he'd brought the goggles along, just in case).

As the night continued, he kept a constant note of where she was—moving Virgil and Fiona ahead when they slowed, or slowing them if they started to pass. It's not like he was stalking her or anything—at least he hoped he wasn't. He was just looking for the right opportunity to start another conversation.

Up ahead, in another parking lot, she had gathered with a large crowd around four half-naked men who were leaping around, whooping and hollering. They wore plenty of beads and feathers and were stripped down to tight buckskin pants.

"What's going on?" he asked.

"Spirit dancers," Virgil said.

"What's that?"

"You tell me."

Luke rechecked the girl's position. She stood near the front, eating frozen yogurt and laughing with her friends.

"What do you mean?" he asked.

"You got that piece of goggle?"

"Sure."

"Take a look."

"You think there's something happening?"

"With them? You bet I do."

Luke reached into his pocket. "Doesn't sound like you think much of Native Americans."

"What's that supposed to mean?"

Fiona patted his arm. "It means you're a bigot, dear. Anti-Indian."

"Anti-Indian? Anti-Indian? Son, I ain't anti-nothin'."

"Unless, of course, it's anti-Pastor Travis," Fiona replied.

Virgil gave her a look then turned back to Luke. "Truth is, these Indians, especially the Cahuilla, they got more going for 'em than most white folks I know. Except—"

"Except what?"

"Just look through that lens and tell me what you see."

As discretely as possible Luke raised the broken half of the goggles to his eye.

There were the usual streaks flying around the crowd—some brighter smears, others darker shadows. Nothing unusual. Except ...

As he focused on the dancers, he noticed a concentration of shadows hovering over their heads, fifteen maybe twenty feet above, forming a core of darkness. From it, fainter arms of darkness whipped back and forth—arms similar to what had given him the creeps that afternoon, and to what attacked them the night before.

"What do you see?"

Luke squinted. "It's like the mountain—only smaller."

The dancers picked up their pace and started to chant. "What else?"

He continued watching as the crowd began clapping to the rhythm of the chant. The core grew darker. But it did not condense like this afternoon. In fact, it actually seemed to grow larger. Its black, flipping arms seeming to lengthen.

One passed directly over Luke's head. He gasped and ducked, pulling the eyepiece away. He was relieved to see that nothing was there—no black, sinister tentacle, no night-flying crow.

The clapping grew louder. Faster.

Luke raised the broken goggle back to his eye.

Another tentacle passed. Closer. Then another, closer yet. And another—almost as if they were zeroing in on him, as if they sensed his watching them and were trying to stop him. But each time they approached they abruptly stopped, always at the same place, a dozen feet away. As if they hit a wall, some sort of invisible barrier.

He glanced to Virgil, who continued watching the dance. Then to Fiona. Her eyes were closed, her lips moving. She had raised one hand to waist level, inconspicuously holding it out.

The dancers continued their chant, faster. They threw back their heads and closed their eyes.

Luke looked back through the eyepiece. The tentacles thrashed even more violently.

He turned to the girl. She was clapping and enjoying the performance with the rest of the group, but—was it his imagination, or were the tentacles that had been trying to reach him moving toward her?

He squinted harder. Yes, they were shifting toward her! How could that be? It was as if they'd seen the direction he'd been looking. Seen his interest in her. And if they couldn't reach him ... was it possible? If they couldn't reach him, were they trying to get to *her*?

The dancers rolled their heads from side to side, pretending to drop into a trance. At least Luke thought they were pretending.

The tentacles continued toward the girl, whipping and snapping over her head, sometimes directly in front of her, just a few feet away.

He couldn't stand anymore. "No!" He broke from the couple and started toward her.

Virgil yelled after him, but he barely heard as he pushed his way through the crowd. He tried keeping the lens to his face, but it only slowed him.

The people clapped louder and faster as the dancers worked themselves into a frenzy.

He was halfway there when he brought the eyepiece back up for a look.

A handful of tentacles surrounded the girl—caressing the space around her, lingering around her hips, her belly, some actually touching and brushing against her bare arms and shoulders.

"No!" He shoved harder. "No!"

She closed her eyes, swept up by the rhythm, the chanting, the dancing.

Luke continued to push. He was ten feet away. There were only a few more groups to fight through.

She began to sway.

Only a handful of people separated them.

"No!"

Her head started rolling. Back and forth. Like the dancers.

"No!"

At last he arrived and grabbed her arm.

Her eyes popped open, startled, afraid. But not afraid of the tentacles. Afraid of him!

"Stop!" he shouted. "You have to stop, you have to get out of here!"

He grabbed her other arm, pulling her away— away from the dancers, the circle, the tentacles.

She screamed and struggled to break free, obviously not understanding.

But he had to help. Whether she understood or not.

Other people moved in. Hands grabbed his own arms, yanking him back.

"No! You don't understand! The darkness!"

They dragged him away, none too gently, and tossed him to the side. He stumbled, nearly falling. But not before he caught a glimpse of the girl.

She had recognized him. And, though her eyes were filled with fear, there was something else. Confusion? Bewilderment? He didn't know.

Then she was gone. Ushered through the crowd. Away from the dance. Away from him.

Still no word on Triple A?" Pastor Lawton dropped his head, trying to stretch the muscles in the back of his neck, anything to relieve the pounding headache.

"Not yet. Sorry."

He closed his eyes, speaking through the pain. "It's all right."

His wife continued on the other end of his cell phone. "I just can't believe someone would slash my tires. And at the Heritage Festival, of all things."

"It's okay, sweetheart. Call me when they get there."

"Are you going to be okay?"

He heard the concern in her voice. Fought back his irritation. "Yes, I'm fine. I'll be all right."

"Okay ... I love you." The concern was still there, but there was nothing he could do about it.

"I love you too."

She hung up. He paused a moment before disconnecting.

"Still no luck?"

He turned to the young blonde in the pew behind him. The breathtakingly beautiful young blonde. "No, not yet."

"I'm sorry to be such a bother."

"No, you're no—"

"If it wasn't for me, you'd probably be there with her now." She threw back her hair which brushed against some very bare shoulders. It wasn't meant to be provocative, he was sure of it. In her line of work it probably just came as second nature. Nevertheless, he looked away.

"Listen—" he cleared his throat—"the decision you're about to make, it's much more important than any festival, or any slashed tires for that matter." The pain made him wince, and he again lowered his head to stretch his neck.

"Headache no better?"

He forced a smile. "Worse."

"Your fight against the casino must really be taking its toll."

"Hmm. If those people were the only problem."

"What do you mean?"

"I mean we've got folks on our own side who are making things difficult—particularly in the religious community." He rubbed his neck, the pain so great his eyes nearly watered.

"Here—" she reached toward him—"let me help. I'm pretty good with—"

"No." It was a bit more abrupt than he wished, but it had to be—given the years in her profession—given the years of his own battle. In fact, that's why they'd moved the meeting out here into the sanctuary, away from the privacy of his office.

And that's why Beth was supposed to have been with them. It was a rule they'd agreed upon when they first married, when he'd first confessed his ... weakness.

For some people their drug of choice was alcohol or gambling or greed. For Pastor Travis it was beautiful young women. And this twenty-five-year-old, top-of-the-pay-scale call girl, who wanted to receive Jesus Christ as her Lord and Savior, was no exception.

"Listen." She gathered her gauzy shawl. "Maybe I should just—"

"No, please." He reached out and took her arm. *Now is the day of salvation*—that was the Scripture running through his head. He could not jeopardize her soul because of his own weakness. He was a pastor, a man of God; he would do this. He *had* to do this.

She glanced at his hand and he immediately withdrew it. "Sorry, I didn't—"

"No, that's okay, I appreciate your concern."

He nodded, then again stretched his neck.

"It's not often that I have men, you know, interested in me—for the right reasons."

He gave a brief nod.

"But really ..." She scooted behind him, her hands suddenly on his neck. He started to stop her, but she'd found the spot. And they were strong hands. Cool and comforting. "I'm pretty good at this."

She was right, she *was* good.

He dropped his neck lower as she continued to rub. "If there's one thing I'm a pro at it's helping people relax."

He wasn't certain, but it sounded like her voice was closer.

"Man, you really are tense. Must be awful carrying all that responsibility around. Being the one everybody looks up to."

Her hands dropped slightly, finding other knots between his shoulder blades. Knots that he didn't even know were there. He closed his eyes, savoring the touch.

"You're doing so much for others ... for me. I mean, let's face it, this is the least I can do for you." Her voice *was* closer. And softer. As pleasing to his ears as her hands were to his shoulders.

He could feel his body reacting. But he had been under such pressure and this felt so good. And she was so young ... and beautiful ...

Her hands moved lower to the center of his back—strong, comforting. He would stop her, in just a moment he would stop her.

Her voice was near his right ear. He could smell her perfume, feel a trace of her breath against his neck.

"Better?" she asked.

He nodded, eyes still closed.

"Good ...," she whispered, closer still. "Good ..."

Another moment and her lips brushed against his cheek. Barely touching. He turned his head, longing for more, cursing himself even amidst the desire. Her lips returned, gently touching his own. And then again. Firmer. Their passion growing—warm, moist, filled with a hunger of their own ...

and you think you were, what, just going to slip this by me?" Pilar paced in front of Bianco's desk, barely containing her rage. "Reserve an entire floor and not let me know?"

He did not look up from his work. When he spoke his voice was preoccupied, almost condescending. "These people merely want discretion."

"Fine. But at least let me notify the VIP team. If they're going to rent an entire floor, you can be sure they expect some—"

"They have no interest in being treated as VIPs."

"They—" She stopped and turned to him. "Peter, what's going on?"

Finally he glanced up. "What do you mean?"

"Who are those people?"

"Investors, private capitalists."

"They want to invest in the casino?"

He held her look but did not answer.

"Investors in what?"

He returned to his work. "There are some things you're better off not—"

"As tribal representative I have a right to know. I have a responsibility."

"For the moment, you'd be doing your people more good by not knowing."

"What?"

He continued his work.

"If you're risking the Cahuillas' investment by—"

For the first time he showed irritation. "Nobody is risking anything, Pilar."

She stood, waiting.

He hesitated, then resumed his work.

"I'll find out, you know I'll find out."

"As I said, it's better for all parties if you don't."

She hovered over his desk another minute. When it was clear the conversation was over, she turned on her heels and stormed toward the door.

"Oh, and Pilar."

She came to a stop.

"Tell your child, if I catch her snooping around here, or anywhere else in the casino, especially during these next few days—there will be serious repercussions."

"And if it should slip my mind?"

Bianco looked up ... and she froze. She'd only seen that expression once or twice before. That cold-dead look. It lasted only a second before he covered it with a smile.

"I've always had a soft place in my heart for Misty. Perhaps too soft." He shrugged. "She's been like a daughter to me, and perhaps I've indulged her more than I should."

Pilar said nothing, waiting for more.

"But on this, there is no discussion. Tell her we are not playing games, Pilar. For her own welfare, make sure she understands."

He held her look until, almost against her wishes, she gave the slightest nod.

He nodded back and returned to his work.

no, this isn't right."

"What?"

"No." Travis pulled away.

"Come on, baby, it's what we both want." She pressed herself to him. "It's what we both need."

Maybe it was the shame of being in the sanctuary, maybe it was the desperate prayer that flickered through his mind as she pushed back his shirt. Whatever the reason, Pastor Travis Lawton suddenly had enough strength to break free and step back. "I'm sorry."

Once again she reached for him.

This time, more forcefully, he pushed her away. "I'm ... sorry."

"What are you afraid of, baby? That someone will see us? 'Cause we can go back to my—"

"No, no ..." He ran his hands through his hair. "I'm sorry." He dropped his head and began buttoning his shirt, then saw he'd started wrong and began again. "This was all my fault, and I'm sorry, I should never have—"

He caught movement and glanced up. She was reaching down to her small handbag on the pew. Why, he wasn't certain. Instead of pulling herself together, she produced a rhinestone cell phone and hit a single button.

"What's that, who are you calling?"

"What?" She turned back to him. "Oh, nobody, baby. Nobody important."

She closed the phone and moved to him, beautiful and barefoot.

But this time Travis stood his ground. This time he would resist.

She placed her hands on his shoulders. "Don't you like me?"

He was careful to keep his gaze only on her eyes. "Cinnamon ... Ms. Watkins—"

Suddenly she pulled her body to his, clamping her lips over his mouth.

Startled, but in control, he reached around his neck and unclasped her hands.

That's when the sanctuary doors flew open and the church was filled with blazing light. He turned from her and saw the reporter who had been at the meeting this morning. At his side a cameraman was busy taping.

"Good evening, Pastor Lawton."

He froze, the half-clad woman clinging to his neck, his shirt still open.

"I'm curious. Is there any statement you'd like to make?"

uke waited.

He rechecked his hair, his shirt, his breath—for the second or third time.

When everything met his approval, he again reached for the buzzer. Before he pressed it, the door suddenly opened and there she stood—thick disheveled hair, tank top with spaghetti straps ... absolutely heart stopping. In her arms she held a black cat.

"It's you." She wasn't angry, just surprised.

"Hi, I—" He cleared his throat and started again.

"How'd you get in?"

"Virgil and Fiona, they know lots of people who work here."

"You came in through the service entrance, then? They don't let minors on the casino floor."

"Right, uh, some busboy from the restaurant. Goes to their church."

He tried swallowing but those liquid black eyes had evaporated all moisture from his mouth.

"Listen, can I, uh—"

"You want to come in?"

"Well, yeah, I mean if it's, uh, you know, okay."

"Depends. You don't plan to attack me again, do you?"

"No, I, uh ... I'm sorry." He lifted the broken goggles in his hand as if they gave all the answers. "It was these."

"These what?" She held her ground, stroking the cat, her eyes continuing his meltdown.

"I saw something in them. Something, I don't know, some sort of dark power or something trying to hurt you or ... something."

She stared, giving him the once-over—his shirt, his jeans, his cowboy boots.

He shrugged, definitely feeling like a moron.

She remained fixed on his boots for a moment, snickering, before finally opening the door. "All right, cowboy. But only for a minute." She turned and entered an expensively furnished living room. "My mom's about off work. She'd go ballistic if she came up and caught you here."

He stepped inside. "Why ..." He tried swallowing again. "Why's that?"

"Probably 'cause you're a guy and she's afraid you'll rape me or something." She picked an apple out of a fruit bowl on the glass table. "You're not, are you?"

"Not what?"

"Going to rape me?"

Luke blinked.

"Hello?"

He came to. "No ... of course not."

Biting into the apple she asked, "Why, aren't I pretty enough?"

"No, of course not. I mean, yes, I mean ... Your mom thinks I'm going to rape you just because I'm some guy visiting?"

"Don't be stupid."

"Then—"

"She thinks you're going to rape me because you're some *white* guy visiting."

He tried to smile, thinking it was a joke.

"Don't laugh. It could happen."

"I suppose, but—"

"How do you think *I* got into this ol' world?"

Again he blinked. Her candor left him totally disarmed. "I'm sorry. I didn't—I mean, I'm sorry to hear that."

"Not me. Better that way than no way."

He could think of no appropriate response.

"So what'd you see with these?" She dropped the cat and reached for the broken goggles.

He gave them up and she held the lens to the light, trying to see through it.

"It, uh, it only works for me."

She turned to look out the room's picture window, past the flashing glare of the red and white casino lights, to the black desert beyond.

"I burnt my retinas or something, climbing like a microwave tower. And for some reason I'm the only one who can see stuff through it."

With the lens still pressed to her eye, she turned to him. "What type of stuff?"

"Mostly darting lights. And shadows. That's what I saw heading toward you. At the festival."

"What?"

"Shadows ... mostly."

She removed the lens and frowned. Then, without a word, she turned and headed for the hallway.

Luke stood in the room, unsure what to do.

Still examining the goggles, she arrived at the first door, pushed it open with her foot, and stepped inside.

Luke hesitated, glanced around the penthouse, then followed.

As he entered, he was unsure if it was somebody's bedroom or an electronics warehouse. Everywhere he looked there were parts of computers, parts of televisions, parts of everything.

She'd already seated herself at a long table that was covered with even more electrical stuff. Beyond the table was a stack of a dozen different-sized TV monitors that formed a type of wall. Most of them were turned on and glowing with pictures.

"Is this your ... room?"

She swiveled the arm of a mounted magnifying glass toward her. Already hunched over, she continued studying the goggles, oblivious to Luke's presence.

He shoved his hands into his back pockets, again unsure what to do.

The girl gave him no clues.

"I'm, uh ... my name is Luke."

"Right."

More silence.

"And you're ..."

No answer.

He tried again. "Your name, I never caught your name."

"Misty."

He nodded. He stood another moment. Then, with nothing else to do, he nodded some more.

She reached for a pair of pliers. Even scrunched over she was so beautiful his throat ached.

She continued tinkering.

He continued standing.

He turned his attention to the TV monitors. Most were pictures of what he guessed to be the downstairs casino — red carpet, splashing water fountains, green felt tables, lots of people, and plenty of flashing lights.

Then there were the cocktail waitresses. They were clothed like Indians. Well, at least the parts of them that were clothed.

One monitor featured a long row of slot machines. Another, a high-angle view of a roulette wheel. Another, a hallway that looked like the outside of her penthouse. Another, some sort of master control security room with rows of more monitors.

And to the far left was a screen showing a small theater with an older stand-up comedian.

Luke leaned in for a better look. "Is that Joey Popiski?"

She gave her usual no answer.

He tried again. "Sure looks like him."

Repeat in the no-answer department.

He grew concerned about the time. Virgil and Fiona had only given him ten minutes—just enough to go up, apologize, and try to explain his behavior. He pulled out his cell phone to look at the clock.

"Don't use that in here."

He looked up, startled, unsure how she knew ... until he caught an image of himself, standing behind her, in yet another monitor.

He shoved the phone back into his pocket and cleared his throat—for what purpose, he had no idea.

Suddenly, a voice demanded, "What are you doing here?"

Luke jumped and turned to see the mother glowering at him from the bedroom door.

"Oh, hi, I was just, uh—"

"He's probably come for sex."

He spun to Misty, who continued her work, then back to the mother. "No, that's not true, I, uh ..."

The mother waited.

He tried again, eyeing the open door. "I just came up to apologize to her."

"Apologize? For what?"

"For—" he swallowed—"attacking her at the festival."

"What?"

"Pretty scary, when you think about it," Misty said, still hunched over the workbench.

Luke tried again. "Look, I know I'm white and everything, but—"

"White?"

"And I know you think that all white guys want to do is, well, you know."

Her hands were on her hips. "What do I know?"

"Listen, I think I really need to be going." He motioned toward the open bedroom door. "You don't mind if I leave now, do you?"

"I think that's a very good idea."

"Yes. Right." He scooted past her. "Thanks." He headed across the living room. "It was nice meeting you. Both of you."

The mother said nothing.

Unfortunately, the daughter did. "Better luck next time, cowboy."

His hand was on the front door, opening it. "What?"

"About the sex. Better luck next time."

He didn't bother responding to the mother's glare as he stepped into the hall and quickly shut the door behind him.

four

the work on the guy's goggles was tougher than Misty had figured. But with a little ingenuity—which unfortunately involved cannibalizing Mom's laptop for the latest processor—she was able to start getting a signal. It wasn't much, but a lot better than before.

'Course she still couldn't see a thing through them, but maybe it would help the boy. At least that's what she hoped. And if it didn't, well hey, at least it gave her a chance to hang with him some more. It's not like he was hot or anything, but he did have a sweetness to him—something rare compared to the wannabe machos who usually hit on her. Besides, what guy had ever gone out of his way to try and "save" her like he had at the festival?

Kinda romantic. Unfortunate that he thought he was saving her from the powers of darkness. But, still, kinda romantic.

She'd just returned from the Surveillance Room—with its 120 monitors overlooking and recording every game the casino ran. Its sole purpose was to catch scammers and con artists. Of course it was a restricted area (as were many places in the casino for Misty), but Chad McKinney had the graveyard shift. And since Chad McKinney had a thing for her and since she needed a lithium battery ... it had taken little effort to charm her way in and lift one from their emergency backup junk.

No sweat.

She was attaching it to the goggles when Mom burst into the room. "You still up?" she asked.

"No, I was sleep soldering."

She swept up the TV remote and clicked it on. "Check out Channel 6."

"Mother. I'm trying to work on—"

"Shh, listen." She cranked up the volume. Some reporter was rambling on about Agua Rancheria and one of their church leaders.

Reluctantly, Misty looked up.

The screen showed a stop-action, frame-by-frame scene of some guy making out with a blonde chick. It froze and zoomed in on his face.

"Got him!" Mom exclaimed.

Misty squinted at the monitor. "Who?"

"Our beloved preacher boy."

"The guy picketing the casino?"

"The guy who *had* been picketing the casino. I don't think we'll be seeing much of him anymore."

Misty returned to her work. "Whatever."

"*Whatever*? This means they won't get enough signatures for the referendum. No way will it be on the ballot." She nodded in satisfaction. "Once again *The Man* has been trapped by his own lies and hypocrisy."

Misty shook her head. "You really are prejudiced, aren't you?"

"What?"

She saw no need to respond.

"What do you mean by that?"

Misty shrugged. "As far as you're concerned, the white man is the cause of all our suffering."

"That's not true, how can you say that?"

She continued soldering.

"I believe most are good."

"Right."

"But you'd have to be blind not to see what they've done to our people. To our land. And if you showed the slightest interest in your heritage, you'd see how they've exploited us."

"I think we're doing okay."

"Here, now, of course. Once we discovered their weaknesses."

Wearily, Misty recited, " 'Sex, greed, materialism—the American way.' "

"There's nothing wrong with providing the means for them to gorge on their own desires."

"While we make off like bandits."

"While we exploit the exploiter."

Misty ignored her and continued to work. There was no reasoning with the woman when she got this way.

d ear Lord, we ask You to use this ugly situation to open our brother's eyes that he might repent and come to fully know You."

Virgil—*Pastor* Virgil—continued praying behind a marred and chipped lectern in the tiny storefront church of his Holy Ghost Revival Center.

"We ask that You remove the blight he has brought upon Your name and upon Your servants. And we ask that You remind each of us how easily we can fall if we are not empowered by Your Holy Spirit. In Jesus' name we pray, amen."

There was a peppering of amens about the congregation.

Luke raised his head. He sat beside Fiona in the second of three rows of folding chairs. Almost immediately, a middle-aged woman, seven or eight seats over, rose to her feet and started to ... well, Luke wasn't exactly sure what she was doing. She was talking, but it definitely wasn't English. In fact it wasn't any language he'd ever heard.

Whatever it was, there were lots of repeated phrases with plenty of harsh consonants.

He turned to the rest of the congregation. The older ones wore suits or dresses; the two or three younger ones sported cargo shorts and flip-flops. But no one seemed surprised at the woman's outburst. In fact many, like Fiona, had their eyes closed. Others smiled. Some gently nodded.

It lasted nearly a minute before she came to an end and sat back down.

Now, except for the roar of the window air conditioner, the small room fell silent. Even Virgil didn't seem inclined to talk—a first as far as Luke could tell.

Finally, a young man, just a little older than Luke, rose to his feet. A handful turned to him, nodding in encouragement. He took a hesitant breath and started to speak. This time it was English. The first few words were timid, but gradually his voice grew louder and more confident.

"Thus saith the Lord. 'I know, My people, that you love Me. Yea, I know that some of you love Me more than your very lives. And this causes Me great delight. For I know the paths I have set before you,' saith the Lord. 'Paths for good and not evil. I know how I would have you walk. Yea, walk in My way,' saith the Lord. 'Stray neither to the left nor to the right. For I have given you power and authority to tread upon the enemy.' "

Once again the congregation had closed their eyes, listening, nodding, occasionally mouthing quiet amens, as he continued: " 'Trust in Me, My children. For I have heard your prayers and I have sent a deliverer. I have placed a deliverer here, among you this day, My people. Yeah, I have sent him and he sits among you, in your very midst, my children.' "

More amens—though a few had opened their eyes, discretely glancing about. More than one pair landed upon Luke.

He fidgeted, wondering what was going on.

As if sensing his uneasiness, Fiona reached out and rested a reassuring hand on his arm. Her eyes remained closed.

" 'He will be My tool, My instrument to unite and deliver this land,' saith the Lord. 'Very soon this shall come to pass. Only trust Me. Trust Me as a child trusts a Father. For I am Your Father,' saith the Lord, 'and You are My children ...' "

The young man stood in silence, waiting. Then, with apparently nothing more to say, he eased himself back down into his chair.

More silence. A few coughs.

Finally, an old lady, sitting up front at a cheap electronic keyboard, played the opening phrase to a song. Once she'd finished the phrase, she began again. This time the group joined her in song. There were no hymnbooks, not even an overhead projector. Yet, somehow, everyone knew the words. They sang loudly and with little concern for pitch.

Luke sat listening. Talk about an education. In fact, the entire Sunday morning had been full of information—starting from the moment they'd heard of Travis Lawton's "fall" over the car radio as Fiona drove them to church.

As far as Luke could tell, Virgil hadn't exactly been torn up about the matter. In fact, as they pushed open the church doors (he made a point of never locking them) and stepped into the dusty room, the man actually seemed lighter on his feet. And, when they pulled back the drapes to let the light pour in, he might even have been humming.

"Does he really hate the guy that much?" Luke had asked Fiona as the two of them removed a dustcover from the sun-bleached altar.

"Who?"

"That Pastor Travis guy."

"No, son, he doesn't hate him."

Luke glanced over at Virgil, who stood in the front door, enjoying the sun, humming away.

"He's doing a pretty good imitation of it."

Fiona looked on with a sad smile. "I don't think it's hate. I think it's love."

"Love?"

"Toward the Lord."

"You lost me."

"I think Virgil and Pastor Travis are so in love with God that they'd do anything to protect Him."

"So it's a good thing?"

"Not at all."

"Loving God isn't good?"

"Loving Him is great. Not trusting that He can protect Himself, isn't."

Luke frowned, trying to understand. But before he could ask any more questions, Virgil called out, "Woman, you gonna stand around jawing all day, or you gonna help me set up these chairs?"

They looked over to see him pulling the first of the metal chairs off a stack and begin unfolding it.

"I'd prefer jawing, if you don't mind."

He snapped open the chair and clanged it onto the concrete floor. "Why am I not surprised."

"But seeing as you'll probably throw your back out again ..." She turned to join him.

"My back is as strong as a mule," he said. "It's like ten mules."

"No, dear, that's your bullheadedness, there's a difference. Luke, give us a hand, will you? Before we have to call 911."

The congregation continued singing as Luke mused over the memory. He watched dust drift through a shaft of sunlight streaming in from the open door behind them. It's not like he was bored with the concept of church or anything, he was just—well, all right, sometimes he was bored. Majorly bored. Sometimes it seemed like the songs just dragged on and on and on some more. And when his minister back home spoke, it felt like he went out of his way to turn a ten-minute talk into forty.

Still, if that was part of the Christian thing, he'd live with it. After all, it was a small sacrifice for what he'd experienced up in Washington State. For what they'd all experienced—him, Dad, Preacher Man, and the half dozen others ...

It had started out as a strange experiment financed by the guy who'd made the goggles—some media billionaire nutcase by the name of Norman E. Obolitz. It was supposed to help them experience the Presence of God. And it did, in the end. But at the beginning it forced everyone to see what they were really like, what their souls actually looked like. For some, like Nubee, Luke's mentally impaired friend, their souls were pretty impressive. For others, well, that was another story.

As the Presence increased, so did the hallucinations or visions or whatever you wanted to call them. Until, at the very end, everyone was catching glimpses of heaven, hell, and everything in between ... including the Lamb that was killed but sitting alive on some throne. Unfortunately, with his eyes getting fried, Luke had missed seeing most of it. But even when he was partially blind, he'd been the one to help them all escape.

And for that, he'd been quite the hero ... at least for a few weeks. But, pretty soon, more out of habit than anything, everybody fell back into treating him like the baby of the family ... again. It made no difference what awesome stuff he'd done, or how sure he was that he'd be doing even greater things. In no time flat, they were back to treating him like some little kid.

A shadow briefly blocked the sunlight. Someone was standing in the doorway.

As inconspicuously as possible, he looked over his shoulder. It was the girl! Misty!

She gave a nod.

He returned it, then faced back to the front, sitting a little straighter.

What was she doing here?

He looked back over his shoulder.

She motioned for him to join her.

He frowned, discretely shaking his head.

But she wouldn't take no for an answer. Again she motioned, this time holding up the broken goggles he'd left with her. Goggles that now had two lenses and a bright orange cable attached to some sort of box. She motioned again.

He turned back to the front, hesitated, then with a sigh of frustration, lightly tapped Fiona's arm. She stopped singing and opened her eyes.

He indicated he needed to step into the aisle.

Figuring he had to go to the bathroom or something, she nodded and pulled in her knees. But to his surprise, as he rose, she took his hand and discretely slipped a pocket New Testament into it.

He looked down at it, then to her.

She motioned that he was to take it and then nodded again, as if she understood.

Understood what?

She closed her eyes and resumed singing.

He glanced around. More than one member of the congregation was stealing peeks at him. Feeling even more self-conscious, he stepped past Fiona, reached the aisle, and quickly slouched toward the back, slipping on his sunglasses.

Pilar gave a start as the cat leaped onto the workbench in front of her. She tried looking past him as he paraded between her and the monitors, his tail catching her nose every second or third pass.

"Balzac ..."

But he did not cooperate.

She reached for the computer mouse, sticky from whatever ice cream or chocolate Misty had last eaten, and clicked the video to *16x speed*.

The images of Bianco's office zipped by.

She felt lousy sneaking into Misty's room like this— especially since her latest lecture about spying on the man. But something was going on and she had to know—not out of childish curiosity, but for the tribe. For the Council of Elders.

Isn't that why they'd assigned her this position in the first place? To make sure Bianco and his investors didn't pull any fast ones?

Up on the screen, he crossed from the minibar to the front of his desk.

She dropped the speed down to *2x* as he reached for the tube. The tube another fellow had brought in earlier and from which they had removed a large document. Together they had unrolled it on the desk and studied it.

Unfortunately, both of their bodies had blocked her view.

That had been—she glanced at the elapsed time—*08:22*. Only eight and half minutes had passed before Bianco was back at his desk, pulling out the document and studying it again.

It must be important.

Now if he'd just step out of the way so she could see it.

Earlier, she'd caught a glimpse of the name on the tube, some logo, and she'd marked the frame number. But it was the document that she needed to see. If he'd just move a few inches to his left, she could—

There!

She hit *freeze-frame*.

A good portion of it was visible. But eager for more, she shuttled the tape ahead, one frame at a time. Unfortunately, he leaned forward, his body again blocking her view.

It looked like the one glimpse was the best she'd have.

She inched the tape backward and jotted down the frame number.

Then, ejecting the cassette, she pulled it from the machine and headed downstairs to Surveillance.

Y ou fixed them?" Luke asked.

"Try 'em on."

Misty's voice was so loud that he threw a nervous glance back into the church. He motioned for them to step farther away.

As they moved down the sidewalk he pointed to the extra lens and elastic head strap. "What's with these?"

"From my old swimming goggles—so you don't look like some cyborg. Only the one lens works. The strap and everything is just to make you look more fashionable. Go ahead, try them on."

"And this?" He lifted the orange cable attached to the pack.

"Try them on."

"All right, all right."

It took a little doing, but with some effort he was able to slip them over his sunglasses.

"You have to wear those all the time?"

"Just in daylight—'cause of my retinas and stuff."

Once the goggles were in position, he blinked but saw no more through the single lens than he normally saw. Just the occasional light smears and darting shadows.

"So?" she asked.

"'Bout the same. Nothing's too—"

"Oh, wait a minute, let me turn them on."

She clicked a switch on the battery pack and his vision was filled with light.

"Whoa!" He threw back his head and groped for the goggles.

"What is it? What do you see?"

The light was blinding, piercing. And impossibly beautiful. Every imaginable color and more!

"Luke!"

He knew he should rip them off, but he could not. He felt the light burning his eye, but it didn't matter.

"What's wrong? What do you see?"

Directly behind him was the source of the brightness. Against all common sense he turned toward it. It burned into his eye, penetrated his head.

And filled him with terror.

He tried to scream, but the sound caught in his throat.

A giant entity was wrapped around the church building. Horrifying in power. Light blazed from it like the sun, shimmering and falling from its shoulders like water.

Luke began to tremble.

"You okay?" The girl's voice was far away. A different world. "Cowboy?"

"Get me ..." He didn't know if she could hear him. "Get me out—"

The creature turned toward him. But its face was too bright, overwhelming.

He felt his knees losing strength.

"Luke ..."

Such beauty. Such horror. He could not look away.

"Get ... me ... out of ..."

He was falling, floating toward the pavement. Breath sucked from his lungs. All strength leaving. All consciousness gone ...

Sitting in the Surveillance Room, Pilar brought up the first frame and zoomed into the logo printed on the side of the tube. The resolution, with its boxy orange and red pixels, was too poor to read.

She hit the *visual enhancement* key and waited.

Toward the front of the glass-enclosed, air-purified room two security officers sat at the big board. They drank their coffee and shot the breeze while only occasionally checking the long wall of monitors before them. After all, it was Sunday morning, and cons seldom worked the tables in the mornings. They preferred hiding amidst the hustle and bustle of the evening crowd.

Pilar sat twenty feet away at a smaller console in the back. She watched as the pixels on her screen tumbled and focused until they formed a triangle with the words: *Bernard Construction.*

She scowled at the name. The casino was always doing construction and remodeling; that was nothing new. But this company she didn't recognize. They were either new or out of the area or ...

She highlighted the name, drag-clicked it to another screen, and ran it through one of their many database programs.

In seconds the answer appeared. There were four Bernard Constructions in the state of California. One up near Redding, another in Modesto, and a couple in San Diego.

But why so far away when there were a dozen reputable firms right here in the area?

She saved the data and returned to the first monitor. She shuttled to the other frame, the one of the blueprint, and zoomed in until it blurred into another haze of pixels.

She hit the enhancement key and waited.

The image came in faster. She leaned in and watched as the blueprint to a building appeared. Beside it, some basic topographical information.

The building was nothing she recognized. At least nothing connected to the casino. And it wasn't much—just a small, one-story structure with no more than five or six rooms. Another building, like a large garage, was attached to it.

Beside it was what appeared to be the foundation for yet another. But longer. Much longer. Perhaps it was a parking lot or driveway. She pulled back. It continued stretching across the blueprint. She pulled back farther and farther.

No, it was too long to be a driveway.

A road?

Perhaps. But where? Why?

uke woke to the sound of squealing tires as his head slammed into a passenger door. He opened his eyes just in time to be thrown in the opposite direction as more horns honked. That's when he saw Misty struggling with the steering wheel.

"What's going on?" he mumbled

"You okay?" she yelled.

A louder horn blasted.

He sat up just in time to see a semitruck bearing down on them. She swerved hard to the right, returning to her own lane, missing the big rig by mere feet.

Suddenly he was wide awake. "What's going on!"

"You're all right?"

"For now! Slow down! *Slow down!*"

"You don't need a hospital?"

"I'm fine, I'm—" he braced himself as she shot through a red light bringing on a new set of blaring horns—"fine!"

Obviously relieved, she hit the brakes. They slowed and a moment later she swerved into a bus-only zone to park. Forgetting to use the clutch, she fought the car as it bucked three or four times before dying ... one wheel on top of the curb.

They sat in silence, Luke staring directly at Tahquitz Peak, which rose over the buildings before them.

Finally, he turned to her and asked, "First time with a stick shift?"

"Not really."

He nodded, unsure how to respond.

"It's one of the casino's cars. I borrow whatever I can without getting caught."

"Getting caught?"

"They frown on letting you drive without a license."

"You don't have a—"

"Not yet. But as soon as the probation time between tests is over, I'll get it. Third time's the charm, they say."

Once again Luke nodded.

"Talk about giving people a heart attack. I thought you'd died or something."

"Yeah," Luke said, feeling the throbbing in his head and beginning to rub his temple. "Me too."

"So what'd you see?"

"What?"

"With the goggles?"

"Light, mostly."

"But you've always seen light."

"No, this was way more intense. It had ..." He dropped off, unsure how to explain.

"It had what?"

"I don't know, like a personality to it."

"A personality?"

"Yeah, kinda like when we were up in Washington—when we saw God and everything."

"You saw ... God?"

"Yeah, sorta." He tried his best to sound nonchalant as he looked for the goggles.

"You saw God?"

He nodded. "Sure. What'd you do with the goggles?"

She stared at him a moment, then motioned behind her seat. "Back there."

He reached for them until she stopped him. "No way."

"What?"

"They just about killed you, that's what. And now you're gonna slip them on and do it all over again?"

It was true. They'd knocked him for a loop, and suddenly he couldn't wait to put them back on. What was he thinking?

He turned back to her. "What exactly did you do to them?"

"I changed their frequency a little."

"Meaning?"

"You probably didn't see exactly what they were meant to see. And, of course, I gave them more power."

"That's for sure."

"By the looks of it, too much."

"Maybe ...," he said.

She turned to him.

He continued, thinking it through. "I don't know if it was the goggles' fault. I mean, they just showed me what was out there." He frowned. "Maybe it's me, maybe I just gotta get used to them." Once again he reached toward the back.

This time she grabbed his arm. "No."

Her firmness surprised him.

"I don't care who's to blame, I'm not watching a rerun of what I saw."

"But if I—"

"No. Let me cut down the power. Add some filtering. At least till your system gets used to them."

Luke wanted to argue, but he knew she was right. As much as he wanted to continue, she was right.

"So when can you fix them?"

"Would you give it a rest for a minute?"

He said nothing, promising himself to try and be more cool.

"So you want me to take you back to the church?"

He shook his head. "Not really."

"How 'bout lunch. I'm starved."

"Lunch is good. Then maybe we can go back to your place and—"

"—fix the goggles," she finished with a sigh.

"If that's okay."

"Sure, why not." She reached down and turned on the ignition—this time remembering to put in the clutch.

Luke looked back out the windshield to the mountain. "People ever climb that thing?"

"What, Tahquitz Peak?" She struggled to find first gear. "Not often."

"Why not?"

"Long story." She found a gear and released the clutch. They shot backward until she hit the brakes, again killing the engine.

"Sorry."

She was obviously embarrassed, but equally as determined. With a little more effort, she got the right gear and they leaped forward ... jerking once, twice, before pulling into traffic.

five

The Land Rover hit a series of ruts, yanking the steering wheel from Pilar's hands. She gripped it tighter, vowing to concentrate harder. She flipped up the sun visor. No need to fight off the lowering sun now that she was deep in the shadows of the San Jacinto mountains. For nearly an hour she'd been negotiating switchbacks and peering over drop-offs as she continued toward one of the range's highest and most remote canyons.

She hated the place. It had been years since she'd been there, and despite the barren, rawboned beauty, she was more than a little edgy.

Earlier, she'd asked the security guys about the captured image of the blueprint. It had taken little effort for her to delete the building and concrete road and simply show them the topographical information. It had taken even less effort to get them to strut their computer machismo by overlaying various topographical maps of local regions until they found a match.

Tahquitz Peak. More specifically, Kiva Canyon.

It was the last place she wanted to visit, but apparently she had little choice in the matter.

Kiva wasn't a large canyon—about a thousand yards in length and a fraction of that in width. *Kiva* was the Cahuilla word for their underground ceremonial centers. And, although it was known by some of the locals and all of the Cahuilla, the kidney-bruising ride on a dirt and boulder road (if you could call it a road) made the place anything but popular.

A few years back it had been a favorite with the spring-break crowd—those looking for privacy to carry out their drinking and debaucheries. But times, they do change. Now, since such gatherings were openly broadcast on cable, there was little reason to hide the activities in such difficult and remote locations.

Of course the canyon was still occasionally visited by teens out to prove they weren't afraid of its legends. But, other than that, the place was pretty much left alone.

And just as well.

It's not that Pilar was superstitious, but the stories drilled into her head since she was a little girl had definitely taken their toll. Stories of a dark, powerful entity who roamed the area, torturing and devouring any soul unfortunate enough to wander into its domain. A sinister creature of shadows whose insatiable hunger for power and sex drove it into the villages at night to seduce and steal young maidens, dragging them away into its lair, where it would ravish and devour them ... one beautiful limb at a time.

The stories persisted to this day, in one form or another—often with a wink when an item would disappear from someone's backyard, or the shake of a head when some chaste and pious young thing stopped being so chaste and pious.

"Just ol' Tahquitz doing his work," the older ones agreed.

But the work was a little more horrific in the fall of '88 when the corpses of five beheaded teens were discovered.

More gruesome yet was that each of their skulls had been smashed against a famous granite wall—the very wall to which legend claimed the Cahuilla, a peace-loving people, once brought their prisoners of war for a similar fate. A fate that—

The impact jolted Pilar from her thoughts. She cried out, instinctively hitting the brakes and the truck slid to a stop. She spun to the windows, then the mirrors. She caught movement in the passenger mirror. A dwarf scrub pine was shaking.

She leaned closer and peered.

The branches nearest the ground were moving. An animal. She must have hit an animal.

Taking a breath for resolve, then another, she reached for her door and opened it. The alarm chimed, reminding her the keys were still in the ignition. She climbed onto the door ledge and called over the roof.

"Hello? Anybody there?"

No answer but the chiming.

She hesitated, then stepped down. Leaving the door open, just in case, she crossed around to the front of the truck—checking the fenders, the bumper, looking for any sign of impact.

Nothing.

She glanced back to the pine. It was still moving. Probably just the wind, or *ya-ee* as her people called it—the breeze that often kicks up at the end of the day.

She shook back her hair, took another breath, and started toward it.

There was no sound but the crunch of gravel under her feet and the chime of the alarm that grew more distant.

"Hello?"

To her left was a drop-off of white granite—so steep that the tops of the highest pines were nearly eye level.

Another gust of wind blew grit into her eyes. She squinted, trying to blink it out. The tree, more like a large bush, was a dozen feet away. And still moving.

She looked to the ground where dirt near her tire tracks had been disturbed. There were scattered drops of blackness. She stooped down, stretched out her fingers. The blackness felt damp. She raised her hand for a better look. Smelled her fingertips. It was blood, just as she suspected.

She rose, more cautious. If she'd injured an animal, every instinct told her to back off, give it space. No telling what it could do in its pain and rage.

She slowed but continued forward. She wasn't sure why. Maybe it was in anger over her fear. She refused to be intimidated, especially by this place.

She heard a sound. Something guttural.

At five feet away she saw the shadow.

She slowed to a creep but continued. She heard it again. A growl.

With every sense alive, ready to leap back, she reached to the nearest branch. It was just on the other side. Watching, crouching.

She inched the branch to the side. Gently, gent—

It lunged at her, fangs snapping, bloody snout snarling.

She screamed and lurched back.

It quickly withdrew, darting down the slope, glimpses of moth-eaten fur, bony legs, ribs. A coyote—its face black-red with blood.

And then it was gone.

Pilar stood a moment. Breathing hard. Letting the adrenalin wash through her body. Bad luck hitting coyotes. They were the clever ones, the sly ones. The ones that legend claimed had outwitted the lesser gods—and even *Mukat* himself.

Having finally shaken it off, she turned and started for the Land Rover.

The shadows had grown. It was getting late. And the sooner she saw whatever it was she was supposed to see, the sooner she could leave.

Being in Kiva Canyon at night was the last thing she wanted.

Because it wasn't just its legends or the ghoulish history of its wall that put her on edge. There was also the other matter.

The one of her rape.

aall right, here we go." Misty turned from her workbench and handed Luke the goggles. "Slip these on."

They'd been there most of the afternoon and now things were finally ready.

He pulled the elastic strap over his head. The room grew darker as he fit them into place.

"Here." She handed him the battery pack, bulky but possible to slip into his cargo pants. "The switch is there on the side."

He felt it and nodded.

"Ready?"

He took a breath, hesitated, then flipped it on.

The goggles buzzed slightly against his cheeks, then bright light filled his vision — though not as blinding as before. He was startled as the glowing figure, off to Misty's left, came into view. Much of its shape was undefined from the glare. What little he could make of it appeared almost human, though bigger. Nearly seven feet. As it turned to him, he felt the same presence, the same power that had drawn and frightened him earlier that morning at the church.

He spotted another, standing near the corner of the room. Just as big. Just as intimidating.

They seemed to know he was watching. But unlike the attacking darkness from the mountain or the Spirit Dancers, they appeared unconcerned.

"Well?"

He turned to Misty and gave a start. Initially he'd been unable to see them because of the other creatures' brightness. But, as he grew accustomed to the light, there was no missing the—well, he wasn't sure what they were. They floated at eye level on both sides of her, a couple feet in diameter, lumpy clouds—concentrations of dark, misty blackness.

He counted two, no, three of them. Unlike the glowing creatures, he felt no attraction toward these things. Only a chill.

"What is it? What's wrong?"

They sensed his watching and turned until he was staring into what could only be faces. Their wispy snouts melded into wide, hairless heads. He saw no ears but several bumps, like warts. And above the snouts, on either side, black recesses that could only be eyes. In many ways they reminded him of ... frogs.

Or gargoyles.

"Luke?"

They drifted toward him. He caught glimpses of their mouths, lips curled back to reveal teeth—no, longer than teeth. Fangs.

Another floated up and over her shoulder, turning to face her. Spindly arms appeared, reaching out to her face, drawing closer.

Luke stood speechless.

"What?" she demanded.

It opened its mouth—as if preparing to bite her.

He had no time to explain. He grabbed her hand. The creature lunged at him and swiped at him with tiny hands, long, skinny fingers. For the briefest moment, Luke thought he saw talons. He flinched but felt nothing as they passed through his arm.

"Come on!" He yanked her off the stool and toward the door.

"What are you doing? Luke!"

They raced through the doorway and into the living room.

"What are you—"

They arrived at the front door and he threw it open. They entered the hall and started to run. It was much darker than the room. Apparently, he'd left the bigger creatures of light behind. He hoped the same was true with the others.

"What's going on?"

"They're all around! We've got to get away!"

"Away from what?"

They arrived at the elevator and he hit the button. He turned just in time to see the dark mists enter the hallway. But not through the door.

They came through the wall.

He spun back and hit the button again. "Come on!" And again. "Come on, come on!"

"What's going on? What do you see?"

He glanced over his shoulder. The creatures glided down the hall toward them. Twenty feet away. Snarling.

The elevator *dinged*. He spun around as the doors opened. Tightening his grip, he dragged her inside.

"Luke!"

He turned, saw they were ten feet away, coming directly at him. He punched the close button. Over and over.

Eight feet.

The doors began shutting—

Five feet.

—and finally closed.

He blew out a breath of relief ... until the things passed through the doors and entered the elevator.

He shrank back to the wall, pulling Misty with him.

"What do you see?"

The elevator began to drop. As it did, the creatures disappeared through the roof, snarling in protest.

But as the car approached the next level, others appeared through the floor. Sometimes only their warty backs or faces slid up through the walls and doors—sometimes he saw entire hunched bodies. They didn't all look the same, but they were definitely related.

One rose through the back of the elevator, so close that part of it actually passed through Luke.

But instead of cold or fear, he suddenly felt desire. Urgent. Demanding. It was as if every nerve in his body wanted Misty and wanted her now. It was so powerful he literally gasped ... until it passed through and disappeared up and out of the roof ... as the elevator continued to descend.

Another with a flattened face appeared, also rising through him, bringing with it a hunger he could not explain—a desire to control, to take charge at any cost ... until it passed and vanished through the ceiling.

The same was true as they continued to the next floor, and the next—the misty forms floating through him, bringing desire, exhilaration ... and terror.

Luke pressed as far back into the corner as possible, shivering. Only then did he notice Misty reaching out and touching his face.

He was drenched in sweat.

"What do you see? Tell me, what—"

The doors opened onto the casino's main lobby. The air was literally black with the vaporous creatures. And they were all turning toward him, leering, snarling.

"Shut the doors!" he cried. "Shut—"

Misty hit the basement button and the doors closed—partial torsos and faces appearing, then slipping up and through the roof.

"Take them off!" Misty shouted.

He barely heard over his gasping. "Wha—"

She reached for the goggles. "Take them—"

"No!" He pushed her away.

"Luke!"

The doors opened again. This time to the service entrance. More creatures, though not as many, turned to face him. And block him.

They moved forward.

"My God!" Luke wasn't sure if his cry was a prayer or an oath. Whatever it was, one of the light creatures from upstairs suddenly appeared beside him. It raised its arm—a swift, sweeping motion. With it came a blazing pulse of light, so powerful it threw the snarling vapors against either wall, creating an unobstructed path.

Luke needed no second invitation. He grabbed Misty's hand and started running.

If you'd just speak to him, let him know he's not alone." Virgil paced the threadbare carpet in his living room, the phone to his ear. "He's not alone, Mrs. Lawton. We're all in this together."

"Is that why nobody's talking to him, why no one's returning his calls?"

"He's not called me."

There was a moment's silence.

"Mrs. Lawton?"

"You know how he feels about your ... differences. About your theology."

Virgil's back stiffened. "And still he refuses to humble himself. Even now his religious pride forces his own wife to make the—"

"He doesn't know I've called."

Virgil sadly shook his head, allowing his silence to speak for itself.

"He was set up," she blurted.

Virgil's response was gentle but measured. "No. Nobody stood half naked in front of that woman but him. Nobody fondled and kissed her but—"

"He's repented!" Emotion filled her voice. "You should see him, Pastor. He's so torn up and broken ..."

Virgil turned and stared out the window toward the mountain. Night was coming fast. "Mrs. Lawton?"

"Please ..." She sniffed, regaining her composure. "Call me Beth."

"There's a difference between repenting 'cause you're serious 'bout your sin, and repenting just 'cause you got caught."

"Please ..."

"I know it's tough. Perhaps if he were to call me himself—"

"No."

"Perhaps I might be able to—"

"No, no!"

"If he were to humble himself, if he were to—"

"He won't do that and you know it!" She sniffed again.

Virgil shook his head over her husband's arrogance. "Then maybe you would like my wife to visit you. Perhaps she can offer you some comfort, woman to woman."

"I'm not the one dying here!"

He nodded, quietly adding, "Nor are you the one full of sin and pride."

He turned to see Fiona enter the room with her evening tea. "Is it Luke?" she asked.

He shook his head. "Turn him to the Scriptures, Mrs. Lawton."

"Travis's wife?" Fiona asked. She reached for the phone. "Here, let me—"

He frowned, turning away from her. "Have him seek the Holy Spirit for the power to—"

"Virgil—"

"—humble himself and admit his—"

There was a soft click.

"Hello?"

No answer.

"Mrs. Lawton?"

Fiona's hand was on her hip. "Now what did you do?"

"Nothing," he said defensively. "Nothing at all."

Is this far enough?"

Luke scanned the night from Misty's speeding car. As best as he could tell there were no more of those black, vaporous things. Not here in the desert.

There were, however, the same two bright creatures of light he had seen in her room. At least he thought they were the same—their glare was so intense it was impossible to tell for sure. The fleeting glimpses he caught of their expressions were also similar. Mildly interested but not terribly concerned. They floated along on opposite sides of the car. One, fifteen, maybe twenty feet from Luke's side, the other the same distance from Misty's. It made no difference how fast or how slow she drove, they remained the exact same distance, unaffected, perhaps even oblivious to her speed.

"I think we're okay now." Luke nodded. "Yeah, we're all right."

"It's about time."

Misty slowed the car and pulled it off to the side of the road. It jerked to a stop and died before she remembered the clutch.

They both leaned back into their seats, catching their breath.

Finally Misty turned to him. "Now will you take off those stupid things?"

He closed his eyes and rubbed his temples. His head throbbed worse than ever.

"Luke?"

"No, not yet."

She sighed in exasperation. "Why not?"

He didn't have a good answer. Common sense told him enough was enough. He only aggravated the creatures when he saw them.

But there was something else.

A desire to know more. A hunger to look where no one had ever looked before.

Then there was the mountain rising behind them. He knew it was there. But between the buildings that had blocked his view, and the fear and panic, he'd found an excuse not to look.

Until now. Until they were out here, clear and open.

He reached for the door.

"What are you doing?"

"Just stretching my legs."

Frustrated, she dropped her head back into the seat. Then she leaned forward and turned on the radio. The station was classical, which she immediately dumped in search of something she could stomach.

Outside, the light creatures remained stationary, standing or maybe floating just above the ground. They dimmed for a moment. Then grew brighter. Then dimmed again.

"That's weird."

"What?"

He touched the goggles. "Could these be shorting out or something?"

"I doubt it."

Again the creatures grew brighter, then dimmed.

"Well, there's something wrong."

"Probably just the batteries. They're only good for an hour or so."

"Do you have more?"

"Not here. But I can wire some in parallel. Soon as we go back, I can—" She'd found a station, urban rap, and cranked it up.

"What?" he yelled.

She shouted something which he couldn't quite hear.

He dropped his head down to the open window. "What did you—" And then he froze.

Just above the dashboard a darkness had formed. Not really a darkness, but a void. And from that void a small black vapor appeared. And then another. And another. Miniature versions of what they'd just escaped from—no bigger than his fist, but definitely similar.

The void or hole reminded him of the opening above the porn shop. An entrance or exit. Only in this case everything was exiting from the darkness and entering the car.

Entering ... and drifting toward Misty. Approaching her shoulders, her neck, her face. She seemed oblivious to them as she closed her eyes, losing herself to the music.

Yet they were all around her and drawing closer.

"Turn it off!" he yelled.

She didn't respond.

"Turn it—" He reached through the window and snapped off the radio.

Instantly, the black hole disappeared. And the creatures with it.

Misty's eyes flashed. "What did you do that for?"

"The things, from the radio, they were—"

The car exploded in light.

And then again.

Luke pulled out his head and spun to the light creatures.

They had moved behind the car. Not only had they moved, but they had stretched out their hands, allowing torrents of light to stream down from their arms like sheets of sparkling water.

They disappeared, then reappeared, just as a wavering puff of blackness slammed into one of the sheets and exploded into blinding brilliance.

And then another.

Luke stared, dumbfounded. The creatures had formed a type of shield, a barrier to protect the car. To protect *them*. But from what?

The images disappeared, longer this time, then reappeared.

Another impact of darkness, another flash of light.

This time Luke was able to track the source. It came from the cloud surrounding the mountain peak. But it was more than a cloud.

It was difficult to see in the night, but just as a creature of blazing light had surrounded the church earlier that day, so a form of blackness surrounded the mountain. Its outline was vague, but it looked like some sort of lizard, though with a longer neck. A neck that arched and lunged forward, exhaling another cloud of blackness.

Luke saw it coming toward them. Black and translucent, wavering and distorting what images he could see through it. He braced himself for the impact, but it never came as the goggles sputtered one last time, then died.

The night had returned to normal. Silent. Peaceful.

Though Luke knew, at least for himself, that it would never be that way again.

The twelve-foot chain-link fence was new. And more than a little suspicious. It was still under construction, which explained why the gate had not yet been put in place—and why Pilar felt little guilt in easing her vehicle through the opening. However, she did have the foresight to turn off her lights before cresting the final ridge that led down into the canyon.

If there was somebody down there, they didn't need to know she was up here.

Along with the night came a thick overcast of clouds—no moon, no stars—which made the place far darker than she wanted. At best, she could only see the black shadows of weathered pines against lesser darkness of granite rock ... until the lights suddenly came into view from the buildings below.

Carefully, she eased the Land Rover back out of sight. As an added precaution, she drove off the path to a flattened area beside the fence, behind a group of boulders, in case someone should be leaving.

She climbed out, gently shut the door, and made her way across the loose, sloping rocks. She watched carefully lest she stumble upon any rattlers who hadn't returned to their holes from their afternoon sunning. The big ones weren't a problem. It was the babies, recently born this spring, who hadn't developed rattles or the common sense to be predictable, that concerned her.

As an only child, she had learned much from her father about life in the desert and mountains. It was part of their ancestry, their life. In fact, by fifth grade, there wasn't a plant or animal she couldn't name.

Then came puberty. And with it, embarrassment over her parents, her culture, over everything she was. By the time she entered high school she'd managed to shirk most of her ancestry. And by the time she was a senior, she was running with the richest and fastest white kids in town—including a relationship with the student body president and all-around heartthrob, Matthew Morrison. A relationship consummated and concluded less than a hundred yards below her.

With heart pounding, she climbed up and over the final outcropping of granite as the lights came back into view. Now she stood directly above the sheer bluff of the 230-foot Smashing Wall. This is where the Cahuilla enemies, as well as others, had met their fate. And, just below, at its base was ...

She took a cleansing breath. Memories welled up so quickly that she could barely push them aside.

Beyond the base was what looked like the building from the blueprint. It was a single-story rectangle, seventy-five feet long and half that wide. She could make out no distinguishing features — except for the camouflage pattern painted on its sides ... and the dirt, brush, and boulders that were scattered across its roof.

Attached to it was another building like a giant garage or work area. Through the large open door, she saw a tanker truck.

Directly beside the structures was a parking lot, where she counted two vans and a pickup.

She repositioned herself, searching for the long strip of concrete she had seen in the blueprint. But the heavy mist and darkness made it difficult to see much beyond the buildings and light.

She thought of climbing down beside the wall, where it was less steep and easier, but decided against it. She was strong but not that strong.

The road which snaked down into the canyon was an equally poor choice, since it would take forever to get there by foot, and there was always the possibility of surveillance cameras.

Besides, what did it matter? The point is she now had proof. Something more than a blueprint to shove into Bianco's face.

She stood another minute, looking down, the wind whipping up the wall, blowing back her hair. Only then did she notice how heavily she was breathing.

She turned and started for the truck when three loud horn blasts filled the canyon.

She spun around but saw nothing.

Then she heard a low, quiet rumble, immediately followed by harsh scraping. She scowled, peering hard into the darkness. She thought she saw movement but couldn't be certain.

Suddenly, the canyon was filled with light.

She squinted against the brightness until her eyes adjusted, and she saw two rows of lights, about twenty feet apart.

They ran the entire length of the canyon floor.

We're coming up on three days now, and you two haven't so much as raised a hammer to the place."

"He helped us set up for worship this morning."

"Not exactly major renovation."

Luke lay in bed unable to sleep. Misty had dropped him off an hour ago, and now he remained unmoving, listening to the muffled voices of Virgil and Fiona as they faded in and out of the adjacent bedroom.

"I tell you, woman, I'm beginning to wonder."

"Wonder what?"

"Maybe I've made a mistake."

"That would be a first."

"Making a mistake?"

"Wondering if you did."

"Listen to me. I'm serious ..."

Again the voices faded, the couple obviously moving about, getting ready for bed.

Luke strained to hear, but it caused his head to throb even worse. And his eye ... it burned and itched beyond belief. Of course he was concerned that he might have redamaged the retina, but that was small potatoes compared to what he'd seen and experienced.

And what he hoped to see more of once Misty found some better batteries.

"Maybe the church repairs, maybe they weren't supposed to be physical."

"You're talking about this morning's prophecy?" Fiona asked.

"And the feeling in my gut, ever since he got off the bus."

"You felt it too? It didn't even dawn on me ..." Once again Fiona's voice faded.

Luke frowned, scooting closer to the wall.

"... this valley for God. Do you think *he* could be the one?"

"I don't know; we've certainly had our share of false hopes in the past."

"Thirty-three years, to be exact."

"But those glasses he has. What he saw at the Festival."

"And don't forget that crow."

"You think God might have sent him? That after all this time it's going to be ... a boy?"

" 'And a child shall lead them ...' "

There was more mumbling as Luke's heart began to pound, as he struggled to fit the pieces together.

Was it possible? What had the guy said in church? *"I have heard your prayers and have sent a deliverer ... here, among you this very day."*

And the way everybody had looked at him. It wasn't just because Luke was new. It was like they were expecting something. *"A feeling in my gut ever since he got off the bus."*

Expecting something from ... *him.*

Could it be? Did they really think he was someone special? Sent for some sort of mission?

He closed his eyes, the possibilities racing through his head. And the images, playing and replaying: black tentacles, misty clouds, frog faces ... turning on *him,* glaring at *him,* attacking *him.*

And giant creatures of light, protecting *him.*

As he lay there he felt an indefinable ... purpose. A swelling that filled his chest, flowed through his arms and down into his gut.

Something was happening. And whatever it was, it involved *him.* Revolved around *him.* That nagging sense of destiny he could never shake, the frustration of always being treated like a child. It was coming together now. Making more and more sense.

"I have heard your prayers and have sent a deliverer ... here, among you this very day."

This very day.

He knew there was no chance of sleep coming now. How could there be? Not with his head spinning with all the possibilities.

He heard the squeak of bedsprings, guessed the couple next door was snuggling in for the night.

"Good night, old woman."

"Good night, old coot."

Then there was nothing but silence.

Except for the thoughts that would chase and churn in his mind throughout the night.

part two

part two

interlude

momtakwit trembled, barely able to breathe for fear of the approaching Starmen. He struggled to hold his ground, but could not as they pressed in from above him and before him. With each backward and unsteady step he drew closer to the precipice of Smashing Wall.

He had taken the datura as he waited for the appearance of Tahquitz—chewed its bitter root and leaves, allowed its powers to course through his soul, to open his mind to the world of spirits. It was an honor allowed to only the few, the chosen.

And since his birth, that had been Momtakwit's desire ... to be chosen.

Now it was that very desire that was about to destroy him.

Instead of Tahquitz, the Starmen had appeared. Their seduction had been clever. As the drug took hold, they appeared around him—beautiful, blazing creatures of light that had beckoned and wooed him to break through Mukat's protective barrier—that translucent bubble protecting mortal from immortal. They assured him it was the only way to receive their promises of power and glory and honor.

But it had been a trick. Darkness disguised as light. A way to lure him into their presence. Vulnerable and exposed.

Yet they did not attack with sticks, or rocks, or spears. No, the weapons which drove Momtakwit to the precipice were his own thoughts. Memories of his own failures.

The dazzling creature to his left pounded him with accusations of past weaknesses. Memories of himself as a child and young man, cowardly acts now so vivid that he could only stagger under their weight.

Another, directly before him, screamed of his immorality. The times in his youth when he had been unfaithful to friends, to loved ones, even to great Mukat.

His left foot slipped. He'd reached the edge as yet a third creature, to his right, shrieked of his dishonesty, his deceptions, his half-truths. Dishonorable things that all Cahuilla despised. That he, himself, despised.

Rocks under his heels gave way. He lunged forward, fighting for balance as the assault continued—accusations striking his soul, his very spirit.

Desperately, he cried out to Mukat. Cahuilla legend claimed that Creator had given up his very life for such failures, for the times of weakness when men chose to follow their own song instead of his.

But Mukat did not appear.

And Tahquitz's warriors attacked with a final fury, illuminating his repulsive pride, revealing the soiling of everything he touched, everything he loved, everything he was.

Finally, the great shaman lost his balance. He tumbled backward, plummeting from the top of Smashing Wall. Falling, falling, falling . . .

six

the elevator *dinged* and the doors opened. The chief of police, Greg Wallace, and a prostitute stood halfway down the hall. Pilar cursed softly as she stepped out to join them. It had been a long, ragged night. They'd busted some college card counters at the blackjack table, thrown out an entire party of disorderly drunks from the Sacagawea room, nabbed a pickpocket, and arrested a married couple selling crystal meth right in the lobby.

And now this.

What a night. Actually the past several nights had been no better. It was like the whole place had gone a little bit crazy.

Then, of course, there was what she had seen in the canyon. She'd deal with that and be in Bianco's face just as soon as he showed up in his office.

"Pilar, good to see you, darlin'."

She nodded to Chief Wallace, an overfed cop right out of *The Simpsons*. The only thing missing were the doughnuts.

Beside him, slouched against the wall, was Pepper, or Sage, or whatever her name was these days—a hooker Pilar had thrown out more times than she could count. But, as with all the call girls in town, if a patron met them off-site and brought them into his room, there was little she could do.

The chief continued, "You know Cinnamon?"

The hooker looked up, her left eye swollen, already blackening. The abrasions on her face had started to scab.

"Sorry I'm late," Pilar said as she joined them. "Had a few other fires to put out. He still in there?"

The chief nodded and Pilar started toward the open door until he stopped her. "They're not done yet. Should be a few more minutes."

She turned back to the hooker. "What exactly happened?"

The chief answered, "Manslaughter or self-defense, take your pick."

"The puke tried to kill me," Cinnamon muttered through a swollen lip. "I put up a fight and he just keeled over."

"Heart attack?"

Wallace shrugged. "Most likely."

A voice called from inside. "Chief, can you come here a minute?"

He turned and entered the room, speaking to them over his shoulder. "Now you girls don't go anywhere."

Pilar leaned against the doorway and addressed the woman. "Busy night?"

Cinnamon mused, "Busy week."

"What do you mean?"

"The past five or six days business has nearly tripled."

"Really?"

"Not just for me. For everybody."

Pilar nodded. "I'm seeing it too. Wonder why that is?"

"Who knows. Something in the air. Some of the girls are getting jumpy. Not me. I say make hay while the sun shines."

Pilar did not respond.

"You see me on the news last night? With the preacher guy?"

"That was you?"

The woman tried to smile but winced at her cut lip. "I hear they've run it a half dozen times." Musing, she added,

"Wonder your boss doesn't want a percentage for all the publicity it's gotten me."

"Bianco? What's he got to do with it?"

She scoffed at the question. "He footed the bill."

"Bianco was behind that?"

"Sure."

"Cinnamon," the chief called from the room. "Will you come in here a minute?"

But Pilar barely heard, her mind already racing. She knew Bianco could play hardball, but this?

"Listen," the hooker coughed. "Sorry 'bout, you know ..."

Coming to, Pilar looked up. "What—don't worry, it happens."

"Cinnamon?"

"Yeah," the woman sighed wearily as she turned and entered the room. "It happens."

a Bible, you brought a Bible?"

"Well, yeah."

"Whatever." Misty hunched back over the workbench making last-minute adjustments. They'd been in her room almost an hour, ever since Fiona had dropped him off after breakfast.

"No, listen, this is what Virgil was telling me." He had flipped open the pocket New Testament and started to read: " 'For our struggle is not against flesh and blood, but against the rulers, against the authorities, against the powers of this dark world and against the spiritual forces of evil in the heavenly realms.' "

"Meaning?"

" 'Spiritual forces,' " he repeated. " 'Heavenly realms.' This is the same sort of stuff I saw up in Washington."

She continued working, unimpressed. "Angels and demons."

"Yes, exactly."

"Wanting to destroy us."

"Or protect us." He didn't bother explaining that was one of the reasons he agreed to return to her place—the "protect us" part. Because, despite the attacks, the two beings of light were always there ... in her room, at the service entrance, standing behind the car. Granted, there had been a couple close calls, but neither he nor Misty had been hurt.

Then, of course, there was the other reason, the main reason ... his special calling. He would tell her, but only when the time was right, only when he thought she could handle it.

"Why?" she asked.

He looked back to her. "Why what?"

"Why do they want to destroy us? These frog faces you're talking about—they having a bad day? Wake up on the wrong side of the coffin? Or are they just bored and looking for something to do?"

Luke paused, thinking. "I don't know. Unless they just naturally, you know, hate God."

"But why attack us?"

"I'm not sure, but from what I experienced up in Washington, God's feelings for us are *real* intense."

"So?"

"So if they can't hurt God by attacking Him, maybe they can hurt Him by attacking something close to Him."

"Us?"

Luke shrugged.

"And those other guys, the big light fellows?"

"Not sure, but maybe they're for our protection. At least, mine."

"What does that mean?"

He started to answer then shook his head.

A bit irritated, she shoved the goggles at him. "Here."

The cable attached to them was split in two—one leading to a new battery pack, the other to a smaller unit.

"What's this other thing?"

"Try them on."

He slipped the strap over his head, adjusted the goggles, then reached for the battery pack and turned it on.

There was that slight buzz against his cheeks followed by the brilliant light.

He turned to see the same two glowing forms he'd seen at the back of the car last night.

"Your big buddies still here?" Misty asked.

"Yeah."

"What about the others?"

He turned away from the glare, allowing his eyes to adjust until, sure enough, hovering near Misty, he saw three dark floating clouds. They were a bit more defined than yesterday—amphibian faces, snarling lips, spindly arms. And they seemed a lot more agitated.

"Well?" Misty asked. "What about it?" There was no missing her sarcasm. "What about your 'spiritual forces of evil in heavenly realms.'"

Suddenly the creatures were thrown backward as if struck.

"Whoa!" Luke cried.

"What?"

"Say that again."

"Say what?"

"That Bible verse."

"What are you talking about?"

Not taking his eyes from the mists, Luke fumbled for the Bible. "This. Read this."

"What? Where?"

He found what she'd just quoted. "This."

Blowing the hair from her eyes and with definite attitude she read, "'For our struggle is not against flesh and blood, but against the rulers—'"

This time the creatures were flung harder, somersaulting all the way into the wall.

" '—against the authorities, against the powers of this dark world and—' "

"Sweet," Luke interrupted.

"What?"

Their mouths were open in what must have been screaming.

"They sure don't like that."

"What?" Misty repeated. "This verse?"

"Read something else."

"Where?"

"It doesn't matter. Anywhere."

The forms righted themselves and cautiously approached.

Misty scanned the page a moment, found something, and read, " 'Put on the full armor of God so that you can take your stand against the devil's schemes.' "

Once again they flew backward, slammed into the wall by an unseen power.

"Oh, baby," Luke chuckled. "You are doing some serious damage."

"Just reading words?"

"No. Those words. I completely forgot. 'The sword of the Spirit.' "

"The what?"

"That's what the Bible calls itself. There's something supernatural about those words. I saw it up in—"

"I know, I know, 'up in Washington.' "

The creatures pulled themselves together—even more angry and outraged. Only this time they kept their distance.

Luke continued watching as he explained, "Remember the story where Jesus was tempted by the devil in the wilderness?"

"I missed that one."

"When Jesus and the devil duked it out?"

"Sorry."

"It's not like they used swords or guns. I mean, they didn't try to nuke each other or anything."

"Your point ..."

"I'm saying that *that*—" he pointed to the Bible—"is what they used. The most powerful person in the universe and the most evil person in the universe chose the most powerful weapon in the universe."

Misty raised the book doubtfully. "This?"

"The sword of the Spirit."

"Interesting."

"Do it again."

"Later. I want to try something. Can you still see them?"

"Oh, yeah. Definitely not as frisky as before, but they're still here."

"Good. Now I'm going to turn this on, and I want you to tell me what happens."

"Whoa, turn what on?" He glanced down to see she was holding the other pack that was attached to the goggles. "What's that?"

"A Facial Recognition System."

"A what?"

"It's software the casino uses to recognize cheaters. It scans their faces and matches them to a database of other faces. If it recognizes them as a con busted from another casino, we throw them out."

"But what has that got to do—"

"We'll capture their features and start our own database. That way you can tell if they're the same ones who—"

"But there were hundreds of them—inside the casino, outside, along the—"

"Right, but you said some looked the same."

"From what little I could tell ..."

"So maybe they're like different races or species or something."

"How does that—"

"See those little crosshairs I scratched in the center?"

For the first time he noticed a large plus sign cut into the lens. "Oh, yeah."

"Line them up on one of your critters."

Luke picked the closest mist, five or six feet from them, and squinted. From what he could make out, it looked as if the thing had pointed ears and enough overbite to make any vampire jealous.

"Got it?"

"Yeah."

Misty reached to the newer pack and pushed a button. Immediately an image of the creature froze, though the original was still behind it, very much alive.

"You just took a picture."

"Sort of—though unfortunately, you're still the only one who can see it. Now I'm going to move that image over to the right and drop it into a storage bin."

Luke watched the picture slide across the goggles until it disappeared off to the right.

"Now look for another."

He obeyed, picking out a second. Its face was rounder, puffier. "Got it."

She snapped the photo and slipped it off to the right.

"Any more there?"

"Yeah." Luke looked around the room. "There were three. But I don't know where—"

He turned to see that another had sneaked up behind them, within touching distance.

"Ah!"

"What?"

He stepped back and the thing drifted closer. He spun toward the light creatures who remained in the corner, unconcerned.

"The Bible!" Luke cried. "Read the Bible!"

"What! Where?"

"Anywhere!"

She reached for the book, fumbled to open it, and read: "'Uzziah the father of Jotham, Jotham the father of Ahaz, Ahaz the father of—'"

As before, the black vapor flew backward, slamming hard into the wall.

Luke took a breath, forcing himself to relax. And then another.

"Quit fooling around and line it up," Misty ordered.

Still unnerved, he dropped the crosshairs over the cloud as it finished righting itself and shook off the impact.

"Got it."

Misty took a third picture, again sliding it off to the right of the screen. This time, however, it flashed, superimposing itself over the first photo which reappeared.

"What did you do?" Luke asked. "It's blinking. The first one and the last are blinking over each other."

"Then we have a match. The features between them are close enough for a match."

Luke nodded, keeping a wary eye on all three of the creatures. "Well ..." He took another breath. "I guess that about does it."

"For this room."

"This room? What's left?"

She gave him a look.

He stiffened. "No. No way."

"No way, what?"

"Not down to the casino. You're not taking us into the casino."

"Of course not." She turned back to the workbench and began shutting things down. "Minors aren't allowed on the floor."

He relaxed but only slightly.

"No." Misty threw him a grin. "I've got some place even better."

can't believe you're still going!"

Pastor Travis Lawton glanced over to his wife at the other sink. She was seven months pregnant. In eight short weeks he would be a father. He watched as she pulled back her thick chestnut hair and began scrubbing her face. In many ways she was more beautiful now than the day they'd met back at Baylor.

And definitely stronger.

Not only had she learned to endure the nonsense of being a pastor's wife, but she'd endured him. His past. His infidelity.

And he never understood why.

"It's because I believe in you," she had said in the counseling that followed. "I know who you are — " she'd tapped his chest — "down there. I know the real Travis Lawton."

It didn't make any sense then and it didn't make any sense now. She had every right to leave him, had threatened a half dozen times. But she had stayed. Not out of codependency. Heaven forbid. Not this tougher-than-nails Texas lady. But because ... well, he just didn't have an answer.

He rinsed his razor and started working above his lip. "I have no other choice but to go," he answered.

"You don't even know if people will show."

"Oh, people will show all right ... just not the ones I want."

"We had six people in church yesterday, Travis. Six."

"They obviously don't have cable."

She blew out her breath in frustration.

He tried to explain. "The initiative is coming up in less than a month. If I back out now, if I don't show up, they will have won for good."

"They've already won. And if you weren't so bull-headed, so full of pride, you'd — "

"Pride?" He turned to her, not believing his ears. "*Pride*?"

She held his look.

"Do you honestly think I have one ounce of pride left? That I'm picketing the casino because I want to? I'm the joke of the valley, Beth. The very proof they want that all Christians are hypocrites." He returned to his shaving. "No, I'm going because it's the only way to stop them."

"You can wait a day or two."

"No."

"Till things are settled."

"Till what is settled?"

"Till we can prove it was a setup. That the casino—"

He turned to her. "Sweetheart ... all they did was provide the bait."

"No."

"I'm the one who took it."

She shook her head. "No, no—"

"I'm the guilty one."

"How can you say that?"

"Because it's true. God knows it breaks my heart and yours. But it's true."

Her eyes shone with moisture, but she did not back down. "You're a good person, Travis Lawton."

"No." He felt his own eyes starting to burn. "I'm a filthy sinner who has returned to his vomit."

"No! That was then, this is now! We've been too far down the road on this thing. We've taken precautions. We've built the right walls. We've beaten this thing, and it will stay beaten!"

He looked on, marveling at her strength, that incredible mixture of satin and steel.

She continued. "You did not bring this on. They found your weaknesses and used you."

"Yes, but—"

"And it's a weakness we've overcome. *Together*. We will not lose that, do you understand me? This was nothing more than a setup."

He glanced down, exhaustion once again settling in. "How many more times, Beth? How many more times do I let you down, do I let God down?"

"I didn't know Christ had a limit on grace. Isn't that what you tell the congregation? If you fall, fall toward the cross?"

"I've failed. I've failed you, I've failed—"

"Cut the self-pity. I'll put up with a lot, but not that!"

He swallowed.

"What happened was a malicious attack that we were unprepared for. It's the exception, not the rule. You're better than that. We both know it. You've been better than that for years."

He reached back to the razor. "Well, that's one in this town who believes it."

"It better be two."

He looked to her, her eyes still moist but chin jutted out in defiance. He had no choice but to nod—more out of respect than agreement.

She blotted her face with a towel. "Maybe if you had some support ... maybe you should call Pastor Virgil."

"Pastor Virgil? Now there's someone with *real* pride. Wouldn't he just love to tear into me with those holy-roller teeth of his."

"But you're both against the casino; you've been from the start. Maybe if he were to be there with—"

"Oh, he'd love to be there, all right. Especially if they need someone to pass out stones to the crowd."

"How can you say that?"

He nicked his face with the razor and winced. "I can say it because it's true." He rinsed his shaver and continued. "No, I'm going. I will be heckled and ridiculed and who knows what, but I'll be there."

"Because?" She looked to him, waiting for an answer.

"Because ... that's what God expects."

Luke and Misty sat so far backstage that it was impossible for the audience of the tiny nightclub to see them. It made no difference that it was 11:30 on a Monday morning (apparently there's no such thing as morning in casinos), Joe Popiski had started his first show. It was a stupid standup routine using bad impersonations of Richard Nixon, Sean Connery, and Edward Kennedy, with enough raunchy humor to embarrass even Luke.

But the routine wasn't the reason they were there.

Thirty minutes earlier they'd met the pudgy comedian at one of the tables and explained their situation.

"You want to spy on my audience with those things?" He had motioned to the goggles.

"Not really spy," Misty said. "Just sort of ... observe."

"Observe?" He turned to Luke. "Observe what?"

Misty explained, "It's more of a camera than anything else. Like night-vision goggles—only you can take pictures with them."

"That's cool." Popiski smiled at her over the rim of his Bloody Mary. "And you invented them?"

"Part of 'em." She smiled.

"Very cool." He grinned.

"Yeah." She grinned back.

Luke couldn't be sure which of the two was flirting more, the old fat man with too much cologne, or Misty. It was probably a tie. And that bugged him. A lot.

Still, it got them what they wanted. And now, as the comic launched into some tired old routine about men not closing toilet seats, Luke donned the goggles.

"You set?" Misty whispered as he adjusted them.

He nodded.

There was the faint click as she hit the switch, followed by the slight vibration. Suddenly his vision was filled with light. But not as bright as before. In fact, as he glanced around, he couldn't even spot its source.

Nowhere did he see the tall, translucent forms. Just their light.

And the darkness.

Plenty of darkness, particularly beyond the stage. Black, shimmering forms hovered over individual patrons as they sat at their tables. He guessed about half a dozen of the things were scattered throughout the audience of twenty people. (Joey wasn't much of a draw ... at least at 11:34 in the morning.) Many of the folks looked haggard, as if they'd been up all night. They probably had.

As before, when the goggles powered up, they drew the attention of the creatures—their vaporous heads turning toward him, snarling. From time to time he spotted pencil-thin wisps of darkness rising from them and disappearing up through the ceiling. He suspected they'd always been there but now, since he could make out more details, he saw them more clearly. And yet, despite the details, what still unnerved him the most was their rage and hatred.

Rage and hatred directed at *him*.

"See anything?" Misty whispered.

"Oh, yeah."

As he stared, the creatures' agitation quickly grew.

Again, he scanned the room, hoping for some sign of the light beings. Again, he saw nothing.

"You okay?"

He gave a nervous smile. "Yeah. Listen, maybe right now isn't such a good time. Maybe we should go and come back a little—"

"Go? We just got here. Come on, line one up."

He didn't know how to tell her that even great warriors know when to fight and when to run. And right now, without any backup—

"Come on."

"Misty ..."

"Come on, come on!" Her impatience was getting the better of him. "Quit fooling around and just do it!"

Finally, with a sigh, he agreed. "All right, but just one. Then we should—"

"Yeah, yeah. Get it in the crosshairs and let's take a picture."

He turned and focused on a round, dark cloud that reminded him a bit of Yoda from *Star Wars*. It floated just above a man with rumpled hair, watery eyes, and a growing collection of empty glasses.

"Got it," he whispered.

Misty pressed the button and the image froze over itself. It then slid off to the right and disappeared.

"Any match?"

He shook his head.

"Find another."

He looked around. Some of the creatures were drifting away from their hosts and starting toward the stage.

"Misty ..."

"Don't be such a wuss," she scorned. "One more."

Reluctantly, he found another, actually two perched above the shoulders of a young balding man and a younger lady, her blouse buttoned so low Luke wondered why she even bothered. It was obvious they couldn't get enough of each other—kissing, caressing, rubbing one another's legs. It was also obvious that the creatures, although aware of Luke's presence, shared in the couple's pleasure. In fact, they actually appeared to be growing in size, as if feeding upon that pleasure.

"You got something?"

He lined up the man's shadow first. "Yeah, take it."

He heard the click and saw the image freeze. It slid to the side and immediately began flashing as another appeared, superimposed under it—one that he'd seen in the room when he was alone with Misty.

"Match," he whispered.

Immediately he shifted the goggles to the woman's creature. "Again."

Misty obeyed. The image froze, then slipped off to the right until it appeared over the other two and began flashing.

"Bingo."

"Another one?"

"Yeah."

He looked up from the couple and quit breathing. He'd been so preoccupied that he hadn't noticed how many of the others had left their hosts and were drifting toward him.

And they didn't appear to be slowing.

He rose from the chair. "We gotta go."

"Luke."

"They're coming."

"Give 'em a verse," she argued. "Hold them off with one of your Bible verses."

They picked up speed, their mouths opening and closing ... as if gnashing their teeth.

"Misty—"

"Quote something."

They were twelve, ten feet away.

His mind raced. "I can't think of ... I don't—" Remembering the pocket New Testament, he pulled it from his pants and shoved it at her. "Here."

"Where?"

"Anywhere, just—"

The book slipped from their hands to the floor.

She reached down to pick it up.

The closest was eight feet away. Luke could clearly see its spine-covered body ... and its fangs.

He threw a glance to Popiski, who was oblivious to what was happening, then back to the creatures.

Their faces twisted and snarled. Some appeared to be shouting, though of course he heard nothing. He saw a few glancing upward and followed their gaze to yet another. It hovered beside a long pipe that held a heavy crimson curtain.

A pipe that suddenly broke free from its support chain and fell toward them!

"Look out!"

He reached to pull Misty away but was too late when, suddenly, the air beside them ripped apart. A shaft of light arced through the opening, striking Luke and Misty so hard it knocked them to the ground ... just as the curtain and bar crashed to the stage, missing them by inches.

The crowd gasped as Popiski spun around.

But Luke barely noticed. Scrambling to his feet, he grabbed Misty's hand and pulled her up, yelling, "Let's get out of here!"

They darted across the stage toward the exit.

Luke glanced over his shoulder. The things were moving faster. All of them.

Faster and directly for him.

He reached the door and threw it open only to see the casino before them with its thick mass of black vapors turning to face him.

"What do you see?" Misty shouted.

He spun back to the stage.

The others were closing in fast.

He turned back to the casino.

The mists were changing, coming together, forming a single dense cloud. Occasionally he caught glimpses of bulging eyes or protruding fangs within the cloud.

"The Bible," he yelled to Misty. "Read something!"

"It's back there!"

"What?"

"On the stage!"

He struggled to think through the panic. For the life of him, he couldn't remember a single piece of Scripture. He turned to her and shouted, "You know anything from the Bible?"

"Me? How would I—"

"Something! Anything!"

"I don't … uh … I …"

The massive cloud approached. Within seconds its darkness would envelop them.

"Jesus loves me!" she shouted.

"What?"

"Third grade, vacation Bible school!"

"I don't—"

She repeated, " 'Jesus loves me—' "

"That's not a—"

" '—this I know.' "

The cloud began to slow.

"Say it again!"

"It's not a verse, it's a song!" She tried singing, her voice thin and trembling, " *'Jesus loves me, this I know …'* "

The cloud continued slowing until it finally came to a stop … not four feet from their faces. It churned and boiled upon itself, but proceeded no farther.

"Keep singing!" he shouted.

"That's all I know!"

He threw in what he remembered, his singing even shakier than hers. " *"Cause the Bible tells me so!'* "

She nodded and repeated, " *"Cause the Bible tells me so!'* "

Ever so slowly, the cloud began to pull back … withdrawing. As if their voices were somehow pushing it.

"All right!" Luke shouted. He resumed singing. " *'Jesus loves me …'* " He took a tentative step forward. The cloud retreated more, slowly beginning to separate. " *'… this I know.'* "

The separation continued … six feet, then seven. Darkness roiled on either side, but a clear path was forming in front of them, less than a yard wide, but definitely a path.

He nodded to Misty, who again joined in, a little stronger, " *'… for the Bible tells me so.'* "

He took another step. The darkness continued retreating.

"Again!" he shouted. " '*Jesus loves me, this I know . . .*' "

And the more they sang, the farther the darkness receded, giving them more and more space to move forward.

"This is nuts!" she cried.

He nodded. " '*. . . for the Bible tells me so.*' "

"Everyone's looking at — "

" '*Jesus loves me, this I know* — ' Keep singing! Sing!"

Reluctantly, she obeyed " '*. . . for the Bible tells me so.*' "

The path continued separating in front of them . . . and closing behind them.

"Where's the nearest exit?" Luke shouted.

"Just ahead. A fire exit."

"Get us there! *Jesus loves me . . .*' "

She nodded and continued. " '*. . . this I know . . .*' Aren't there any other words to this thing?"

He shrugged. " '*. . . for the Bible tells me so.*' "

They arrived at the door. Luke pushed hard against it, tripping a fire alarm as they stepped out of the casino and into the bright noonday sun.

He glanced over his shoulder and saw the cloud sealing up behind them. Sealing up and closing in!

"Run!" he shouted.

"What?"

He grabbed her hand and pulled. *"Run!"*

Pilar was furious. "What do we need with a runway?"

"It's for airplanes. Comes in handy for taking off and landing." Bianco stepped from his restroom. "And if you would have asked me, instead of sneaking around, I'd have been happy to — "

"We don't need an airport," Pilar interrupted. "We've got the Palm Springs airport less than thirty miles—"

"Not big enough for the larger planes."

"Larger planes?"

"That's right."

"What about Ontario? LAX? What's wrong with our helicopter service?"

"Look, I'd love to stick around and spar, it's always such a pleasure, but our very important, non-VIPs are scheduled to be landing in ..." He checked his watch and swore. Looking to Tweedle Dee, he asked, "Got the limos prepared?"

"All set, Mr. Bianco."

He nodded and headed for his desk, Pilar on his heels. "That's what you built it for? For them?"

"Who?" He turned so abruptly she nearly ran into him. "Is my tie straight?"

Instinctively she reached out to adjust the knot, then caught herself. "Who? These ... invisible VIPs."

"Among others. Come on, is it straight?"

Reluctantly she fixed it.

"Thanks." He turned to grab his suit coat off the chair—his very expensive suit coat. With the usual pristine care, he slipped it on and turned to her. "Mind the store while Daddy's gone." He started for the door.

"What about the hooker?" she demanded.

"Ah, right, call girls." Bianco turned toward Tweedle Dumb. "Put in a call to the escort service. Make sure their best talent is available for the next seventy-two hours."

"Boss, you can't expect them to just stop working for three days."

"Put them on a retainer."

The big man nodded and reached into his suit pocket for his cell.

Bianco continued toward the door. Pilar remained right behind. "I'm not talking about them. I'm talking about the prostitute and the preacher. Saturday night. You set that up?"

"Yeah. A hospitality comp." He stepped into the hallway and started toward the elevators. "Gift from Casino Rancheria."

"But—" She stopped at the door. "Mr. Bianco?" He continued walking, accompanied on either side by his brute assistants. "Peter?"

He waved without turning and disappeared around the corner.

They'd barely taken off in another car from the casino, before Misty began grilling him. "What happened back there?"

He continued checking the sidewalks, the storefronts, anywhere the dark clouds could be hiding.

"Luke?"

He did not answer.

"Luke!"

From time to time he thought he spotted one, but couldn't be certain.

Instead, he was struck by the people ...

A group of children laughing, playing tag in a small park, completely clueless to the evil he'd just witnessed. An old man and woman, out for a stroll. Over on Misty's side, two young mothers were shopping, struggling to keep their toddlers under control. So much life here. All around him. So much goodness. And for reasons he could not explain, its innocence and beauty made the back of his throat ache.

"Okay, fine!" Angry at being ignored, Misty snapped on the radio. Nice and loud.

Once again the air above it parted and a dark hole appeared. From it blacker wisps floated. Smaller versions of what they'd left behind.

Luke lunged for the knob and shut it off.

She glared at him and reached for the radio when a blasting horn forced her to look up and swerve, missing a car in the intersection by less than a yard.

Luke adjusted his goggles. "Red lights usually mean stop."

"What went on back there?"

"I'm guessing a major battle. And by the looks of things, we actually won."

"What?"

He sat back in the seat, more than a little satisfied. Sure, he had plenty to learn and was plenty scared. But the bottom line? They stepped aside for him. They pulled back and separated for *him*. And if he had that type of authority, then maybe, somehow, it was time for him to exercise more.

"Do you see anything now?" she demanded.

He shrugged. "The usual."

"*The usual*? What's that supposed to mean! What about the singing? What was that about?"

He spotted a black cloud floating above the sidewalk to his right. It hovered over a homeless young man who was in a hot debate with himself. As with the other mists, a filament-thin stream rose up and away from it. Spotting the car, it turned toward Luke, baring its fangs, but it did not attack.

With rising confidence, Luke continued, "It was our worship."

"Worship?"

"We were singing to God. They hate it when we do that."

"It was some stupid kid's song."

"Doesn't matter, it was still worship. I should have remembered that from before."

"Before? Let me guess ..."

"Washington. I learned lots of important stuff up there. And it looks like I'm going to have to start using it."

He caught a glimpse of Misty shaking her head.

"What?"

"Never mind. Take those stupid things off. We're hitting the desert; you won't need them."

Luke scanned the area. "I need to see what's going on."

"They make you look like a dork."

"It's a small price for ..."

"For what?"

He did not answer.

"For what? What's that supposed to mean?"

"It means ..." He hesitated. Like it or not, it was time to explain. "It means that in church yesterday, before you showed up, there was this prophecy thing."

"Prophecy?"

"Yeah, some guy started saying all this stuff about me. Like how I was going to save the valley and everything."

"Pleeease ..."

"No, think about it. With all my past experience and with me being the only one who can see through these things, not to mention all that's been happening since I showed up ... don't you see a pattern?"

"I see you becoming stuck on yourself."

"I'm serious."

"So am I. You think you're hot stuff 'cause you're the only one who sees things that do or *do not* exist."

Luke started to argue, then stopped. Why bother. If she didn't get it, she didn't get it. At least for now. He looked out the back window to check on the mountain. The glare of the sun made it impossible to see anything. He rolled down the passenger window and stuck out his head.

Now he saw plenty.

"Stop the car!"

"What?"

"Stop the car! Stop!"

Misty pulled to the side and brought them to another jerking, engine-killing stop ... as Luke threw open the door and scampered out.

"What are you—"

He turned to the mountain and stared. The darkness surrounding the top had grown. It had lowered to cover nearly half the peak. And it seemed to be increasing before his very eyes—slowly, stretching farther and farther down its slopes.

The multiple sweeping arms he had seen earlier, the ones leading to and from the city, were also there. They still flowed in two directions—some toward the peak, some away from it. But it was the ones flowing up into the darkness that caught his attention. They were the ones that seemed to be feeding it. Just as the smaller mists inside the nightclub had grown from the people's hungers and lusts, so this cloud seemed to grow from the pencil-thin tributaries attached to those mists.

The people feeding the mists, the mists feeding the cloud.

But there was something else ...

At first Luke thought it was merely a thicker arm, a wider tributary. But, instead of leading to the city, it stretched up and into the air, where it suddenly stopped.

How odd. The thickest of all the flows feeding the darkness was attached to absolutely noth—

Wait a minute. That wasn't true. It was attached to something. A plane. A private jet was approaching the mountain. And the closer it drew, the more darkness it seemed to be pumping into the cloud.

Luke turned and headed back to the car. "The mountain!" he exclaimed. "Something's happening with the mountain!"

"Get in," Misty ordered with a heavy sigh.

"What, why?"

She motioned him inside.

"Are we going there?"

She shook her head. "Not me. I don't go near the place."

"Then what—"

"Get in the car, oh great one. I've got somebody for you to meet."

seven

blistering heat reflected off the tarmac as Peter Bianco extended his hand. "Senor Velasco."

"Mr. Bianco."

The man's grip was firm and steady. So was his gaze. He looked much younger than his voice. Part of it was the Armani suit, though Bianco guessed he spent an equal amount of resources on keeping his body in shape.

"How was your flight?"

Velasco turned, gazing up at the sky above the rim of the canyon. "So far ... uneventful."

Bianco laughed. "Exactly as it should be. We have the best uneventfulness money can buy."

The man turned back to him. "Yes, well, that is what we are here to find out, isn't it." His voice was steely, and Bianco realized the tone for the rest of their meetings had just been set.

"I assure you, Senor Velasco, you will not be disappointed."

Three others had exited from the Gulf Stream V. Two men and a woman, all in their thirties and dressed equally as expensive.

Without waiting, Velasco turned and started toward the limos.

Bianco followed, motioning to the ground attendant, who signaled the private jet toward the hangar. He said nothing more. If Velasco wanted cool, he'd have cool.

As they approached the limos and the chauffeurs opened the doors, two horn blasts cut through the air, echoing against the canyon walls.

Velasco slowed to a stop. Bianco continued around to the other side of the vehicle.

"What was that?"

Bianco turned. "Pardon me? Oh, that? Just the alarm."

"Alarm?"

"Of course." Bianco nodded back toward the runway.

Velasco followed his gaze.

A camouflaged tarp of painted rock, dirt, and vegetation appeared along the entire length of the landing strip. With a slight rumbling and scraping, it slowly slid across the surface until the runway was completely hidden.

Velasco removed his sunglasses. "That is ... remarkable."

"It's the same technique we use to cover our swimming pools. Though, perhaps, a bit more sophisticated."

Velasco turned to him.

"Although we can buy the silence of authorities, we can not blind the eyes of their satellites." With a shrug Bianco climbed into the limo. "It's simply another way to keep things uneventful."

Stunned into silence, Velasco turned back to the nonexistent runway.

If the man wanted cool, he would have cool.

misty sounded surprised. "You're saying those goggles are helping him see what your grandfather saw?"

Her wizened grandmother gave Luke a second, or was it a third, look-over. "Maybe I am, maybe I'm not. I only know he's right when he speaks of two *nukatem* ... good and evil."

"*Nukatem*?" Luke tried not to fidget under her gaze.

The grandma nodded. "Spirits around us. The first of all beings created by Mukat."

He glanced to Misty. "And Mukat is ..."

The old woman answered impatiently, "Creator of all things."

"Right." Luke pulled up a chair at the table beside her, doing his best to appear relaxed. "And this Tahquitz, or whatever you call him, he's also a nukatem?"

"The most powerful of all nukatem. He was the one who led their revolt against Mukat and killed him."

"Killed him?" Luke tried to scoff. It came out more of a squeak. "How do you kill God?"

"Precisely. That is why there are those who say He came back to life."

"And this ... Tahquitz?" He leaned back in his chair, still trying to appear at ease.

"He's the one my grandfather tracked into the mountains to battle. The one whose power he prophesied would be broken by another from my line."

Luke hesitated. There was that word again ... *prophecy*. He glanced to the goggles on his lap. "And that's what I'm seeing on the mountain, this Tahquitz guy?"

"That has been his home for centuries. Each nukatem has regions, areas that are under their control. That is his. That and much of our valley."

Luke tried to chuckle. "You sound like my pastor friend."

She turned, her milky cataracts holding his look. "In this matter Virgil is correct."

"You know him?"

"We have been friends for many years. And in this matter we agree."

Luke spotted a bowl of peanuts on the table between them. "And these nukatem things?"

"As you saw, there are good and there are evil. Many are loyal to Mukat and want to help protect us. Others are loyal to Tahquitz and wish only to destroy us."

"But why us?" Misty asked. "What have we done to them?"

The old lady tilted her head quizzically.

"We're just people," Misty explained. "Why don't they pick on cats or dogs or toads?"

"We are of Mukat's heart. His beloved. And if Tahquitz cannot harm Mukat, than he will try to inflict injury by destroying his beloved."

Luke nodded in satisfaction. Hadn't he explained that very thing to her just a few hours earlier? Maybe now she'd start giving him credit.

The old lady continued, "And if the evil nukatem cannot get past those whose duty it is to protect us, then they will try to attack from within."

"Within?" Luke asked. "Within what?"

She turned to him. "Within ourselves."

"I don't understand."

"They take the very gifts Mukat has given and twist them into curses—perverting them into hungers that can never be satisfied."

He thought back to the nightclub, the casino, what he'd felt as the things passed through him on the elevator. He tried to sound casual, but she definitely had his attention. "Such as?"

"Many, many things. Sex, greed, gluttony, gambling, alco—"

"Gambling?"

Her face crinkled into a smile. "I am afraid we Cahuilla have always enjoyed our gambling. Even as children."

"Like *Peon*." Misty grinned.

Luke turned to her. "Peon?"

"It's a game we played as kids, where you guess which bone is hidden under which pot."

The grandmother smiled. "Yes, child, like Peon."

"But Amma? Those things you mentioned—sex, greed, gambling, and all that?"

"Yes."

"Aren't those the same things people are blaming the casino for?"

"That and much more, you are correct."

Misty looked at her, thinking.

"And," Luke added, "they're the same things I've been seeing."

Amma turned back to him. He was pleased that he at least had *her* respect. "These things, their manifestations—you are certain they are what you are looking upon?" she asked.

"Sure. Not only have I seen them, but we just finished kicking some of their butts over at the casino. Isn't that right, Misty?"

The best he got from her was an eye roll.

The old woman motioned to the goggles. "And you both saw such things with those?"

"Actually," Luke corrected, "I'm the only one who can see them."

"Without *kikisulem* you saw them?"

"Oh sure, of course. Why not? What's, uh, Kiki-whatever?"

"A tea," Misty explained. "Made from the datura root. One of the most powerful hallucinogenics in the world. Our shamans used it to see into the spirit world."

Luke felt his heart beat just a little faster. "There's a drug that helps you do that?"

"Yes," the old woman said, "but it is most powerful. Not something for children to play with."

Luke stiffened. "Who said anything about children? And who said anything about playing?" He held her look as long as he could, before glancing away to the table, then to the bowl of peanuts.

She replied more quietly, "It is a most dangerous medicine."

"I'm sure it is ..." Then, looking back up, he added, "But if it could help someone who has been given special abilities ... to better use those abilities. If it could help someone who's been chosen, to better see what they're supposed to see ..."

The old woman reached out and touched his hand. "You will see what Mukat wishes you to see."

He frowned, not necessarily pleased with the answer.

"Remember, my young friend, there are evils far greater than what you have witnessed."

"Such as?"

"The evil that caused Tahquitz to revolt in the first place."

He reached into the bowl of peanuts, nonchalantly picking one out. "Which is?"

"I'm afraid that is something you must learn on your own."

He shrugged, popping the peanut into his mouth. It was bland with no husk or salt.

He heard Misty giggle and caught her glancing away.

"Do you like my peanuts?" the old woman asked.

He gave another shrug. "Yeah, they're okay."

"Please, have as many as you like."

"Thanks." He grabbed a handful and started tossing them into his mouth.

Misty giggled louder. He gave her a scowl, but it didn't seem to help.

"Yes, my young friend," the old woman repeated. "There are some things you must learn on your own."

hypocrite!"
"Go back to your whore!"

The stream of insults was constant as Travis Lawton paced the hot sidewalk.

Constant, and for the most part, warranted.

But still he continued to walk, back and forth in front of the casino, carrying a placard reading:

ILL-GOTTEN GAIN
EQUALS
ILL-GOTTEN PAIN

No one from the church had joined him. Not a soul. And he didn't blame them.

Beth was right, he was a fool. But he'd gone this far; there was no way he could back out now. Not for the people of the valley. Not for God.

"You call yourself a Christian?"

"Hypocrite!"

"Take the log out of your own eye!"

By the second hour he began keeping score of the most popular insults.

By the third he saw no need. *Hypocrite* won hands down.

And they weren't wrong.

It was interesting that during the entire morning only one person had offered the slightest word of encouragement. And it wasn't even a word. Just some homeless fellow in an ugly Hawaiian shirt and worn leather gloves who had offered him a sip of his Burger King soda.

"Uh, no thanks." Travis had smiled, wondering how many diseases were on the straw. He motioned to the water bottle by his backpack. "I'm good."

The man shrugged and shuffled off, slurping loudly through the straw.

It was just past noon when the reporter and cameraman arrived. The same reporter who had set him up in the church.

"Pastor Lawton!" he called. "Pastor Lawton!" He snaked through the crowd and arrived, shoving a microphone into his face. "How do you believe your actions have affected your support?"

Of course Travis had a thousand things to say—a thousand answers he'd run over and over in his mind. But he knew he'd only make things worse. Besides, it wasn't about him. It was about the casino. What it was doing to the community.

So, instead of answering, he merely shook his head and continued to walk.

The reporter pressed in. "Oh, come on, Pastor ..." The tone was condescending, an obvious attempt to goad him. "Surely you must have something to—"

That's when the reporter either tripped or was jostled from behind—it made no difference. The point is the mic, which was already too close, hit Travis's face, slamming his lip against his teeth.

Instinctively, Travis pushed it away.

The reporter, who'd been catching his balance, shoved the mic back at him.

Travis pushed it away. Harder.

The reporter countered until Travis, catching himself, turned away and stormed off.

"Pastor Lawton! Pastor Lawton!"

He continued walking, fuming—not over being struck, but at the realization that he'd once again given the reporter another sound bite.

Sound bite, nothing. With the right commentary and stop action, it could look like he'd provided him a major brawl.

Peter Bianco saw the confrontation coming before he could stop it.

Earlier he'd given considerable thought about which entrance to use. Velasco's privacy called for them to whisk him through the back service entrance with its stark concrete walls, laundry carts, and sterile fluorescent lights.

However, the need to impress Velasco demanded that they use the front entrance with its full-on glitz and glamour.

For better or worse, Bianco chose the front.

As a result, patrons were already craning their necks to see if they recognized the VIPs crawling out of the limos. Employees were already exchanging alarmed looks that they hadn't been notified. And, of course, Velasco was already growing furious.

But it didn't matter.

Bianco's private financiers had gone to great expense to ensure there would be equality in the partnership. And he wasn't about to hide the casino's high profile and power from the man just because he was a little shy.

It's not that he didn't respect his privacy. Peter Bianco was a second-generation casino boss. He understood the need more than most. With a father whose connections to the Mob allowed him to run one of the largest Las Vegas casinos in the sixties and early seventies, Bianco had seen far more back entrances than he could count. Publicity was good for singers and starlets. Not so good for men suspected of whacking their competitors.

Of course those days had come and gone. Thanks to the State Gaming Commission everything was legit and aboveboard. Now things were owned and run by the government and big financial empires. And if you couldn't trust the government and big financial empires, who could you trust?

He had just stepped around the limo to join Velasco when he spotted the scuffle—a news crew and a picketer.

No. It was the reporter ... and the preacher!

What was Travis Lawton doing showing his face now? Didn't he know he'd been beaten?

Apparently not. He'd just turned from the reporter and was angrily stalking away, when his eyes met Bianco's and widened. Before Bianco could react, the preacher, adrenalin still pumping, shouted at him, "Ill-gotten gain means ill-gotten pain!" The fool was quoting his own placard.

He came closer, eyes on fire. "Ill-gotten gain means ill-gotten pain!"

Instinctively, Bianco took Velasco's arm as Tweedle Dee and Tweedle Dumb appeared from nowhere, their bodies forming a protective wall of flesh. They moved up the red carpeted steps, passing under the giant stone-carved faces.

But the preacher wasn't finished. "You may be able to silence me, Bianco! With your tricks and your money! But you can not silence God!"

They reached the entrance.

"Do you hear me? You can not silence the Almighty!"

The doors whisked open and they were struck by the cold blast of air conditioning. The preacher's voice faded under the sound of voices, bubbling fountains, and slot machines.

As they walked across the crowded floor, Velasco leaned over and demanded, "Who was that man?"

"Who?"

Apparently he saw no need to repeat himself as they continued past the statues, flashing lights, and scantily clad hostesses.

"Oh, that. Just some kook. One of our friendly protestors."

"I am surprised you would allow such things."

"It's America." Bianco forced a chuckle. "Freedom of speech."

A well-endowed hostess passed. "Good afternoon, Mr. Bianco."

"Hey, Jody. How are you today?"

"I couldn't be better."

He gave her a wink. "I'll say."

She smiled and glided through the crowd.

Velasco remained on point. "Nothing is for free."

Bianco leaned closer. "How's that?"

"Everything has its price. Even a man's silence."

"I'm afraid not everyone can be bought."

"If he will not sell his silence, then perhaps he should be forced to donate it."

Bianco directed them toward the elevators off to their left. "Senor Velasco, I really don't—"

"Ours is an important relationship, Mr. Bianco. Nothing must jeopardize it. If you cannot assure the man's silence, I will be happy to provide those who can."

They arrived at the elevators and Bianco pressed the button. "No, of course, I'll handle it. If you consider him a problem, I will be happy to handle it."

Velasco nodded as the elevator arrived and its doors opened with a cheery *ding.*

S o you're telling me this stuff your great great whatever took, this datura, that people still use it today?"

Misty continued studying the text on the monitor before her. "Some, yeah. I got friends who mess with it. Pretty powerful stuff, though."

"Any chance of, you know, visiting them?"

"Who? My friends?" She glanced at him. "Why?"

He shifted beside her at the workbench and adjusted his goggles. "I don't know, maybe, so I could—"

She turned to him in surprise. "You want to try some?"

Luke swallowed. "It's not that I *want* to—but if it helped your grandma's granddad know what was coming down, and if I'm supposed to be part of the solution, then maybe I should—"

She turned back to the monitor. "Sorry. If you're going to be our valley's savior, you'll have to do it in a drug-free environment."

"But if it could help . . ."

"You heard what Amma said, it's not for kids. Now can we get back to work?"

Luke scowled. Why was she being so difficult? She saw the signs as clearly as he did—the prophecies, the goggles, the way her grandmother kept eyeing him.

"Now . . ." She motioned to the pocket New Testament he'd opened on the workbench. "What else do you got?"

He looked back down, adjusted his goggles, and read: " 'To the angel of the church in Ephesus write . . .' And then there's another one: 'To the angel of the church in Smyrna write . . .' And another: 'To the angel of the church in Pergamum write . . .' And another: 'To the angel of the church in Thyatira write . . .' And another—"

"Hang on, cowboy." Misty glanced from the Internet Bible she had up on the screen. "Where are you?"

"The last book in the Bible. Revelation. Jesus is dictating all these letters to the angels of these different churches."

"Meaning?"

"Meaning that it sounds like each church has its own angel. Just like what I saw outside Virgil's church."

Misty gave a vague nod.

He was grateful to see she finally agreed he had a point about something.

She turned back to the screen. "Okay, my turn. There's this guy, Daniel, in the Old Testament. And he prayed real hard and stuff."

"The guy from the lions' den."

"Whatever. Anyway, it looks like an angel appears to him too. Check it out." She began to read: " 'Do not be afraid, Daniel. Since the first day that you set your mind to gain understanding and to humble yourself before your God, your words were heard, and I have come in response to them.' "

"Cool."

"There's more. 'But the prince of the Persian kingdom resisted me twenty-one days. Then Michael, one of
the chief princes, came to help me, because I was detained
there with the king of Persia.'"

"'Prince of the Persian kingdom ...' So Virgil and your
grandmother are right, there really are territories and
stuff."

Misty nodded. "Could be. Not only that, but the first
angel, he had to call on this Michael dude to help him fight
it." She turned to Luke. "So there's battles and stuff too."

"That's what I've been trying to tell you."

"But the thing is, all that fighting, it started with this
Daniel guy. Just because he prayed."

Luke saw where she was going. "You're wondering if
we really have that much clout ... just by praying?"

"Or singing, or reading that thing." Misty motioned to
his New Testament.

Luke nodded, quietly adding, "Just like in Washington ..."

She gave a heavy sigh, and he knew it was best to
change subjects. He glanced down to another place he'd
marked. "Okay, I got something else."

"Shoot."

"This is Jesus talking, probably about kids. 'See that
you do not look down on one of these little ones. For I tell
you that their angels in heaven always see the face of my
Father in heaven.'"

"So if that's true," Misty said, "then we really do have
like our own personal angels?"

"Sure sounds like it."

"Do you ..." She glanced around the room. "Can you
still see them—the good guys, I mean?"

"Oh, yeah." He gave an authoritative nod. "There's one
over there at the window, and another one right beside
you."

Misty stiffened at the close proximity.

"Are they ..." She lowered her voice, why, Luke couldn't imagine. "Are they the same ones, you know, that were here before?"

"Hard telling ... they give off so much light and stuff." He tried his best to sound bored. "But, I suppose. Yeah, sure, why not."

She gave him a withering look before turning back to the monitor. He shrugged, figuring it was just jealousy.

But, as he suspected, curiosity soon got the better of her. She looked back up, then ever so tentatively reached out her hand, testing the air.

He watched in amusement.

"I think ..." She frowned. "I think I can feel something."

He couldn't help laughing. "Actually, you're reaching in the wrong direction."

"Are you sure?" Now she was trying to save face. "Because I could swear I—"

Suddenly she screamed, and they both jumped as the cat leaped up on the workbench.

"Balzac," she scolded. "Get down from here! Get down!" She gave him a push and he jumped to the ground with a complaining grunt.

She turned back to Luke. "So they're both here?"

"Yup."

"And those other ... dark thingies?"

Luke squinted against the light, looking to the far wall, the darker corners. As far as he could tell there wasn't a one in sight. "That's weird."

"What?"

"They've all left." He scanned the room again. Then, with even more confidence, concluded, "I guess we gave them the willies."

"We?"

"All right." He adjusted his goggles. "I guess *I* gave them the willies."

She gave him another look.

"What?"

She nodded to the Bible. "You don't suppose spending the last half hour reading that helped, do you?"

He shrugged. "Maybe, a little."

Misty shook her head. She was about to say something when her cell rang. It was the evil emperor's theme from *Star Wars*. She pulled the phone from her pants and answered with forced weariness, "What is it, Mother?"

A moment later she replied, "Nothing."

Then, with more frustration, she repeated, "We weren't doing anything." Cutting Luke a sly glance, she added, "Just sitting around having a Bible study."

She must have gotten the rise she wanted because she broke into a grin. "Chill, Mom, it's just the Bible."

Another moment, then: "What? Now? Okay, but I'm bringing him with."

Another pause. "*Mother.*" And then she hung up.

Removing the goggles and rubbing his eyes, Luke asked, "What's up?"

"We're going downstairs to the Surveillance Room." She rose from her stool and started for the door. "Mom wants me to run a program for her."

She was nearly out of the room before Luke asked, "So do you want me to come with?"

"Unless you're planning on staying and going through my underwear drawer."

"Don't be gross."

"Don't be stupid. C'mon."

He turned from the workbench and followed her into the living room. "And it's cool with your mom?"

She opened the front door. "Why would it be cool? She hates you."

from his office, Peter Bianco stared at the wall of monitors. He hit *replay* and watched the preacher confronting him from yet a different angle.

He glanced at his watch. He was scheduled to meet with Velasco in an hour. Plenty of time to come up with a plan.

"If you can not assure the man's silence, I will be happy to provide those who can."

He sighed heavily. The preacher was no threat. He'd already been beaten. But apparently Velasco disagreed. And with a multibillion-dollar venture on the line, Bianco had to listen.

Velasco would expect no less.

Neither would Bianco's investors.

He rewound the tape and watched again. How do you silence a man who will not be silenced ... without making him a martyr and strengthening his cause?

Bianco leaned back in his chair with another sigh. His eyes drifted across the monitors until they stopped at the Starlight Room.

Popiski was giving his third and final performance for the day. It would be evening soon, and the big names would be hitting the stages. In just a few minutes the comedian would be off work for the day.

Or would he?

Bianco glanced back to the tape of the shouting preacher. He froze the picture and turned back to Popiski ... an idea taking shape.

they were at the back console of the Surveillance Room.

Pilar stood impatiently behind Misty, who worked the keyboard. On one of the two screens before them was the image she'd pulled from a surveillance camera at the entrance of the casino—the best angle she had of Bianco's mystery guest.

The other monitor was running their Facial Recognition Software.

"And you've been through every database?" Misty asked, her fingers flying over the keys.

"All we subscribe to."

"Other casinos?"

"Check."

"National and international?"

"Check."

"Convicted felons?"

"Check."

"Stanford, MIT, all the—"

"Yes." She cut her off. "Every database we have access to."

The kid beside her broke in. "Hold it, wait a minute." His confidence had definitely swelled since their last meeting. "Why colleges?"

"Just the best ones," Misty explained without looking from the screen.

"Why?"

Pilar answered, "They send out card counters to cheat at the blackjack tables. By counting the cards and knowing what's been played, they increase their odds."

"People do that?"

"They *try* to do that. But we have the face of every student-body member from every suspected school."

The boy whistled softly.

"So tell me," Misty sighed, "how am I supposed to help if you've checked every database?"

Pilar recognized the tone. Knew it was a setup. She also knew there was nothing she could do about it. "I thought maybe you could check out some of the others—you know, the databases we don't have access to?"

"You want me to hack into other people's programs?" Here it came. "You want me to do something illegal? Mother, I'm surprised at you."

To avoid responding, she turned to the boy. He was holding those stupid goggles up to his face again. Scanning the dozens of monitors up on the front wall.

"I'd prefer you not use those in here."

"It's okay," Misty said. "He can't see anything on the monitors. No electronics. Everything has to be live."

"But do you really have to use them?"

"More like he can't stop."

"What exactly do you see again?" Pilar asked.

"Mostly angels, demons, that kind of stuff." The kid's feigned nonchalance about the goggles was as irritating as Misty's attitude. The only thing worse was when he turned and stared at *her* through them.

In spite of herself she shifted uneasily. "And you're the only one who can see through them."

He gave a single nod.

"How convenient."

Misty threw in her own sarcasm. "Sure comes in handy if you're our chosen Messiah though, doesn't it, cowboy."

"Our what?"

"Never mind. Here we go."

Pilar looked up to see another program running beside the image of Bianco's guest. Faces strobed faster than she could count. "What's this?"

"Homeland Security."

She caught her breath. "You hacked into a government facility?"

"Relax, I do it all the time."

The words gave her little comfort.

Several seconds passed and they continued to watch until the program finally came to a stop. Two words appeared at the bottom of the screen: *No Match*.

"Zip," Misty said.

"What does that mean?"

"It means your boy has never broken a law and isn't a threat to the US."

Pilar raked her hands through her hair. "I find that pretty hard to believe."

"You're telling me Mr. Bianco might actually associate with unsavory characters?"

"Spare me your irony." Pilar continued staring at the screens. "So that's it, there's no other place to look?"

"The mystery man has never done anything illegal inside the United States."

"And outside?"

"You didn't say anything about outside."

"Is there a way to check?"

"Mother, I can't sit here and go through every country."

"Right, but—"

With a sigh dripping in inconvenience, Misty began working the keys.

"Now what?"

"Hang on."

Pilar watched as more faces flashed on the adjacent screen.

"What is it, what did you log on to?"

Misty gave no answer.

"What about a disguise?" the kid beside her asked. "Couldn't he wear like a disguise?"

Pilar shook her head. "The software compares eyes, nose, and cheeks—areas difficult to disguise without surgery." She turned back to Misty. "Would you *please* tell me what you logged into."

"You don't want to know."

"Misty."

"Interpol."

"I've checked—"

"You checked their public information files, not their classified stuff."

"You're hacking into their—"

The pictures came to a stop.

"Bingo."

A gentleman with a mustache and sunglasses came into view.

Misty hit a few more keys. A dotted square appeared around the middle of the face. She rotated it until it was at the same angle as the image from the surveillance camera.

She hit another set of keys, removing the sunglasses and mustache.

Instantly, the image lit up.

One more flurry across the keys and a full-front view and profile of the man appeared upon the screen. Below it, the following data:

```
GENERAL INFORMATION
NAME: Gabriel Garcia Velasco
FORENAME: Not Available
SEX: Male
HOME: Bogotá, Colombia
BIRTHDATE: December 11, 1967
LANGUAGE SPOKEN: Spanish, Castilian
PHYSICAL DESCRIPTION
HEIGHT: 1.75 meter = 69 inches
WEIGHT: 72 kg = 159 pounds
COLOUR OF EYES: Dark Brown
COLOUR OF HAIR: Black
PERSONAL INFORMATION
WIFE: Maria Sanchez Velasco
BIRTHDATE: September 10, 1969
CHILDREN: Manuela. Born May 7, 1981
Octavia. Born September 23, 1983
RELIGIOUS AFFILIATION: Catholic
OCCUPATION: Agricultural Consultant
TERRORIST AFFILIATIONS: None
```

PRIOR CONVICTIONS: None
ASSETS: Undetermined
SUSPECTED CRIMINAL ACTIVITY
Possession of illegal firearms
Attempted murder
Murder
Second in command of Fuego Drug Cartel

eight

reporter Michael Fortenbra knocked on the bungalow door. He could still feel the heat of the day radiating from the door's planks and the stucco wall. The smell of Star Jasmine hung in the cooling air.

"Just a minute." Pastor Travis Lawton called from inside. There was no missing the preacher's Boston accent. The same one Fortenbra had heard earlier on the phone when the man had asked for the meeting.

To be honest, he was suspicious of Lawton wanting to talk. Particularly to him. Particularly here, at the guest bungalows on the far side of the casino complex. Then again, these were where all the celebs stayed who wanted their privacy.

And the preacher could, no doubt, stand for some privacy.

Nevertheless, Fortenbra had made certain his cameraman, who had been explicitly *not* invited, knew exactly where he was going. He'd also called Tanya, his wife, promising that the story had no more juice, and that he'd be home in time to celebrate their anniversary.

The bolt to the door unlatched, and as it opened he saw a man much heavier than the preacher. And older. He wore a dark suit and looked familiar, but Fortenbra couldn't place him.

"I'm sorry, I must have the wrong—"

"No, no, please—" the chubby man motioned to him—"please, come in."

"I was looking for—"

"Pastor Lawton, yes. Please."

Fortenbra didn't like the vibe he was getting.

Again the man motioned for him to come inside, and again he declined.

"Is he here?"

"Yes, come in and I will—"

That's when he noticed the sweat and shifting eyes.

"No, that's all right. Tell him I'll be waiting over by the pool."

"He's here. He's just—"

Fortenbra turned to leave. "That's okay. Tell him—"

"Mr. Fortenbra?"

He turned around just in time to see the faint muzzle flash of a handgun with silencer. The impact struck his chest, knocking him off balance. He felt no pain, not yet.

The second shot, into his face, ensured he never would.

don't you see the connection?" Luke demanded as they moved down the hall.

"Enlighten me."

"This Velasco jerk shows up at the same time Tahquitz, or whatever it is, is getting bigger and bigger—and everything around town is getting uglier and uglier."

"Uglier?" Misty asked.

"Isn't that what your mom said? That the past few days everything's been going crazy? And now suddenly I show up with these goggles and, and—"

"And all the answers."

"No, that's just it. I don't have the answers. Not yet. But with the extra help—"

"I'm not taking you to my friend."

"Misty." He adjusted his goggles. Despite the pain, they'd almost become a permanent fixture.

"I'm not your drug dealer."

"But if it would help me see. If it would help me understand more of what's going on and what I'm supposed to—"

"I can't believe you're asking this. You have any idea how scary that stuff is?"

"Not any scarier than these glasses."

She blew the hair out of her eyes as they rounded the corner and headed for the elevators.

He tried again. "Look, you'd be right by my side. It's not like anything could go wrong."

She remained silent. A sign, he hoped, that she might be weakening.

"It wouldn't have to be a lot. Just enough to take a peek. Just to see what's happening so I'll know how to help and do whatever I'm—"

She turned on him. "Will you stop with this Messiah thing!" Her voice cracked. "Just stop it, okay! It's not funny anymore!"

The emotion surprised him. Just when he figured she hated his guts, she pulled something like this. Girls, go figure. He paused, taking a moment to regroup, to find some way to make her see.

As they continued down the hall, he occasionally sidestepped a black cloud that appeared and disappeared through the walls. For the most part, the things seemed far more intent on what was going on inside the rooms than what was happening out.

He knew the two glowing creatures were around somewhere. He didn't always see them, but some part of their shimmering light was always present.

He reached under the goggles and wiped his right eye. It burned all the time now, often tearing up. He was doing it serious damage, no doubt, but it seemed a small price to pay. Because the more he saw, the more he wanted to see.

No. The more he *had* to see. For himself. For Misty. For all of Agua Rancheria.

His cell phone chirped. He pulled it from his pocket and saw Virgil and Fiona's number. He'd call back later. They'd been good about letting him have the day off, as long as he checked in from time to time. Of course he was feeling guilty that they'd still not done any work on the church. But what had Virgil said? *"Maybe his help wasn't supposed to be physical ..."*

The evidence had clearly stacked up.

Not far ahead, the elevator doors opened. An old guy in a crew cut emerged. On either side of him were two big guys.

But it was the shadow wrapped around the guy that made Luke catch his breath. It wasn't one of those small clouds with an amphibian face. No, this was an intense blackness that encompassed the entire man before it stretched back to his shoulders and up through the ceiling.

"Well, hello, Misty." The man gave a nod to Luke. "New boyfriend?"

"Yeah, right," she smirked.

They approached and slowed to a stop.

Now Luke could see more details within the blackness — wiry arms, long talons, fangs. And, yes, gargoyle faces with bulging eyes. Lots of them.

"Nice sunglasses, son." The man motioned toward the goggles. "Little early for Halloween though, isn't it?"

Luke tried to answer but couldn't find his voice.

As if sensing his fear, the shadows thickened.

"Or is it another one of Misty's inventions?"

Not only did they thicken, but they began stretching forward. Toward Luke.

He took a half step back.

Misty threw him a concerned look.

The shadows continued reaching. And with their approach came an icy coldness.

Luke took another step back, his heart beginning to pound. He gave an involuntary shudder. And then another, clueless over what to do ... until he remembered the song. He opened his mouth and took a breath. But his voice would not come. He coughed, clearing his throat. Finally the words came out, hoarse and raspy: " *'Jesus loves me, this I know ...'* "

The cloud's advance slowed.

"What's that, son?"

He coughed and sang louder, " *'For the Bible tells me so.'* "

The blackness came to a stop, roiling and boiling, less than a yard from his face.

Still singing, Luke reached out to Misty, trying to pull her back.

" *'Jesus loves me, this I know ...'* "

But she'd have none of it.

The man turned to her. "Just a suggestion, but your friend here might want to increase his medication a bit."

All three men laughed. The leader shook his head and began to pass as Luke pressed against the wall.

The shadows retreated as well, apparently also wanting to keep their distance.

But Misty wasn't finished. "You'd be the one to know, wouldn't you, Mr. Bianco."

She got no rise as he continued down the hall.

"About medication, I mean. You know ... *drugs.*"

The man slowed, then turned.

Alarmed, Luke resumed singing. Louder. " *'Jesus loves me, this I know ...'* "

"What do you mean?"

She held her ground.

"Is there something on your mind?"

Luke reached out to her arm. " *'For the Bible tells me so.'* "

She shook him off.

The man repeated, "Are you trying to say something?"

"*'Jesus loves me—'*"

"Why ask me?" she said. "Why don't you ask—"

Luke grabbed her arm, shouting, "*'—this I know...'*"

"Luke—" She tried to break free, but he held on, turning and directing her down the hall. "Let go of—"

"*'... for the Bible tells me so!'*"

"Misty?"

Luke didn't know if they were coming after them or not. He didn't bother to turn and see.

"*'Jesus loves me...'*"

"Let go of—"

"*'... this I know...'*"

They continued down the hall, faster.

"Misty?"

They continued. Not running, but not strolling, either.

ravis Lawton trudged across the church parking lot, rubbing the back of his neck. The pain had returned full force.

It had been another long day—the last two hours spent painting over the obscenities scrawled across the back of the church. Obscenities and, of course, the always favorite: *hypocrite.*

Oddly enough he didn't resent the word. It merely stated the obvious.

"Woe to you, teachers of the law and Pharisees, you hypocrites! You are like whitewashed tombs, which look beautiful on the outside but on the inside are full of dead men's bones and everything unclean."

That was him. Loving pastor, holy crusader, man of God ... on the outside. Filthy sinner, full of lust, pride, and who knew what, inside.

It had pretty much always been that way. Even as a teen. In fact, he often wondered if that's why he entered the ministry in the first place. To expunge his filthiness. To scrub himself clean through extra work and service and commitment.

As if the extra work for God would somehow bring him closer to God. At least that's what he hoped.

And that's why he had such little patience for preachers like Virgil. Those who talked about God as if they were best buddies. As if you could just saunter on up for a hug anytime you wanted. Who cared about theology. Who cared about rules. Just be bathed in his Holy Spirit, and that was that.

But that wasn't that.

There was holiness.

There were rules.

And despite all the lovey-dovey gobbledygook, the closer you adhered to those rules, the closer you adhered to Him.

Or, in Travis's case, the worse you failed, the farther away you fell.

He arrived at his car, a silver Honda Civic, and unlocked it. He climbed into the front seat, belted in, and pulled out his cell to call Beth.

She answered on the first ring. "Hello."

"Hey, hon. All through here." He turned on the ignition. "I'm on my way—"

"Yes, I heard the news."

"I'm sorry, what?"

"In fact, the police are here right now. I think they—"

"The police are there? At our house?"

"Yes, they think Travis is somehow involved."

"Sweetheart, it's me, it's—"

"Yes, that's right. I understand."

His mind raced, trying to piece it together. "Beth, are they right there, are the police in the room with you?"

"That's right. We're all waiting for him here."

"For what? What do they think I—"

"I know. Killed right there on the casino grounds, can you believe it?"

"Killed? Who? Beth? Who was killed—"

"Terrible, just terrible." Turning her head from the phone, she asked, "What was the reporter's name again?"

A male voice mumbled something.

She came back on. "Michael Fortenbra. They say his name was Michael Fortenbra."

"The reporter?" Travis caught his breath. "He was murdered?"

"Uh-huh."

"And they think ... they think *I* did it?"

"It sure looks that way."

With his free hand, Travis dropped the car into gear. "I'll be right there. I'll—"

"No, I don't think that's such a good idea."

"Why? What—"

"Lots of people's minds are already made up. Fact, I'm pretty sure they'll arrest him as soon as he shows here."

"But I'm innoce—"

"And if he's being set up *again*, like at the church ... well, you can bet somebody pretty powerful will have tried to make it an open-and-shut case."

Travis started to answer but kept silent, listening for more.

"I'm afraid whatever he does, whatever *we* do, it'll have to be on our own."

He closed his eyes, trying to think.

"Listen, I've got to go. Be sure to tell Fiona and Virgil hi for me. We've had our differences, but they know more folks than just about anybody else around. In fact, I'll mention that to Travis. Maybe *they* can help."

"Right." His voice was hoarse. "I understand."

"Okay then. Bye-bye, I'll talk to you later."

"Good-bye ...," he whispered.

And the phone went dead.

Travis sat in the car, everything eerily quiet except for his pounding head.

And the approaching siren.

He looked up. Saw red and blue flashing lights reflecting off houses two blocks over.

He hesitated, then finally pressed the accelerator. Dirt and rock spit from the tires. He turned, sliding in the loose gravel, until he was headed for the back exit.

The siren grew louder.

He reached for his lights, then stopped. He'd turn them on later, when he was farther down the road.

When he'd had time to think.

Y ou're involving us with a drug trafficker?" Pilar trembled with rage.

"I'm exploring various business opportunities, that's all."

"That's why you built an entire runway? For him? Because you're *exploring* opportunities?"

Bianco sat on the edge of his desk. "I told you, he likes his privacy."

"The man's a drug lord!"

"Who also has other financial investments which are perfectly legal."

She turned her head, not believing what she heard.

"Listen, Pilar, I assure you everything we are doing is legal and aboveboard."

"Like setting up that preacher with a hooker?"

Bianco shrugged, which infuriated her even more. "The man is a murderer! You think you can play with fire and not get burned? How naive is that?"

He reached for the hand-carved humidor on his desk. Opening it, he produced one of those Cuban cigars he was so proud of, along with a sterling silver cutter. Snipping off the end, he asked, "And even if we were playing with fire, what difference would that make to you?"

"I beg your pardon?"

"Even if we were involved in something illicit, like drug trafficking, which we're not—wouldn't we simply be taking another one of the white man's vices and turning it against him?"

She could only stare.

Finding no lighter in his pocket, he rose from the desk and moved behind it to open a drawer. "Take a look around you, Pilar. We are an entertainment corporation. Our job is to provide people with the distractions of their choice. Food, booze, sex, gambling, you name it—any and all forms of entertainment."

"This man deals with drugs. There's a difference."

"Is there?" He found a match and lit the cigar.

"Yes! Drugs bring crime, corruption, addiction. There's a huge difference."

"Really?" He puffed on the cigar until the flame caught. "Now who's being naive?"

Pilar's jaw slacked.

"It's simply a matter of degree."

She wanted to argue, but his reasoning was so foreign it caught her off guard.

He waved out the match. "Nevertheless, these are moot points since, as I've said, our business is entirely legal."

Pilar held his gaze, not entirely believing him. "And the Tribal Council. What am I to report to them?"

"Those issues have already been covered."

"What? But I'm their representative. I'm—"

"Those issues have already been covered."

Again she was surprised into silence.

"Now, if you'll excuse me, I have some preparation to do."

Pilar stood as he sat behind his desk and returned to the work before him. Finally, realizing she'd been dismissed, she turned and angrily stormed toward the door.

"Oh, and Pilar."

She stopped.

"Until we reach an agreement, I trust you will hold this information in the strictest confidence. You *and* Misty." He looked up. "Because you are right. These are ruthless men. They do play for keeps. And if their anonymity was somehow compromised, well, I would hate to see anything happen to you ... or your child."

The words hit hard. She swallowed, doing her best to recover. "Are you threatening me?"

"Me?" He forced a chuckle. "Of course not. We're all family here. But you need to know there are some things even I can't protect you from."

I'm still not crazy about this." For the third time in ten minutes, Misty found herself rising from the wobbly table and trying to pace—though the scattered books, magazines, and empty pizza boxes made it difficult.

"It'll just be a little," Luke repeated. "Just to see what's going on."

"I'm afraid there's no such thing as a little with this stuff." Derrick Anderson, one of Misty's dropout friends, turned off the hot plate he used as a stove. He crossed to the table with a blackened saucepan in hand.

"What do you mean?" Luke asked.

"It's like opening a door, dude." He poured the greenish brown liquid into a mug, using a tablespoon to hold back the leaves, buds, and roots he'd been boiling. "You can open it a lot or you can open it a little. Either way, it's still open."

"Luke ..." The concern came out before Misty could stop it.

He turned to her and smiled. The condescending, cocky smile. "Don't sweat it. It's cool."

She watched as he grabbed the mug with one hand while adjusting the goggles with the other. She'd really grown to hate those things. And hate what they were doing to him.

It was like he'd become a different person. Not that she was crazy about the original one. Heaven forbid. And the fact that he was all she could think about at night when she stared up at the ceiling—well, that made her even less of a fan.

But this ...

To be honest, she still wasn't sure how he'd talked her into it. Still, with all that was happening (including opening her big mouth in front of Bianco), maybe they really could stand for a little extra help. Especially if Luke was supposed to be involved in some way. Yes, she had reservations. Big time. But there were those prophecies, and there were those goggles, and there were his visions ... and there was Amma.

"Drink up," Derrick prodded.

Misty looked at Luke.

He hesitated. For the briefest second she thought he might not go through with it. Then he glanced over, gave her that hotshot grin of his, and raised it to his lips.

"Here goes nothing—" he grinned bigger, probably just to irritate her—"or everything."

She watched, biting her bottom lip, as he took a sip.

He winced and made a face.

Derrick chuckled. "Didn't say it would taste good."

Luke nodded. Then, taking a breath, he tilted back his head and gulped once, twice, three times before emptying the mug and finally lowering it.

"All gone?" Derrick asked.

Luke nodded, wiping his mouth and making another grimace at the taste.

"All right." Derrick turned with the saucepan and crossed back to the sink. "Seriously, dude, I'm impressed you'd even go near this stuff."

Dirty dishes clinked as he rummaged through the pile.

"What do you mean?"

He found a traveling mug with big red letters—
D.A.R.E.—stenciled across it. "You say you're Christian,
right?"

"Yeah, so?"

"So this is *pharmacia*, man." Carefully he poured the
remainder of the tea from the pan into the mug.

"Pharma ... what?"

"Pharmacia. Using drugs to see the spirit world."

Luke looked at him, not understanding.

"It's supposed to be like a major no-no for you guys."

"It is?"

"Sure." Derrick grabbed the mug's lid and screwed it on
tight. "Rates right up there with sorcery and witchcraft.
Back in the old days, the Bible says folks were supposed to
be killed for doing it."

"No way."

"Yup."

Luke exchanged a nervous glance with Misty, then
looked away.

Derrick crossed to a stained refrigerator and grabbed
the handle. Its seal cracked and popped as he opened the
door. Inside there was a half gallon of milk, a few slices of
bread in an open brown wrapper, and the shriveled remains
of old plums ... or new prunes.

Trying to look cool and sophisticated, Luke leaned back.
But Misty could still hear the nervousness in his voice. "So
when ... you know, when will this stuff kick in?"

Derrick set the mug in the fridge and shut the door.
Dragging a chair across the floor to join him, he chuckled.
"Oh, you'll know, dude. Believe me, you'll know."

Luke forced another grin, not quite as big. "Cool."

Virgil groaned as he rose from his knees inside the tiny
closet under the stairway. But this was no time to

indulge in stiff knees and arthritic joints. He had to tell Fiona.

He waited for the dizziness to hit, pressing his hands against the walls for support—walls covered with photographs of the people in the community he prayed for daily.

But the word he'd just received from the Lord had nothing to do with these people. It had everything to do with the boy. With Luke.

The dizziness came—five, six seconds before it finally faded. When he could trust his legs, he pushed open the door and stepped out.

"Fiona?"

There was no answer.

"Fiona?"

He hobbled down the hallway into the kitchen. The lights were out, the dishes done.

"Woman!"

He turned and entered the living room.

"Woman, where are you?"

The lamp next to her reading chair cast an orange glow over the room, but she wasn't there. Through the window he noticed the porch light burning and shuffled toward the screen door.

"Woman!"

It creaked mournfully as he pushed it open and stepped into the cooling air. He spotted her on the swing, open Bible on her lap. When she looked up, tears were in her eyes.

"Luke's in trouble!"

She nodded.

"Have you tried his cell phone?"

"He's not answering."

"Come on then, we gotta find him." He turned and started down the porch steps toward the car. Checking his pockets for keys, he grumbled and turned back to the house.

She was already there, shoving them into his hands. "You go," she said. "I'll stay and pray."

He looked at her, then at the keys. With a grunt, he turned and headed for the car.

Just let yourself, go, dude. Don't hold back."
Luke turned to see Derrick sitting on the sofa beside him. Beyond him was Misty. She seemed anything but relaxed, so he leaned over and gave her a reassuring smile.

She looked away.

He eased himself deeper into the sofa and gazed up at the stars. He hadn't noticed before that the ceiling was gone. He wondered what Derrick did when it rained.

But they were beautiful. Not only their sight ... but their sound.

Each brilliant pinpoint of light was singing. Not words, not exactly. But long, sustained chords. Weaving in and out of each other. And the way they intertwined, sometimes quickly, sometimes slowly, formed patterns and phrases.

And smells.

Somehow they too were connected to the music. Sweet and fragrant, like flowers. Their intensity depended upon the power of the phrases. Shorter, louder sounds produced stronger scents. Softer, flowing ones brought a more delicate aroma.

Luke smiled. This was good. Very good. And safe. As far as he could tell there were no menacing shadow creatures. No gargoyles. And no black tentacles.

Just the stars ... which rapidly grew in brightness and size. No, they weren't growing, they were approaching. The stars were coming nearer!

But he wasn't frightened. How could he be with such beauty and splendor?

And the closer they approached, the more he sensed their ... *glory*. That was the only word for it. Each seemed to have a distinct glory. A majestic personality that shimmered and dazzled as beautifully as their light.

They arrived, hovering just beyond the ceiling, radiating such sparkling effervescence that he could literally feel their light brushing against his face. Not only their light, but their song and their fragrance—soaking through his skin, his clothes, warming his entire body.

And with the sensation came the power. The same feeling of power he felt when he wore the goggles. Only much stronger.

He began to see their faces. Their bodies. Human, but more. Awesome in their perfection. And, as their features came into focus, so did a sense of their willingness to share their glory. Not only a willingness, but a desire. It was amazing. They *desired* to share their glory with him! Luke nobody-out-of-the-ordinary Kauffman.

Then again, maybe it wasn't so amazing. He'd always known he was someone special. Everything he'd experienced these last few days had only confirmed it.

And now this.

But there was something else. As he looked into their faces, as he heard their voices, he realized they were not only offering to share their glory, but that they were actually singing to him. They were *worshiping* him! Adoring *him*!

He leaned farther back into the sofa. It just kept getting better and better.

In the center of the group, just to the right, he noticed the most beautiful man (if men can be beautiful) that he had ever seen. But more than beautiful. And more than a man. There was such raw animal magnetism to him, such power, that Luke actually caught his breath. And in the man's eyes and song was the assurance that Luke could be exactly the same. That he could have the same powers of attraction—over Misty, over any girl he ever wanted. Consuming them. Overpowering them. No one could resist him.

It was like the elevator, when the cloud creatures had passed through him. But so much stronger ... and much more promising.

With effort, he pulled his eyes away and turned to another man—equally as beautiful, equally as powerful. But it wasn't a power to control girls. It was a power to control everyone. Not their emotions or their bodies, but their minds. And the more he looked into the man's eyes, listening to his song, the more he was promised ... and the more he hungered.

Another drew his attention. And another. And another. Their songs, their fragrance, their eyes offering unlimited fame, wealth, pleasure, intelligence—and with each promise came the insatiable hunger.

But the next move had to be Luke's.

No words were exchanged, yet he knew it, he sensed it. Despite their powers and promises, the star creatures could come no closer. It was up to Luke to join them. To rise from the sofa and break through the bubble that encompassed him. Odd, he hadn't noticed it before, the thin layer of light that curved around him. But it made little difference. It was so frail he was certain he could break through it.

All he needed was the will.

He looked back to the starmen. He didn't have to move, he knew that. All he had to do was will it. All he had to do was make the decision to rise and join them.

And he did.

Immediately, he felt himself growing lighter. The pressure of the sofa faded. He was rising. Toward the men, toward their promises.

Effortlessly.

Just an act of his will.

Until he felt a tug on his ankle. Not really a tug, but a weight. He looked down to see Fiona clinging to him.

What on earth?

He tried speaking to her, ordering her to let go, but he had no voice.

And she would not look at him. Instead, she kept her eyes clinched tight, clinging to his foot, kneeling at her bed—her bed and yet his sofa—rapidly moving her lips.

He tried to shake her off, but she held on tight.

He felt another tug on his other leg. He looked down to see Virgil. The man was driving their VW bug—clinging to the wheel and yet clinging to his leg.

The star creatures' song grew louder, more imploring. Luke looked up to see that some were actually reaching down to him.

Okay, fine. If the pastor and his wife wouldn't let go of his legs, then he'd take them with him. It took more energy than he expected, but focusing all of his attention upon the creatures, and exerting all of his will, he resumed rising.

He was six, maybe seven feet off the sofa when he reached the bubble, the thin veneer of light. He pushed at it but couldn't pass through. He focused harder, willed more intensely, but it proved a barrier he could not penetrate.

How was that possible? How could mere light form a—

And then he saw that it wasn't just light. But words. Physical letters strung together into words ... and sentences.

He frowned, confused. Where did they come from? How did—

He looked back to Fiona. Saw the open Bible on her bed. The one she was reading aloud from: " 'For *he will deliver the needy who cry out, the afflicted who have no one to help.'* "

Somehow they were rising from her mouth and wrapping around the bubble, thickening it, strengthening it.

But there were other words. Not from the Bible. Not from Fiona.

From Virgil.

"All hail the pow'r of Jesus' name!
Let angels prostrate fall."

He was singing. The same song he'd sung earlier. Not pleasant, not beautiful like the star creatures, but singing nonetheless.

"Bring forth the royal diadem
And crown Him Lord of all!"

As with Fiona, each note, each phrase strengthened the barrier.

Luke tried ordering them to stop but could only cough and grunt.

The light creatures beckoned from the other side, urging him forward. Apparently only he could break through.

He willed harder. The surface of the bubble bulged but never gave way.

"He will take pity on the weak and the needy and save the needy from death."

"Bring forth the royal diadem
And crown Him Lord of all!"

Luke was frustrated. Angry. Who were they to hold him back? Who were they to prevent him from achieving his fullest ... *destiny.*

He closed his eyes, directing all of his will into his throat, into his voice. He took a deep breath and shouted, though it came out a raspy whisper. "Let ... go of me!"

Their grip weakened.

"Let go! I want ... loose!"

And suddenly he was free. He looked up to the creatures, willing himself forward, pressing harder against the bubble's surface.

This time it tore. Effortlessly.

He rose quicker. Faster. Toward the glorious men. Their eyes sparkled in delight as they leaned down, stretching to embrace him with their powerful arms, their razor-sharp talons.

Talons?

He looked back into their faces.

They were transforming. Long aquiline noses were flattening into animal snouts, bulging eyes, mouths revealing bloody, needle-sharp fangs.

They no longer sang but howled. Screams shrieking at the light that surrounded them. Not the blazing, glorious light, but the red glow of fire. It was everywhere. Like water. Immersing them. Burning their flesh, which dripped and melted like wax from their flaming bodies, falling into a burning pool.

No fragrant aroma now. Only the acrid stench of burning tissue and sulfur as its dense yellow cloud surrounded him, gagging him, causing him to vomit. Deep, gut wrenching.

Between convulsions he tried to breathe, to cry out. But the air was flame, leaping down his throat.

He felt the claws piercing his shoulders, drawing him in, their flaming arms wrapping around him. Suffocating him. Molten flesh covering him, igniting his own body. Not only his body, but his emotions, his mind. His soul.

nine

isty slid the car into Virgil's front yard of dirt and sand, honking all the way. She jerked to a stop, throwing Luke's head to her side, causing him to retch again. Fortunately, he had nothing left to retch. It was all over his shirt and cargo pants.

A cloud of dust enveloped them as she honked again—louder, longer.

Angrily, she threw open her door and raced around to his side. Only then did she notice there were no other cars. Maybe no one was home.

But as she yanked open his door, she caught movement on the front porch.

"What's going on?" Fiona's voice shouted. "Who is it? Who's out there?"

"It's Luke!" Misty yelled. "There's something wrong with him!"

"Luke?"

Misty reached across to unlatch his safety belt. He gave a groan—part gasp, part whimper.

"It's okay," she said, fighting the latch, "you're going to be okay."

"What is it? What happened?" The old woman shuffled quickly toward them.

"Luke's sick!" Finally the latch released. "Come on, cowboy." She tried pulling him out, but he was lead.

He turned to her. Mouth and chin wet. Eyes wild, darting.

"It's okay, it's okay."

"Luke?" Fiona was behind her now.

Misty slipped her shoulder under his arm and pulled. "Come on now. Come on."

He tried to help but with little success.

"What happened?" the woman demanded.

"Datura."

"What?"

"He took some datura. I told him it was stupid, but he wouldn't listen."

She gave up on his arm and focused on his legs. She lifted one up and pulled it over, then the other.

"How long ago? How much?"

With both of his feet on the ground she yelled, "Take my arm! Take it!"

He obeyed and she pulled. It was a clumsy maneuver causing her to slam his head into the roof.

"Sorry."

She finally dragged him out and leaned him against the car, pausing to catch her breath.

"How much?" Fiona repeated.

"I don't know. I heard something about six ounces." She had no idea what the typical dose was but the woman's gasp—

"Dear Jesus ..."

—told her it was probably enough.

"Luke?" Fiona moved within inches of his face. "Son, can you hear me?"

At first nothing registered.

"Luke!"

Startled, his eyes focused. He began moving his lips. Two words escaped. "Help ... me ..."

"We will, son, we will." Fiona turned to Misty. "Let's get him into the house."

She nodded and moved to one side as Fiona moved to the other.

"Can you walk?" Fiona asked. "Luke, can you walk?"

He gave no answer.

"Luke?" Misty shouted.

He rolled his head to her.

"We're going to get you to the house. But you gotta help. Okay?"

He nodded and looked ahead, squinting. That's when he caught sight of the mountain. And that's when he went crazy.

His body stiffened. His eyes widened. *"No!"*

"What is it?" Fiona asked. "What's wrong?"

"No!"

He wrenched free from them and stumbled away. Struggling to keep his balance, he took three steps, four. Then stopped and looked back at the peak.

"No!" He snapped back his head, flinching. "Stay away!"

"Luke!"

He staggered backward, raising his hands. "No! No!" He swung his arms, clawing at the air, fighting an invisible attack.

"Luke!" Both women raced to him.

The attack intensified. His arms flew. "No, no, no ..."

Suddenly the group was bathed in headlights as another car swung into the yard.

"Noooo!"

He threw himself to the ground, rolling back and forth. Thrashing. Kicking. Fighting for all he was worth.

Misty and Fiona tried to help, but neither could find a safe way to reach him.

"What's happening?" The driver clambered from her car. "Fiona, what's going on?" She ran toward them. Pregnant, late twenties, not bad looking.

"It's Luke!" Fiona yelled. "He's fighting off spirits."

"What?"

"He's fighting demons!"

travis stared at the road, his mind swimming. Why would anyone want to kill the reporter? He was the hero. Everyone was on his side. Travis was the one left out to hang and dry, not the reporter. If the guy had any enemies he'd done a pretty good job at hiding them.

"The police are here right now ... They'll arrest him as soon as he shows."

Why? Surely they didn't think he was responsible?

He closed his eyes against the pounding headache. Then, remembering the shoving match earlier that afternoon, he let out a groan.

He glanced back into the mirror, grateful that the flashing red and blue lights were nowhere in sight.

For the moment.

But they would find him. They'd have the make of his car, his license. And, according to Beth, they would arrest him.

But that wasn't the end of the world. It's not like he had a reputation to protect or anything. Not anymore. Let them come. He would be arrested, he would eventually be proven innocent, and then—

"You can bet some pretty powerful people will make it an open-and-shut case."

As he approached an intersection another patrol car came into view a block down the street. Instinctively, he turned to the right. He eased down the road, then pulled in front of a parked pickup and turned off his lights.

The patrol car slowly passed.

He sat for a moment, heart pounding, head throbbing.

He couldn't risk being on the road, that was certain. And he couldn't stay in the car.

But where to go? Everything in this area of town was residential. Low-income housing. Many, employees of the casino. And, at the moment, he wasn't exactly the home-crowd favorite. So where could he—

He stopped, remembering Virgil Foster's storefront church. This was the area—just a few blocks over.

"Our doors are always open, can't lock up God." Isn't that what he always bragged?

With a heavy sigh, Lawton grabbed his keys and opened the car door. Truth be told, it would be the perfect place to catch his breath until he could gather his wits. Because if there was one place no one would think to look for him, it would be in Pastor Virgil's Holy Ghost Revival Center.

Pilar entered the Surveillance Room rubbing her eyes. If she'd thought last night was bad, by the looks of things tonight was going to be worse. As if Bianco's new business partner wasn't enough, now there was the murder of the reporter. Cinnamon or Pepper or whoever she was had been right. Things had gotten out of control.

"Preston," she called to one of the surveillance officers at the big board. "Have you filed the p.m. tapes already?"

The skinny kid, just out of puberty and sporting an out-dated mullet, asked, "You want the one of the bungalow? The minister popping the reporter?"

She was struck by his casualness. "Uh, yes."

"It ain't there."

"What?"

"We got no tape. The camera went out."

"Are you serious?"

"Early this afternoon."

"How can that be? How can—"

He turned back to the monitors. "Bad luck, I guess."

Pilar stood, frowning. "Will you bring it up, please?"

"The camera?"

"Yes."

"I just told you we've got no signal."

"Bring it up."

"But—"

"Now."

"All right, all right." With more than a little attitude, Preston punched a set of buttons. The image on the largest screen flickered, then went black.

Pilar stared.

How was that possible? Over the course of a year they lost three, maybe four cameras. Four out of nearly two hundred. And to lose this one. At this particular time, at this particular location?

She hesitated, then turned and headed for the library vault. She'd see for herself if the tape was missing.

the streams of blackness snaked all around—whipping wildly in every direction from the mountain. Both feeding upon and pouring out its evil into the city.

Pouring out its evil into Luke.

The currents overwhelmed him. Desires pounded against his consciousness, pushing him down somewhere deep into himself. But they were more desires. Like the clouds he had seen so many times before, these had specific shapes. Although blurred by their speed, there was no missing the bulging eyes, the fangs, the hunched-over bodies ... and the claws.

Claws that ripped into his self-control. Tearing at his will and pulling him down, down, down.

He was part of the mountain's darkness now. And the darkness was part of him.

Merely a spectator, he no longer had control of his body. He'd been imprisoned in some remote corner where he could only watch. He tried fighting back up. But with each attempt, the currents pushed him farther, the claws pulled him deeper.

Then there were the voices.

Hissing, snarling, shrieking the worst obscenities imaginable. Some he didn't even understand. All directed at him. His weaknesses. His failures. His hypocrisy.

Through the fog he caught glimpses of Misty, Fiona, and Travis's wife. They were kneeling over him, faces bent down, filled with concern.

"Luke, can you hear me?"

"Luke, can you get to your feet?"

He could barely make out their voices over the screaming.

"Luke?"

He tried to answer but couldn't. He was paralyzed. Pulled too far down to move his mouth.

"Dear Lord ..." It was Fiona. She had begun to pray. Not only did he hear her voice, but with her words came flashes of light, stabbing him with their brilliance.

"We ask that You—"

"*Stop it!*" A voice shouted from his mouth. His mouth, but not his voice.

The women looked startled.

"*You have no authority over us. We are his choice. His will.*"

The voice began cursing—the same words he'd heard in his head but now shouted through his mouth. He tried stopping them, clenching his jaw. But they continued.

"No!" she cried. "Dear God, we—"

More burning light. More obscenities.

"—ask for Your power and authority in this matter."

The brightness increased. So did the pain.

"And in Your name—"

He suddenly felt panic. The stronger creatures scrambled down from the surface, shoving the weaker ones to the top.

Another voice shouted. More powerful. Guttural. As it yelled, Luke felt his head turning toward Misty.

"And what does this thing, this tramp of a child know of His name?"

He was looking directly at her now.

"You with the fantasies of filth. Your dreams of boys taking your lovely body into their strong, masculine arms and—"

"Stop it!" Fiona shouted. "We demand that you—"

But the voice continued taunting—shocking the women with growing explicitness.

Misty recoiled, shaken, as if it revealed her most secret thoughts.

Again Luke struggled to surface, and again he was thrown into the dark corner.

And still the voice raged.

Mortified, Misty rose unsteadily to her feet.

Fiona tried to help. "It's okay, dear, they're just trying to—"

But the voice continued. Laughing. Mocking. Revealing deeper and darker desires. Dreams dreamed in secret. Unmentionable embarrassment.

The girl backed away.

More laughter and more insults.

Luke continued struggling for the surface to stop them.

Misty turned toward her car.

At last he could feel his mouth, his tongue. With all of his strength he shouted, "Misty ..."

But it turned into a gagging cough.

"That's it, son!" Fiona encouraged. "You can fight it! You can fight them!"

More roars and shrieks in his head ... until he was slammed down so hard that he lost consciousness. For how long, he did not know.

When he awoke, the voices were still shouting.

He heard an engine and turned. Misty's car was taking off.

He struggled to speak and again he was choked into a gasping whisper, "Misty ..." before he was thrown down.

Virgil opened the door to his church. It gave its customary squeak and groan.

He peered into the darkness. "Somebody here?"

There was no response.

He flipped on the switch, momentarily blinded by the light. As his eyes adjusted he saw the room was exactly as they'd left it.

"Look, I don't mind you comin' in, 'specially if it's to seek the Lord." He stepped farther into the room. "But you gotta know this ain't a homeless shelter. There's one farther down the road a piece and I'll take you there, but this ain't it."

Still no answer.

He glanced to the stack of chairs, the covered altar, the corners of the room.

"Nothing to be afraid of, friend. You're not in trouble or nothin'. I was just driving by and caught movement through the window. So come on out and we'll find you a nice—"

He stopped as Travis Lawton rose from behind the altar.

"Hello, Virgil."

"Pastor ... What are you doing here?"

The man rubbed the back of his neck. "I've been asking myself the same question."

"I don't understand."

"The police are looking for me. Hadn't you heard?"

"The police?"

Travis nodded. "That reporter who did the piece on me with the ... uh ... prostitute. Somebody killed him this evening, and they think I had something to do with it."

"He's ... dead?"

"Yeah."

Virgil blinked, trying to piece it together.

Travis moved from behind the altar and Virgil stiffened. The action was not lost on the younger pastor and he slowed to a stop, a little saddened.

"How ..." Virgil cleared his throat. "How long?"

"How long what?"

"How long have the police been looking for you?"

"I'm not sure. An hour, maybe two. I thought of turning myself in, but ..." He shook his head and dropped off.

"But what?"

"My wife believes somebody set me up. That they made it look like I did it, so they—"

"But you didn't. Right?"

Travis stopped and looked at him.

Virgil fidgeted, then shrugged. "If you're innocent, then I'd say that's all the more reason to turn yourself in and get things straightened out."

"I don't—" Travis swallowed. "Whoever is behind this, I don't think they'd make it that easy."

"It may not be easy, but it's the right thing to do. It's the only thing to do. Justice will prevail, son. It may take its sweet time, but it always pre—"

"I don't think so."

"But ... it's the law. What other choice do you have?"

Travis gave no answer.

"Listen." Virgil stepped closer. "It's always best to come clean with these sorts of things. Come clean and just tell them—"

"I don't think ..." He took an unsteady breath. "I don't think I can."

Virgil scowled and Lawton looked down.

"Well, here then." Virgil reached into his pocket and pulled out his cell phone.

"What are you doing?"

He opened the lid and pressed 911.

"What are you—"

"Just helpin' you do the right thing, brother—what you should have been doin' all along."

"No." Travis moved toward him.

Virgil countered, keeping the stack of chairs between them.

Travis slowed. "Look, you don't understand what's happening. You don't—"

"I understand that the officials are after you. And that if you're an innocent man, I know that justice will pre—"

"No, you don't understand." He took another step.

Again Virgil countered.

At last the operator answered, "Nine-one-one, what is the nature of your emergency?"

"Hi, there. This is Pastor Virgil Foster, who's this?"

"Margaret."

"Well, hello, Margaret." Keeping a careful eye on Travis, he continued, "Listen, I'm at The Holy Ghost Revival Center with Pastor Travis Lawton. I believe the police are looking for him."

"Virgil, please, you—"

"Is he there with you now?" the operator asked.

"Yes, he is, darlin'."

"Are you in danger?"

"Virgil—"

"I don't think so, least not at the moment." As he spoke, he watched Travis slowly seem to shrink. "We're at 1730 Sycamore. You know where that is?"

"We'll send a car immediately."

"Wonderful. That's just wonderful. Say, Margaret, when's the last time you been to church?"

"Sir?"

"Church, you ever go to church?"

"I'm, well, I'm Catholic."

"Oh." He made sure she heard the disapproval in his voice. "Well, if you ever feel like swinging by and visiting us, our doors are always open."

"Sir, I need to—"

"We meet eleven o'clock every Sunday and nine-thirty for Sunday school."

"Sir, I need to dispatch the car now."

"Oh, right, right. Well, it's been a pleasure talking to you, Margaret."

"You're sure you are safe."

"I'm in the house of the living God, child. I couldn't be any safer."

"All right, then."

"And maybe we'll see you some Sunday."

He waited a moment. There was no answer. Knowing she'd hung up, he closed the phone and looked back to Travis. The man had grown smaller, leaning heavily against the altar.

"Not a thing to worry about, son. They'll be here in a few minutes, and it'll all be over."

Staring at his hands, Travis quietly mumbled, "Or just begun."

"What's that?"

Travis looked up, his face drawn. "Guess you're pretty pleased with yourself, aren't you?"

"I'm only helping you do the right thing."

"I don't mean that. I mean you've finally won, haven't you? You've finally proven that your way is the right way."

"It's never been about competition, son."

"Of course it has. Since the moment I arrived, you and I, we've never stopped competing against each other."

"I'm not sure what you're talking about."

"Sure you're not."

"Listen, I'm not the one who got his hand caught in the cookie jar."

The kid faltered but Virgil wasn't done.

"Nor do I, in my wildest dreams, think I can go off and save the world on my own power. You need the Spirit of God for that, son. There's no way of overcoming the flesh of the world without God's Holy Spirit baptizing you in His power to—"

"Please." The weakness of Travis's voice brought Virgil to a stop.

In the distance, a siren approached.

Once again Travis shook his head, quietly repeating, "You've finally won."

Virgil stood a little straighter, a little taller. "No, son, not me. The Lord Almighty, He is the winner."

mother, what are you doing?"

Startled, Pilar looked up from her daughter's monitors.

"I ..." Knowing the best defense was an offense, she immediately changed tack. "Do you have any idea how late it is? Where have you been?"

Misty shuffled in, exhausted and hollow-eyed.

"What's wrong? Are you all right?"

It was her daughter's turn to deflect questions. "You're not spying, are you?"

"Of course not. You know what I think of that."

"Right. So who are you checking up on?" The girl's banter remained, but her fire had definitely dimmed.

"Are you okay?"

She gave the briefest nod as she surveyed the screens.

Pilar turned back to them and explained, "There's some really strange stuff going on right now and—"

"Bianco's office?" Misty interrupted. "You're trying to find my patch into his office?"

"The reporter, the one who did the story on Pastor Lawton—"

"The guy with the hooker?"

"They found him dead in Bungalow Six."

"What?"

Pilar nodded. "Shot in the face."

For once Misty did not have a comeback.

Pilar continued, "All the evidence points to the preacher. Phone calls, appointments, that sort of thing . . ."

"But?"

"Something's not right." She ran her hands through her hair. "So, I thought, maybe . . . well, that maybe—"

"Did you pull up the surveillance tape?" Misty asked. She climbed onto the stool beside her. "We've got coverage of the bungalows, you know."

"The camera's out."

"No way." She reached past her mother for the keyboard.

"Yeah, it went out this afternoon. And if you ask me, that's quite a coincidence."

"You think?"

Misty's fingers flew across the keyboard until a blank image came up on the screen.

She hesitated, then attacked the keys again.

"What are you doing?"

"Shh."

"Misty—"

"Hang on."

A moment later the entire Surveillance Room came up on the screen. All 196 monitors with their blue-green glows.

Pilar looked at her daughter. "You're surveying Surveillance?"

Misty didn't answer but asked, "What time?"

"What?"

"When did he shoot him?"

"Between eight and nine p.m."

Misty nodded, entered more keystrokes, and the picture rewound, coming to a stop at 20:00:00.

She leaned forward, carefully studying the screen, then hit a few more keys. The image zoomed into one particular monitor. The monitor for the bungalows.

It was up and running.

Pilar swore softly.

Misty fast-forwarded the picture until at 20:18:22 a shadowy form entered the frame.

"That's him," Pilar whispered. "The reporter."

Misty dropped to normal speed as the figure knocked on the door and waited.

Pilar shifted her weight. She threw a glance to Misty, who watched intently.

The reporter knocked again.

More waiting ... until the door finally opened. There was a glimpse of another form, a face. But only for a moment before it stepped back into shadow. More talking. Eventually the reporter turned to leave, then turned to the door again ... when, suddenly, he staggered backward.

Pilar caught her breath.

An arm extended from the dark. There was a brief flash as the reporter jerked again, his head flying back ... before he collapsed onto the ground.

Misty hesitated, but only for a second. Immediately she reversed the tape.

"What are you doing?"

She did not answer but inched the tape backward, frame by frame, until the face from inside the bungalow came back into view.

She froze it and zoomed in.

But the closer she zoomed, the more detail was lost until the face was nothing but a blur.

Pilar watched as Misty entered more keystrokes. The fuzzy image sharpened, the pixels coming together, tighter and tighter, though still too blurry to identify. She turned to another screen and began working the keyboard all over again.

"Misty, what are you — "

Pilar came to a stop as the Facial Recognition Program popped up on the screen. A list of several categories appeared. As if reading her mother's mind, Misty clicked and highlighted the first: *Casino Management.*

Faces flew past, including her own, but there was no match.

Making her way down the list, Misty highlighted the second category: *Casino Employees.*

More faces flipped by, several per second, until one suddenly froze. A familiar face to both of them. Below it, the name: *Joey Popiski.*

Pilar could only stare. Then, coming to, she reached for the phone beside Misty.

"What are you doing?"

"I'm calling the police. They've gone after the wrong man."

"Not on this phone, you don't."

Pilar looked at her, then the phone. She hung up and reached for her cell.

"Mother ..."

Again she hesitated and looked at her daughter.

"Could we use just a *little* common sense here, please?"

She hesitated, glancing around the room, then snapped it shut and started for the door.

"Where are you going?"

"Down to the police station. I need a *private* chat with the chief." Turning, she added, "Private as in don't tell a soul."

"Mother ..."

"No one."

Just call on Him, son. You have the authority to—"

"Shut up, old woman!"

"Luke ..."

"He can not hear you. We are the ones who—"

"Call upon His name. Call upon His name and He will deliver—"

"SILENCE!" The voice roared from Luke's lungs. But it wasn't his voice, it was the power of the darkness. Of the mountain.

He stared up from the depths, trying to see through his eyes. He no longer had his goggles; they'd taken them off. Truth was, he no longer needed them. Everything was folding upon itself, turning inside out. The two women, the house, the very ground he was lying on. Like some Picasso painting, he saw them not from one angle, but from several. Inside and out. At the same time. And everywhere, on all sides, was a dark swirling mist.

Maybe it was the drug, maybe it wasn't. He couldn't tell.

He lifted his head toward the mountain. Not only did he see the peak with its consuming blackness, but he saw the evil deep within it.

And he saw the source ...

It was the mountain, yes. But at its center was a deep yawning pit that stretched forever. A tunnel. Glowing in redness. Filled with burning liquid. Vapors rising from it. This was the source of the black mists. The amphibian faces.

"Luke ..."

His head swiveled to Fiona. Although the darkness surrounded them, it did not touch her. It lurked inches away, quivering on all sides, but it could not touch. By contrast, she almost seemed to be glowing.

Maybe she was.

"Can he hear us?"

He turned to the other woman, Travis's wife. Darkness surrounded her as well. But she was also untouched.

"You have the authority!" Fiona shouted. "Just call on His name. He has all the power you need!"

"No." The voice was internal now. Addressing only Luke. *"You have chosen us, we are your power. We are your passion."*

"Call on Him! It must be your choice!"

"You have already chosen."

"Call on Him!"

"You are ours. You have given yourself to us. There is no second chance."

But it was a lie. Luke immediately recognized it. Life had been full of second chances ... with his dad, his sister, himself. That was the love Preacher Man kept talking about back home. The grace he always rambled on about.

"We all screw up, son," he'd said. "Only difference between us and the world is we know we're a mess. That's why we need a Savior."

Yes, there were second chances. His sister had experienced it before her death. He and Dad had experienced it when Preacher Man had led them to the Lord.

"You have already chosen."

No, it was a lie. He had made a mistake. A huge mistake. But that's all it was. He had made the real choice much earlier. Back in that hot tub. Back when Preacher Man did his baptism thing with him.

"Your fate is ours!"

Using all of his will, he sucked in a breath.

"No!" The creatures closed in, clamping his throat, making it impossible to breathe out, impossible to speak.

But he continued to fight, struggling, willing, until finally, he gasped out a choking, "Yes ..."

"No!" Their screams raged in his head, slamming him back down into the darkness.

"That's right," Fiona cried. "In the name of Jesus—"

The voices went crazy: *"No ... Noo ... Nooo ..."*

Once again, Luke struggled for control, trying to rise, "Yes ..."

"Stop it! What are you doing?"

"Yes." His voice grew louder. "Help me. God, please help—"

The shrieks became deafening.

"That's right," Fiona encouraged from someplace far away. "Call on Him. In the name of Jesus ..."

"Yes," Luke gasped. "Help me. Jesus, please—"

Suddenly the air sizzled, filling with white light. So bright, he could no longer see. He could only hear: *"UNFAIR! He is ours! Unfair! Unfair!"*

The screams convulsed his body, knotting it in pain. He guessed he was writhing on the ground, though he couldn't be sure. One thing he did know, he would not give up.

"Yes," he gasped louder. "Help me, help—"

The light grew brighter. So powerful it blew his hair, his clothes.

With excruciating effort, he turned toward it.

"NO ... NO ..."

The light pummeled against his face, so intense he could not open his eyes.

But he had to.

Summoning all of his courage, all of his will, he fought to open them a crack ...

And there before him stood a man carved in blazing light. Tenderly, He stretched out His hand to Luke's face. A hand glowing with a brilliant-white hole in its center. His father had talked about seeing this Man when he had died, when he had gone to heaven. The Man with the holes in His hands.

Luke struggled not to flinch as the fingers brushed against his cheek.

And with that single touch, more light exploded. All around him. Through him. The crushing darkness disappeared. Instantly. Completely. And his consciousness immediately shot back up.

He was in control again.

He opened his eyes. But he was no longer outdoors. Now he stood with the Man inside a fancy office. Bianco, the guy he'd met in the hallway, sat before them on a leather sofa, listening to Velasco, the drug czar.

At the moment, Velasco sounded anything but pleased. *"And you believe having him arrested will be the end of the matter?"*

Bianco shrugged. *"What more can be done?"*

Velasco looked down at the drink in his hand. *"Our friend, the chief of police, he has been adequately compensated?"*

"Along with others — since day one."

"Perhaps you should offer him a bonus."

"A bonus?"

"For insuring the preacher's silence."

Bianco scowled. *"I don't understand."*

"The preacher, he is a man of God, is he not? Caught in the act of adultery, and now murder."

"Yes."

"It would seem such a person would be overcome by shame — unable to endure the public humiliation of his failures."

"I don't —"

"It would be of little surprise if such a man tried to end his own life." At last he looked up at Bianco. *"I am sure there are many ways suicide could happen — especially when one is all alone in a prison cell."*

The image of Bianco and Velasco suddenly dissolved.

As did the light.

As did the Man with the holes in His hands.

"Luke? Luke, can you hear me?"

He blinked until he saw Fiona kneeling before him. She broke into a smile. "Praise God! Thank you, Lord!"

He turned to see Travis's wife on the other side. "Are you okay?"

He tried to speak. "Your hus—" But his voice was leather dry, his body spent with exhaustion.

"Not now," Fiona said. "Don't—"

He shook his head and tried again. "Your husband ... they're going to kill him."

"What?" the wife exclaimed. "What did you say?"

"We have to ..." He took another breath, struggling against the fatigue that rushed in. "... stop them ..."

Misty would have loved to patch into Bianco's office. But they'd discovered her camera just a few days ago and were making it impossible for her to get anywhere near the place to plant another. Of course, he still hadn't found the microphone which she'd had the foresight to plant on the opposite wall weeks earlier. But sound without picture wasn't nearly as exciting.

Still, it was better than nothing ...

With a sigh, she hit a set of computer keys and brought up the audio software. Another click and she'd accessed her mixing board—all thirty-two channels' worth.

The VU bar on Channel 4 was bouncing to beat the band. Good. There was some action. Better yet, as she pushed up the fader, she heard no music. The guy usually kept music going so she couldn't hear his conversations. Talk about paranoid.

But now he was brimming in overconfidence. Obviously convinced there were no more bugs, he'd gotten careless. That was all she needed.

Misty smiled and brought the channel to full volume.

"... at 2:30 tonight?" a heavily accented voice asked.

"Right." Bianco answered. "That will get us there a half hour before its arrival."

"Provided everything goes as planned."

"Everything will go as planned. Believe me, Senor Velasco, we have invested far too much to insure anything else."

"It is true, you have fulfilled your end of our agreement with near perfection."

"And now it is your turn."

"And now it is my turn."

"To us."

There was the clink of glasses.

"May tonight be the beginning of a long and fruitful relationship."

part three

interlude

momtakwit, the great shaman of Dog Clan, lay at the foot of Smashing Wall—defeated from his battle with Tahquitz and his warriors.

For the moment, he still breathed, his fall broken slightly by the branches of a scrub pine. Each breath flared white-hot pain through his side. Yet he was alive. For how long, he did not know. But as he lay under the stars, shivering in the desert wind, he knew it would be just a matter of time before he joined his ancestors.

And then he heard the voice:

"Grandfather ..."

At first he thought it was ya-ee playing tricks with his tattered mind. But it grew louder.

"Grandfather ..."

Was it the last of the datura, still in his soul? Perhaps. But it sounded like the voice of a little girl. A very persistent little girl.

"Grandfather ..."

He rolled his head toward the sound. More pain shot through his body.

There, running toward him across stones that glowed gray-white in the moonlight, was a child. She scrambled over rocks and boulders, until she finally arrived at his side.

"Who ..." His voice was dry as sand. "Who are you?"

"*I am Iktomi.*" She stooped to him, breathless from her run. "*I am your granddaughter.*"

He closed his eyes. "*I have no granddaughter.*"

"*Yes. In time you will have a child. And she will bear a daughter.*"

He grunted, wincing in pain. "*More trickery from Tahquitz. It is not enough he used my pride to kill me; now he must taunt my dying breaths.*"

"*No, Grandfather, it is not true. He has not killed you. You will rise and return to the village.*"

"*No.*" He turned from her. "*I am not worthy. Leave.*"

"*No, you must return. You must return and have children. And their children will have children. And through them, with the help of our white brother, you will vanquish Tahquitz. Together we will complete the task you have begun.*"

With effort he reopened his eyes.

"*Do not give up. For yourself. For all Cahuilla!*"

He heard the caw of a crow and looked up. A giant bird circled the mountain. From its belly spewed a thick black stream. He watched the stream fall until it struck Smashing Wall. Suddenly the entire mountain began to tremble.

"*Grandfather!*"

The shaking grew worse and worse. Any minute boulders would loosen from above and tumble upon them.

"*Grandfather, what is happening?*"

The fear in the little girl's voice moved him. She was so frightened. It was not right that one should die like this. Not at her tender age.

"*Grandfather ...*"

Fighting against the accusations still whispering inside his head and the searing pain in his chest, he rolled onto his side. He bit his tongue, swallowing back a cry.

"*Grandfather ...*" Her voice tore his heart.

The ground shook harder.

Struggling, he rose to his hands and knees. With her help, he stood upon his feet—her tiny shoulders bearing much of his weight.

The crow cawed louder. Despite the shaking and roaring of the earth, he could still hear it. Only when he looked back up did he realize it was no crow.

"Tematsuwet!" he gasped.

"Who?"

"Stealer of souls. He has come to join forces with his brother, Tahquitz."

The earth pitched and rolled. He shouted to be heard. "If they unite, we shall be destroyed; all Cahuilla will meet destruction! There will be no end to their power!"

"What do we do?" she cried.

Dirt and rock streamed down from above.

He leaned upon her and motioned them forward. The first step wracked him with pain; every movement made his head spin. But they continued forward.

"Where will we go?" the little girl shouted. "What must we do?"

The words came with great effort. "We must ... pray, Iktomi. Pray hard ... pray ... deep."

The canyon was narrow and soon they reached its center, as far from the falling rocks as possible. Only then did the great shaman's legs give way, throwing him to the ground. He struggled, rising to his hands and knees. But the little girl was gone. He searched in every direction, but she had disappeared.

All that remained were her pleas for him to return to their village.

And the possibility for a second chance ...

ten

how is he?" Beth asked as Fiona entered the tiny kitchen.

"'Tuckered out, but praise God, he's through the worst of it." She motioned to the cell phone in Beth's hand. "Any luck?"

The woman shook her head. "He's not picking up."

Fiona tried to hide her concern.

"Was that ... I mean what we saw in your yard, was that ..."

"Spiritual warfare?" Fiona asked.

Beth nodded.

"At its extreme, yes."

"I didn't know—I mean you read about it in the Bible, but for today, I didn't know it still happened."

Fiona pulled out a chair from the table and joined her. "When Virgil and I first started out in ministry we were short-termers in the Philippines. We saw it more times than we wanted."

Beth nodded. "One time's more than enough for me."

"I hear that."

A brief silence hung over the conversation.

"But how ... I mean, he's just a boy. And an American at that."

Fiona almost smiled. How much Beth reminded her of herself at that age. "His little friend said he'd taken some jimsonweed."

"Jimsonweed?"

"Datura. It's an Indian hallucinogenic."

"So he was just having a bad reaction."

"Partially. But there was more."

"Those awful voices? Telling that poor girl's secrets?"

Fiona nodded. "Coupled with the boy's own gifts."

"Gifts?"

"The best Virgil and I can tell, he's strongly gifted in the prophetic—with or without those goggles."

Beth shifted in her seat but remained respectfully silent.

"You don't believe that, do you?" Fiona asked.

"We've always been taught that the spiritual gifts no longer apply to today."

"Yes, I know." Now it was her turn to remain respectfully quiet. Finally, changing the subject, she said, "Beth, may I ask you a question?"

"Certainly."

"Why here?"

The young woman blinked. "Pardon me?"

"Why did you come here, to the house, I mean?"

"I don't ... know. We needed ..."

Fiona looked on, waiting for more.

"We really don't know anybody in the community, well, except in our church—and they haven't exactly been supportive." She nervously pushed her hair behind her ear. "Not that I blame them. I mean, Travis can be a bit ... abrasive at times."

"No need to tell me," Fiona chuckled. "He and Virgil are cut from the same cloth."

Beth gave an uneasy smile. "I just thought, I mean, since you're so well-known and respected in the community—"

"Well-known, anyway."

"I just thought maybe there was some way you could ... help us."

Fiona watched as the young woman glanced away, trying to hide the moisture filling her eyes. When she spoke again her voice had thickened. "He really is a good man. A *great* man. I mean, he's got his share of problems ..." She stopped, her bottom lip trembling.

"We've all got our share of problems," Fiona agreed.

Beth nodded and sniffed. "But he really loves God." She sniffed again. "And he's really, really trying to make a difference."

Fiona reached into her sleeve and produced a handkerchief. She handed it to the woman, who looked up, tears spilling onto her cheeks.

"Thank you ..."

Fiona nodded. She wanted to say more but didn't trust her own voice.

misty had just slid underneath Bianco's favorite limo when her cell phone went off. She cringed and glanced between the wheels. As best she could tell, the parking garage was empty, no one had heard.

She wiggled her hand into her tight back pocket until she pulled out the phone and demanded, "What?"

"Are you okay?" It was Luke. He sounded exhausted.

"Am *I* okay, what about you? That was some pretty weird stuff you pulled."

"Yeah ... sorry."

"Sorry? That's it? You're sorry?"

"I didn't — "

"What you said was way over the top."

"I guess."

"You guess?"

"I mean, yes, it was, but it wasn't me. It was those cloud things. They were the ones talking."

"Please ..."

"I'm serious. Some of them got inside me and started ranting and raving."

Her voice dripped in sarcasm. "You were talking, but you weren't talking."

"Most of the time I couldn't even hear what they were saying."

"For real?"

"For real."

The thought gave her a vague comfort. "You sound awful."

"Yeah ... Listen, you know that preacher guy? The one that got busted with the hooker? Something's not right."

She stared impatiently up at the car frame before her. "Tell me about it, cowboy. We're already on it."

"I think your mom's boss, I think he set him up."

She scooted farther up the car. "Right, like I said, we're already—"

"I think they're going to kill him."

She stopped. "What?"

"I can't explain it, but it was like I was in his office or something."

"You were in his—"

"No, I mean I was and I wasn't. It's a long story. Anyway, I heard him talking."

"Bianco?"

"To that drug guy."

"And ..."

"And they were making plans to have him killed. They're going to make it look like a suicide."

"Come on, how are they going to get past—"

"They've bribed the chief of police. They're going to have *him* do it."

For the first time she had no comeback.

"Misty? You there?"

"Listen, if you're making this up, so help me—"

"No, it's true. I swear to God. They're going to kill him and it's going to be tonight!"

Her mind raced.

"Misty?"

"Yeah, listen, I'll call you back."

"But—"

"I'll take care of it."

"It's going to happen and it's going to happen—"

"All right, all right. I'll take care of it."

"You promise?"

"Yeah, I promise." She changed subjects. "Listen, I'm going to need your help on something."

"I don't think I can. I'm pretty wasted."

"Whatever. I'll be there in twenty minutes."

"I doubt Fiona's going to let me out of her sight."

"You'll figure out something."

"But—"

"Twenty minutes. And don't worry about the preacher guy. I've got it covered."

"Mist—"

She disconnected and took a breath. She started to call her mom then stopped. She'd get to that in a second. Right now she had to finish attaching the tracking device. If Bianco and the hotshot drug guy were heading for some big meeting tonight, she was definitely going to know where.

d id I wake you?"

"No, I uh ..."

The man was lying, but it made no difference to Bianco. He spoke into the phone, running his hand over his crew cut. "Good."

He heard the irritated mumble of a young woman's voice. The receiver was covered and there was an exchange of muffled words. Finally:

"So what can I do for you, Mr. Bianco?"

214the seeing

"I may have another job for you."

"Mr. Bianco—"

"I know, I know. But I wouldn't ask if it wasn't important."

There was no answer.

He sweetened the pot. "And after this, I promise, you can write your own ticket."

The man still wasn't taking the bait.

Bianco continued, "Not only will I count you a friend to myself and to Casino Rancheria, but I promise that friendship will continue with my many associates—Las Vegas, New Jersey, not to mention the club scene in LA and New York."

Another moment passed, briefer, before the man replied, "What do you want me to do?"

Bianco smiled and turned to one of the many monitors on the wall before him—the one he'd clicked to *freeze frame*. The one picturing the girl crawling out from under his limo.

More out of habit than reason, he reached to his stereo and cranked up Miles Davis. Then he explained.

Y ou're not listening. I'm telling you, you've got the wrong guy."

Chief Wallace leaned back, the old office chair groaning under his weight. "Pilar ... the reporter left specific word with his cameraman that he was going to meet Travis Lawton. He not only gave the time, he gave the exact location."

"Right, but our surveillance footage shows—"

"Your surveillance camera was out."

She looked at him, surprised.

"I already talked with Bianco. He says you have no tape of the bungalows. The camera was down the entire evening."

"Doesn't that seem just a little strange to you?"

He held her look, then carefully he chose his words. "No, it doesn't seem strange, Pilar. Given the circumstances, it doesn't seem strange at all."

A chill crept across her shoulders.

He sat up, the chair groaning. "So, given the evidence and the fact that there is no surveillance tape, I'd say—"

"That's not necessarily true."

"Pardon me?"

"It's from fairly long distance and we're not entirely sure, but by running it through our Facial Recognition System—"

"You have tape? Where? How?"

"Like I said, we're not entirely sure. It's pretty blurry but—"

"Because if you're withholding evidence on a murder ... that's serious business."

"As serious as arresting and holding someone you may know to be the wrong man?"

A moment passed. Once again the chair creaked.

She leaned forward. "I'm suggesting to you that somebody has set him up. The same somebody who set up his tryst with the prostitute."

"Someone from the casino."

She said nothing, letting the silence speak for itself.

He cleared his throat. "Peter Bianco and the casino have been good friends to this town. They put us on the map, for crying out loud. Employed nearly a fifth of our people. Our economy has skyrocketed."

"Not to mention the crime rate."

"Actually, the crime rate has been steadily falling."

She gave him a look.

If he saw it, he didn't let on. Instead, he repeated with measured tones, "Casino Rancheria has been very good for this town. Very good for everybody. You. Me. *Everybody*."

He waited until her eyes returned to his. "What's the old saying about not biting the hand that feeds you? Or is it, 'cutting off the hand that offends you'? I get those two mixed up."

She noticed her mouth becoming strangely dry.

"In any case, I have no intention of doing either. Nor, I presume, do you." He smiled.

Realizing she'd hit a wall far bigger than she'd bargained for, she thought it best to bring the conversation to an end. "All right—" she nodded—"all right, I think I see your point."

"Good ... I figured you would."

She gathered herself and rose.

"And about this alleged tape."

She started to correct him but realized he'd just given her a way out.

"If it should ever actually surface, I would expect you to give me a call. Immediately." With emphasis, he added, "The sooner the better."

She understood. Loud and clear. "Right." She turned and started toward the door. "Thanks for your time, Chief."

"Certainly. Glad to help. Oh, and Pilar?"

She stopped.

"I wonder if you'd do me a favor."

She turned to him.

"Along with Lawton's arrest, we picked up Virgil Foster."

"The pastor?"

"Caught him driving on a suspended license. We were about to call his wife, have her pick him up. But since you're heading back that way, would you mind dropping him off?"

She was unsure how to respond. It seemed a strange request, but not unreasonable.

The chief continued, "He's raising quite a ruckus about his rights and all ... and the sooner we get him out of here, the more peace we'll have." He chuckled. "Lawton too. They're the only ones in the holding cell, and he's giving the guy no rest."

Pilar looked on.

"You don't mind, do you?"

Coming to, she forced a smile. "No, sure. That'll be fine."

"Great. I'll have Officer Shipley escort you. Believe me, you'll be doing us all a favor by getting him out of here. More than you know."

Officer Geoffrey Shipley, a just slightly slimmer version of the chief, though still under the mistaken idea that he was God's gift to women, escorted Pilar down the hall-way to the holding cell. They'd dated once or twice in her early years, in Pilar's weaker moments, and there wasn't a time she saw him that she didn't regret it.

"You're looking good, Pilar."

"Thanks."

"I mean real good."

She saw no need to repeat herself.

He must have caught her coolness because he regrouped and tried a different tack, this time sounding a few rungs higher on the evolutionary ladder. "So how's Misty?"

"Fine."

"Great."

Silence.

"And the job?"

"Fine."

"Great."

Silence.

"That's just ... great."

It appeared he was finally getting the message.

They continued down the corridor, footsteps echoing against cheap wood paneling and cracked linoleum—Shipley's keys jangling in authority from his belt, right next to his nice shiny black gun.

"Chief says I'm up for a promotion. In six months I'm going to be assistant chief of police."

"Everyone needs a dream."

He seemed unsure how to respond and fell into longer silence—until Pilar's cell phone rang. It played Misty's ring from the *Wizard of Oz* ... "If I Only Had a Brain."

She pulled it from her pocket and answered, "Hey."

"Mom, they're going to kill that preacher guy!"

"I'm sorry, what?"

"The preacher guy, they're going to kill him."

"Who is? Where?"

"The cops."

"What are you—"

"Mom, I'm not fooling."

She threw a look to Shipley, who was discretely pulling hair over his bald spot.

"Misty, if this is some sort of—"

"Mom, I'm telling you the truth. This is not something I'd make up."

"Is that Misty?" Shipley asked.

Pilar glanced to him.

"Tell her hi for me."

She nodded. "Officer Shipley says hi."

"You're still there?"

"That's right."

"Great!"

"Why's that—"

"You gotta get him out of there. Now."

"Misty—"

"Look, I know you hate his guts, but you—"

"Who? Officer Shipley's?"

The man brightened at the sound of his name, sucking in his gut a little.

"No, yeah, him too. I mean the preacher."

"I never said any such—"

"He's white, all right."

"I'm not sure where you get your information, but I don't—"

"Mom, they're going to kill him. They're going to kill an innocent man and make it look like suicide!"

Misty had gone into her drama-queen mode, but there was something in her voice that said she really believed it. Then, of course, there were the chief's last words. *"You'll be doing us all a favor by getting him out of here."*

"And what makes you so sure of all of this, young lady?"

"Look, I know, all right. I wouldn't make this stuff up."

"But, even if it's true—"

"It's true, it's true!"

"Even if it's true, what am I supposed to do?"

"I don't know. Something. Anything. Just get him out of there!"

"Mist—"

"I'm not lying, Mom. This is for real."

"All right, all right, I believe you." She threw another look to Shipley.

"Do you need help?" Misty asked.

They arrived at a green steel-grill door. He flashed her a smile as he reached for his keys.

"No, I think I can handle it."

"Are you sure, 'cause—"

"I can handle it."

"Good, 'cause I gotta pick up Luke."

The phrase gave her even less comfort. She glanced at her watch. "It's one-thirty in the morning. You're not going anywhere this time of—"

"I'm already in the car. Gotta go."

"Misty. You're not go—What car? Misty? *Misty?*"

The line went dead and no amount of shouting would bring it to life. She sighed and angrily closed the phone.

"Kids." Shipley shook his head as he unlocked the door and stepped through.

"Tell me about it," she fumed.

"I'll be right back."

"Where you going?"

"To get him." He started to shut the door.

"Wait."

He slowed to a stop.

"Can't I go back too?"

"It's just ... a holding cell."

"I know, but I've never seen, you know, where you work and all." She did her best to sound interested. She wasn't sure she pulled it off. She did, however, notice a slight swelling to his chest.

"Well, sure. Come on back, let me show you around."

"Thanks." She stepped through as he turned to close and lock the door behind them.

Luke walked down the unlit road, taking one measured step at a time. He wasn't drunk, but definitely unsteady.

After what he'd experienced, who wouldn't be?

Not that they were completely finished. He could still hear distant whisperings, could still catch darting mists out of the corners of his eyes.

Without the goggles.

It had taken little effort to crawl out of the bedroom window. The real effort came in willing himself to go in the first place. Because, for him, it was over. He knew that. He'd blown it. Big time. Truth be told, he was lucky to have escaped with his life.

Then there was the matter of Misty. It's not that he didn't trust her. He just didn't know what she had planned. And the last thing he needed was another adventure.

Still, they were going to kill the pastor. And though she said she had it covered, he had his doubts. With Misty he always had doubts.

He saw approaching car lights and pulled the sunglasses from his pocket. He had the goggles but no way would he wear them. Not now.

The car passed with a gentle *whoosh* and everything returned to peaceful silence ... except for the quiet whisper of voices.

And his uneasiness.

He still sensed he was in the middle of some unfolding plan. The only difference was he no longer wanted to be a part of it. The only difference was that his pride had finally given way to humility ... and fear.

Another pair of headlights appeared. They passed, radio blasting, until he heard the screech of brakes. He looked over his shoulder to see the car sliding to a stop. Gears ground until they found reverse and the car backed up ... so recklessly that he had to leap out of the way to avoid being hit.

"Hey, what are you—"

"There you are!" Misty shouted through the passenger window. She reached over and popped open the door. "Hop in."

"Where are we—"

"You got the goggles."

"Yes, but—"

"Hop in."

He approached cautiously.

"Will you hurry up!"

Even now, after all they'd been through, it was almost good to hear her voice.

"Move it, cowboy!"

Almost.

He looked inside, saw something like a portable TV with an antenna on the seat.

"What's that?"

"Get in and I'll tell you."

"But—"

"Get in!"

Almost against his will, he stepped into the car as she picked up the box and dumped it on his lap.

"What is it?"

"Shut the door."

He pulled it closed and Misty returned to her gear grinding. "Bianco and his drug buddy are leaving in a few minutes. We're going to track them with that."

"What do you need me for?"

The car jerked forward.

"If I've got somebody keeping an eye on it, I can drive better."

Luke nodded, though as they lunged again, he doubted his help would make that much difference.

Pilar had no choice.

By the time they'd rounded the corner and headed toward the holding cell, she'd run every possibility though her head.

Ignore Misty's plea?

Maybe. But everything in her gut said her daughter was telling the truth. Or at least that she thought she was.

Try to talk sense to Shipley?

She stole another glance at the man who by now was practically strutting. Logic hadn't worked with the chief. No reason it would start with his wannabe.

Sweet-talk him?

She seriously doubted she had that much control over him ... or over her stomach retching should she try.

That left only one choice. Again she glanced at the shiny black gun in Shipley's holster.

Great, she thought, *just great.*

The holding cell and the two men inside came into view. Lawton sat at the back looking worn and drawn. Virgil was pacing near the front. He was the first to spot them.

"Pilar, that you?"

"Hello, Virgil."

"Thank God Almighty. Listen, will you tell this gentleman here that I'm supposed to get my phone call?"

"Relax, old-timer." Shipley flipped through his keys. "We'll have you out in no time."

Virgil continued, "TV always shows that if a man gets arrested, he gets his phone call. And I haven't had mine. A man's supposed to have his phone call. Will you tell him that? Tell him I'm supposed to get my phone call."

Shipley shook his head and glanced to Pilar. "As far as we can tell the guy's got no mute button."

Pilar looked up guiltily from his gun and forced a smile.

"My Fiona's gonna be worried sick. And Luke. I was out searching for him. Lord knows what's happened to the boy. And if I don't get—"

"He's with Misty," Pilar answered.

"I'm sorry, what?"

"He's with my daughter."

Virgil scowled. "That's supposed to make me feel better?"

"Hasn't done much for me."

"Here we go." Shipley found the right key. He inserted it, turned it, and swung open the door.

"You letting me make my phone call?"

"You can make all the calls you want."

Virgil was surprised into silence ... but only for a second. "What about Pastor Travis here?"

"For him, it's another matter." Shipley tried removing the key but it was stuck.

"The man's got a right to a phone call."

Shipley pulled harder. He leaned down, practically shoving his hip into Pilar. The hip with the gun hanging from it. "Will you give it a rest, old man?"

"I don't understand. Why would you let me make a phone call and not my associate here?"

Still fighting the key, Shipley's patience was wearing thin. "Listen, if you don't put a sock in it, nobody will be making any phone calls. Not now or ever."

"Is that a threat? Pilar, is he threatening me?" Then to Shipley. "First you deprive us of our constitutional rights as shown on TV, and now you're threatening us. Listen, son, the chief and I go way back. Why, I baptized his nephew just a few—"

Still struggling with the key, Shipley sighed. "Pilar, will you *please* tell the man he is free to go."

It was now or never. The door was open, Shipley was preoccupied, and the gun was ... well, it was right there in front of her.

With a deep breath and one quick move, Pilar snapped off the holster's retaining strap and slid out the gun. She was surprised at how cold and heavy it felt.

She was not as surprised at Shipley's response. "Pilar!"

She stepped back from him, raising the weapon.

"Have you lost your mind?"

"Don't move."

"Pilar!" He started toward her.

Clumsily, using both hands, she pointed the gun at him.

He froze. "Whoa, whoa, whoa, be careful with that thing!"

Only then did she notice how violently she shook.

The room grew deathly still. There was no sound except for her heavy breathing. And Virgil's helpful comment: "Listen, I can always make that phone call later."

eleven

I'm not going."

Pilar turned to Travis in surprise. "Pardon me?"

"You two go on without me, I'm staying here."

She looked at him, then the gun, then finally to Virgil. The old man shrugged.

"Pilar." Shipley held out his hand. "Be reasonable, nobody's trying to kill him." He took a step toward her. "Least of all—" she whirled the gun back on him and he ended his sentence with a squeak—"me."

Still shaking, she answered, "I believe there is plenty of evidence to the contrary."

He took a diminutive step backward.

Travis continued his line of reasoning. "Even if they were trying to, you know, hurt me, my duty is still to obey the laws of the land. I mean, I had my doubts back at the church, but 1 Peter, second chapter, verse thirteen could not make it any clearer."

Pilar stared in disbelief as he quoted: "'Submit yourselves for the Lord's sake to every authority instituted among men.'"

Helplessly, she turned to Virgil.

He gave another shrug. "The kid's got a point."

"They're trying to kill him!"

Again Shipley stepped forward. "Nobody's trying to kill any—" again she twirled the gun on him and again he ended with a pathetic chirp—"one."

Now it was Virgil's turn to reason. "Seriously, Pilar, what do we have to base that on? The word of a fifteen-year-old girl who—"

"Sixteen. She's sixteen now." Pilar winced at how much she sounded like Misty.

"All right ... A sixteen-year-old girl who is known to have, well, a rather overactive imagination, or do we believe the authorities who—"

"And the kid," she interrupted, "your houseguest. He believes it too."

Virgil stopped. "Luke's in on this?"

She nodded.

Travis stepped in. "I don't care if the whole world's in on it. I am not going to defy the government authority placed over me by—"

"Zip it, Travis!" Virgil turned back to Pilar. "Luke believes this?"

She reached into her pocket, pulled out her cell phone, and hit Misty's number. "Listen for yourself."

misty dug into her jeans for her cell as Luke braced himself for a near-collision with a passing mailbox.

"Hey, Mom," she answered. "What's up?"

Luke continued staring at the road, hoping by sheer will to keep them on it.

"Sure, he's right here. Hang on."

She passed the phone over to him and he answered, "Hello?"

"Luke, is that you?"

"Virgil?"

"Are you all right, son? I was prayin' and the Lord, He impressed on me you were in some sort of danger. Is everything okay?"

"Yeah. I'm all right—"

Blinding lights and a blasting horn forced Misty back to her side of the road.

" —for now."

"What's this about Pastor Travis's life being in danger? 'Bout people here trying to kill him?"

"I had like a, I think I had a vision ... sort of."

"The impression I got, son, was that you opened up a door you shouldn't have. That your very soul was in danger."

"Yeah, that too. But afterward ... afterward I saw how they were going to kill that pastor guy."

"You saw?"

"Yeah. The man with the holes in his hands showed me."

"Holes in his ... Jesus? Son, Jesus Christ appeared to you?"

"Yeah, I think so."

"And He showed you Pastor Travis was gonna get killed?"

"Yes, sir."

"You're sure of this?"

"Believe me, I wouldn't make up something like that."

"Well, me and Misty's mom, we're already at the police station."

"You're there now?"

"Yup ... bustin' him out as we speak." Luke heard muffled voices in the background. "Listen, son, she wants to talk to Misty a minute."

"Hang on." Luke handed Misty the phone.

She took it. "Yeah?"

As she spoke, he glanced out the windshield. They'd already entered town and were approaching the casino.

"Got it covered," she replied. "We're already tailing Bianco and his drug pal."

Luke checked all directions. As far as he could tell, they weren't following anybody.

"How would I know where?" Misty snapped. "That's why we're tailing them." She pulled the phone from her ear. Even with the windows down and the radio blasting he could hear her mother shouting.

Finally Misty responded, "Mom ..."

More muffled shouting.

"Mom ... you're breaking up. Mom?"

She threw him a look. "Mom, I can't hear you. Mom ..." She waited a moment, then hung up.

"You lose the connection?" Luke asked.

"Yeah, right." Misty shoved the cell into her pants. "Years ago." She slowed the car and pulled to the curb, this time managing not to kill the engine. Without a word, she reached over to the monitor on Luke's lap and snapped it on.

The small screen lit up, displaying a blue-green map.

"What is this?" he asked.

"GPS."

"And this?" He pointed to a flashing red dot on the screen. It was moving, but just barely.

"That, my friend—" she looked out the windshield as a limo emerged from the casino parking garage nearly a block away—"is our mark."

"Our mark?"

She pressed the accelerator, popped the clutch, and killed the engine.

"What do you mean, mark?"

Blowing the hair from her eyes, she started up the car. Then, with a single leap, they began pursuit.

Y ou can't make me leave if I don't want to."
Pilar turned the gun from Shipley and pointed it at Travis.

Incredulous, Virgil asked, "You're going to shoot him if he doesn't escape?"

She swallowed. "I don't know what I'm going to do." With sweaty thumbs, she pulled back the hammer.

Travis's eyes widened.

She continued, "But I guess we'll find out."

With a sigh of contempt, the young pastor turned and started through the cell door. "Insanity ... absolute insanity."

Virgil followed. "Probably ... but not as insane as you wanting to hang around and get yourself killed."

Shipley tried to follow but Pilar blocked him.

He looked up. "Come on, you're not going to lock me in my own cell?"

"It's nothing personal, Geoffrey."

He tried again, until she brought the gun around on him.

He stopped, then stepped back, making it clear he wasn't pleased.

She didn't much care as she closed the cell door, locked it, and effortlessly pulled out the key—leaving Shipley looking at the floor, shaking his head.

"Okay." She turned to the other two, motioning with the gun. "Let's go."

The preachers traded looks and started walking.

"Say, Pilar?"

"Yes, Virgil."

"About that gun, would you mind uncocking it."

She scowled at the hammer, unsure how. "Um, I ..."

He turned, reaching for it. "Here, allow me."

They stopped as she handed him the gun. With great care he released the hammer, then handed it back to her. "There you go."

"Thanks."

"Don't mention it."

Travis's frustration did not lessen. They resumed walking, rounded the corner, and headed for the steel-grilled door.

"I can't believe it," he said to Virgil. "I can't believe that a man of God would let her get away with this."

Virgil gave another one of his vintage shrugs. "The Lord works in mysterious ways."

"But the Bible clearly states—"

"Yes, I heard you. Chapter and verse. But right now, the good people here would like to kill you, so I think right now would be a good time to shake the dust off your sandals and depart their company."

They arrived at the door. Pilar stepped past them and unlocked it.

"Now what?" Travis pouted. "We're just going to stroll on out the front door?"

"Unless you have a better idea."

Apparently he didn't.

She motioned him forward and they continued down the hall.

"Pilar?"

"Yes, Virgil?"

"I'm guessing the front entrance isn't going to be your first choice. I mean with the chief's office being there and all."

"Maybe she's planning to shoot her way out," Travis said. "Is that it, are you planning for some shoot-out that will get us all—"

"Listen, moron!"

Virgil winced as she swung the gun back at Travis.

"I'm bustin' my butt getting you out of here while my own kid's in danger. So I suggest you be a little more appreciative of—"

"Misty's in danger?" Virgil interrupted. "With Luke? What are they doing?"

"We're about to find out. Soon as we get him out of here, we'll—"

"I'm not being unapprec—"

"Where are they? What are they—"

"Shut up! Both of you, shut up!"

Virgil opened his mouth, saw her reaching for the hammer, and decided to obey.

They arrived at a T in the hallway. To the left was the entrance and front office. To the right, a couple unlit back offices and what appeared to be an emergency exit.

She motioned them to the right.

They reached the door and stopped. A large flat bar stretched across it with the words *Emergency Only* printed on it.

She ordered Travis forward. "Let's go."

"But—" He motioned to the sign, started to protest, then thought better of it. With a sigh of resignation, he pushed the handle and immediately set off the alarm.

Pilar helped shove them both through the door. "Come on!" They stumbled out onto the side lawn. "My car's around back. Let's go! Let's go!"

S top the car!"

"What?"

Luke grabbed the wheel.

"What are you—"

"*Stop the car!*"

Misty hit the brakes, fighting to keep the vehicle on the road as they slid to a stop.

And just in time.

They missed the huge figures towering in front of them by only a few yards.

"What are you doing?" she yelled.

"Look!" Luke pointed toward the glowing starmen, four or five of them in the middle of the road.

"What?" Misty demanded. "Look at what?"

He turned to her. "Don't you see them?"

"See what?"

"Them! They're right—" He turned back to the figures, but they were no longer there. "What the—"

He pressed closer to the windshield, searching.

"Luke ..."

He stuck his head out the passenger window.

"Are you having a relapse?"

But he knew they were there. He could still sense their presence.

"Hey. Luke."

He closed his eyes and opened them, trying to refocus. "They were right here, they were ..."

Against his better judgment, he threw a glance up the mountain. He and Misty were halfway up Tahquitz Peak, still following Bianco. But without the goggles all he saw were thunderheads piling around the summit.

"Put them on," Misty ordered.

He continued to stare.

"Luke, put on the goggles."

He shook his head. "No. No more."

"Luke ..."

Again, he shook his head.

"All right, fine." She reached for the gearshift.

"What are you doing?"

She motioned to the monitor on his lap. "Where are they now?"

Luke glanced down at the flashing pinpoint of light. "About a mile ahead. Listen, I don't think—"

"I'm not crazy about going up here any more than you. But something major is coming down and we need to—"

"But not this way, we can't—"

"Why, because of your invisible buddies?" She revved the engine up high.

His panic increased. "You can't just drive through them without—"

"Watch me." She inched out the clutch, and they started forward.

He closed his eyes, bracing for the waves of lust and greed and power to flood through him.

But he felt nothing.

Not in five feet, not in ten, not in twenty.

He looked over his shoulder. There was still no sign of them. Only the roaring whine of the engine and the smell of a burning clutch.

"Maybe they're the good guys!" Misty shouted. "You know, like the ones hanging around us earlier."

Luke frowned. What he saw were much bigger than the ones he'd seen in her room or when they were out in the desert. Yet they were made of the same glowing light. The same glowing light that had invaded him and taken control.

So how could he know the difference?

Maybe he couldn't.

But there was something else troubling him ...

If the ones standing in the middle of the road were the good guys, why were there so many of them? Out here on a secluded mountain? Away from town?

Misty ground the gears into second and they continued winding up the road.

Unfortunately, Luke already suspected the answer.

He stole another look up to the mountain ... just as the first flash of lightning lit the sky, illuminating the peak and clouds surrounding it.

ahquitz Peak?" Virgil exclaimed from the front seat. "They're going to Tahquitz Peak?"

Pilar kept her eyes glued to the road. "That's my bet."

"I don't like the sound of that—not one bit!"

"And you think I do?"

Travis watched from the back as Virgil looked to Pilar, hesitated, then decided not to respond. A first for the old man.

Turning to the side window, Travis stared at the mountain above them, its top covered in clouds. "What could be up there," he asked, "except the beginning of a good thunderstorm?"

"Demons," Virgil answered. "Evil powers and principalities taking their orders from the depths of hell."

Travis leaned back into his seat. "Why am I not surprised?"

Virgil turned to him. "What's that supposed to mean?"

He sighed, seeing no need to answer.

"As much as it kills me to admit it—" Pilar glanced at him through the rear mirror—"Virgil might have a point."

Travis frowned. "What do you mean?"

"For centuries my people have believed it is the home of an evil, malevolent spirit."

Virgil nodded. "A stronghold over the entire valley."

"Why?" Travis asked. "Because there have been a few unfortunate incidents?"

"You call beheaded teens an unfortunate incident?" Virgil was getting worked up again. "And the college kids with all their sex and drugs in the seventies? And the Hollywood debaucheries in the forties and fifties?"

"Virgil ..."

"And now the casino, destroying our entire community! You call these unfortunate—"

"Virgil!"

He stopped, startled at her outburst. Realizing he might have made his point, he looked back out the window, silent but still worked up.

Pilar explained, "We're going up here because my boss, the one who set you up for murder, is about to receive the first shipment of what I expect to become a huge drug operation."

"What? Up here? In this remote location?"

"Can you think of a better place?"

Travis paused, thinking it through. "Well ... then we've got to stop them. We've got to contact the authorities."

"I believe we've already tried that."

"On a local level, yes, but what about federal?"

She glanced at him. "One thing you can say about Peter Bianco, he's thorough. With this type of money I'm sure he's greased all the right palms at all the right levels."

"But we have to stop them. We have to—"

"First we'll save my kid. Then we'll figure out how to stop them."

"Unless you brought your picket signs," Virgil quipped.

"What's that supposed to mean?"

"Maybe a nice demonstration will impress them. Or another referendum. That's really been helpful so far."

Travis bristled. "Why would I need to do that when you've got all those wonderful snake-handling skills?"

Virgil turned on him. "Listen, Pastor, why don't you take some of that arm of the flesh of yours and—"

"Boys," Pilar interrupted. "Boys ..."

Virgil hesitated, then looked back out the window, sulking more than ever.

Travis made his feelings equally clear with a heavy sigh.

For the first time blessed silence stole over the car ... but only for a moment.

"Pilar?" Virgil asked. "Can I borrow your phone?"

"What happened to yours?"

"It's back at the station. Can you believe it, they still didn't let me make my call."

She reached into her pocket and handed it to him.

fiona scooped up the kitchen phone on the second ring. "Hello?"

"Woman ..."

Relieved to hear her husband's voice, she demanded, "Where have you—"

"Somethin' pretty serious is about to happen. Up on Tahquitz Peak."

"Tahquitz Peak? What?"

"I'm not entirely sure. But I'm bettin' dollars to donuts it's got somethin' to do with all our prayers. It just might be the showdown we've been hopin' for all these years."

"Are you serious? Tonight?"

"Yup. We're heading up there right now to take care of business."

"We?"

"Pilar, Pastor Travis, Luke—"

"Luke's in bed."

"Guess again."

Fiona gave a sigh of exasperation. "What can I do?"

"Right now I'm thinkin' the best thing you can do is pray. Pray like you've never prayed before."

"Yes."

"And get some others to join you."

"Yes." She looked up to see Beth's anxious expression. "I've got Beth Lawton here with me now."

"The wife?"

She heard the hesitancy in his voice and asked, "Is that a problem?"

"No, of course not, I was just—"

"Just what?"

"It might not hurt to have somebody else, you know, a bit more ... connected."

"Connected?"

"Well, yes, to God."

"Honestly, Virgil, sometimes you can be so—"

"I just don't want to take chances. This could be the big moment we've been praying for and I—"

"All right, all right, I'll handle it."

"You hear what I'm saying?"

"All right, I'll handle it."

"Good."

"You be careful now."

"Should be a walk in the park."

"Not if that pride of yours gets in the way."

"Just be praying, old woman."

"You too, you old coot. You too."

The line went dead and Fiona slowly hung up.

"Was that Pastor Virgil?"

She looked up at Beth. "Yes. In a car. With your husband."

"Travis? Travis is with Virgil? In the same car?"

Fiona nodded, almost amused.

"Where are they going?"

Fiona hesitated. "Beth ... would you mind grabbing the phone book? Up in the cupboard by the sink?"

The woman moved to the cupboard and reached up to pull down the book.

Fiona continued, "I don't have my glasses, but in the back I have the home numbers of most of the church leaders in our area."

Beth set the book on the counter and flipped to the back. "Here we go." She started to read, "Richard Swenson ..."

"That's right."

"Reverend Susan Lewis ... Father Riordan—" She looked up. "You've got a priest on this list?"

Fiona ignored the comment. "I want you to read off their numbers while I dial them."

"It's almost two in the morning."

"I think they'll want to be in on this."

"What?"

"It's time for a little ol' fashioned prayer meeting ..."

Slow down!" Luke ordered. "We're almost on top of them, slow down!"

Misty obeyed. They eased around a towering bluff of rock and mountain as a chain-link fence came into view—shiny, new, twelve feet tall.

She started to stop.

"I think we're okay." He continued watching the monitor. "Keep going."

Lightning flashed as they crept forward. They approached the fence's entrance, its gate already open.

Neither said a word as they quietly inched through.

Misty fumbled for the lights and turned them off. Now there was only the blue-green glow from the monitor on Luke's lap.

"Where are they?" she whispered.

He studied the screen. "Just to our right. A hundred yards."

She leaned forward, peering into the night.

Lightning flickered, revealing a flat area to their left. She pulled into it, next to a wall of rock.

"What are you doing?"

"We're walking from here." She turned off the engine and opened her door. "Grab the goggles."

"I'm not—"

"Just in case, grab them."

He hesitated—then scooped them up. He climbed out and gently shut the door.

"This way?" she asked, pointing across the road.

He nodded and they started forward.

Another flash of lightning filled the sky. It silhouetted the rocks and cliffs around them, the fence to their right. As far as Luke could tell, they'd reached the summit of the pass. The mountain still loomed hundreds of feet above them, but the road had leveled off and was about to drop down.

A clap of thunder followed, so loud Misty instinctively moved close to Luke's side. Normally, he'd have enjoyed the proximity ... if he wasn't so scared himself.

Trying to calm them with small talk he asked, "How come there's no rain?"

"What?"

"There's a thunderstorm, but no rain."

"What do I look like, the weatherma—"

Another flash caused them to start. Then, in the fading flicker, they spotted the limo. Thirty feet ahead. As darkness returned, only the tiny glow of a decorative swan light on the outside door panel remained.

Luke slowed.

Misty urged him along. "Come on."

But his mind was made up. As the thunder rumbled, he came to a stop.

"What are you doing?"

"What are you going to do once we get there?"

"Demand an explanation."

"And if they don't feel like giving one?"

"We'll cross that bridge when we get to it. Come on." She took his arm and gave a tug, but he did not move.

She turned to the limo, then back to him, then gave an exaggerated sigh. "I gotta say, I liked the other one of you a whole lot better."

"Other one?"

"Yeah, the messiah and raving egotist. At least that one had some spine."

He knew what she was up to and didn't fall for it.

"Are you coming or am I going by myself?"

He held his ground.

She glanced back to the limo. Exasperated, blowing the hair out of her eyes, she turned to him. "Can we at least get closer, hide over by those rocks and try to get some clue about what's going on?"

He looked to the outcropping of rock a dozen feet from the limo.

She gave another pull. "Come on."

Against his better judgment, he let himself be dragged forward.

More lightning flashed as they moved to the side, picking their way over boulders and circling around to the car. When they arrived, they crouched behind the rocks, as close as they dared get. Well, as close as Luke dared get.

"Let's go," she whispered.

"This is good enough."

"I swear to God, cowboy, if we miss something just 'cause you're a chicken, I'm—"

"Trust me, young lass, you won't be missin' a thing." The voice of Sean Connery made them both jump and spin around.

Joey Popiski stood behind them. Grinning. In his hand was a sawed-off shotgun.

twelve

"Where's Bianco?" Misty demanded.

The comedian shrugged. "He's not here."

"Of course he is. That's his car. We followed him from the casino. We—" She came to a stop as he opened the palm of his hand, revealing a small electronic box.

"With this?" he asked.

"He ... set us up?"

"Bright child."

"Why?"

"Come on." He motioned them toward the limo.

They stepped from the rocks into the clearing.

"Where are we going?" Misty asked.

"For a little ride."

"Why, so you can whack us like you did that reporter?"

Luke winced.

The man hesitated for the briefest second. "What ... are you talking about?"

"You know what I'm talking about. We saw it all on the videotape."

"Videotape?"

"The one from the surveillance camera."

He frowned.

Misty continued, "What'd they do, tell you they were going to shut it off?"

His scowl deepened.

She did not back down. "Well, they lied, didn't they?"

He took a moment to size her up, then answered, "*Somebody's* lying." He motioned them toward the limo. "Come on."

Misty hesitated.

He pressed the shotgun barrel into her shoulder. "Now."

Irritated, she turned and continued toward the limo, Luke at her side. "What exactly do you think you're going to do with us?" she demanded.

"Shut up. The less you talk, the easier this will be."

"Easier for who?"

He gave no answer.

"All right, all right—" she slowed—"it's not on tape. We lied. It's not on tape, but we saw it. A bunch of us. We *all* saw it."

"Yeah, right. You saw nothing."

"Of course we did."

"How? It was after sunset. Nobody was around."

"How did we see it?" she asked. "How did we see it?"

He waited.

She turned to Luke. "Tell him how we saw it."

"Me?"

Her expression made it clear that it was his turn to take the ball. "Sure, go ahead."

Lightning flashed, followed by low rumbling. A slight wind had kicked up.

"So, go ahead. Tell him."

"I, uh ..."

"About the goggles." She motioned to them in his hand. Apparently an idea was forming. "Tell him about the goggles."

"The goggles?"

"How they're not only for night vision but telephoto. How you borrowed them from your dad who's a Navy Seal."

"A Navy Seal?"

She gave him a look.

"Oh, right ... You mean how he uses them to see in the dark for like a half mile away?"

"Or farther ..."

"Or farther." Now he was getting it. "And how I used them to see you kill the reporter."

"Uh, Luke ..."

But he was on a roll. "'Cause I'm the only one they work for and—"

"Luke—"

"—if you let us go, I promise never to tell anybody, and you'll be—"

Her angry frown slowed him to a stop.

"—totally ... safe." He smiled weakly as Misty dropped her head to her hand, slowly shaking it.

He glanced to Popiski, hoping for the best.

The man's grin said he was out of luck.

"Here." Popiski reached out his hand. "Let me see those."

"They really don't work," Misty lied. "He just carries them around to impress—"

"Let me see."

Reluctantly, Luke handed him the goggles.

Popiski took them and motioned with the shotgun. "Keep going."

They continued toward the limo, Luke muttering, "Well, that didn't turn out so good."

"You think?" Misty scorned.

"There's nothing here," Popiski said.

Luke threw a glance over his shoulder to see the man holding the goggles to his face. "That's what Misty was saying. They really don't—"

"You have to turn them on," Misty interrupted. It was obvious a new plan was forming in her mind.

Popiski scowled, pulling them from his face and examining them.

She slowed to a stop. "Here, let me show you."

She reached for them, but he pulled back.

"What are you afraid of, you're the man with the gun."

"Just tell me."

"You have to hold them to your face. Real tight."

Cautiously, he brought them back to his eyes. And for the brief moment that his vision was blocked, Misty motioned for Luke to attack.

But where? How? Popiski still had the shotgun, or hadn't she noticed.

"You see anything yet?" Misty asked, motioning for Luke to hurry.

"Nothing." He started pulling them away.

Well, it was now or never. And, though *never* sounded far more appealing, Luke leaped at the man. Popiski gave a startled *oof* and staggered backward, raising his shotgun. But Luke dug in, pushing until Popiski stumbled over a boulder and they fell, the gun flying from his hands.

Unfortunately, Luke was no fighter. He was unsure what to do next.

Misty wasn't. "Hit him! *Hit him!*"

He swung his fist, punching hard—into what, he wasn't sure. The man was all chest and arms and blubber. But he hit something hard enough to cause the man to gasp. Encouraged, Luke hit it again ... until the man flipped him over and climbed onto his chest, pinning his arms, nearly suffocating him with his weight until—

Thud!

Popiski yelled, grabbing his head.

Misty stood above him, holding a rock.

He turned to her, swearing.

She responded by hitting him again.

Taking advantage of the moment, Luke tried to push him off. The man looked down and punched him hard in the mouth. Then again, catching his cheek just below the left eye.

Luke felt no pain, not yet. Only anger. He squirmed, trying to free his arms, when car lights bounced and blazed into his vision.

Popiski looked up, then scrambled off Luke's chest, pushing a knee into his stomach in the process. He crawled to the shotgun, grabbed it, and turned it back on them.

Pilar hit the brakes, throwing both men forward. The Land Rover barely stopped before she had the door open and was racing toward her daughter. "Misty! What are you doing?"

That's when she saw the man staggering to his feet and wielding a sawed-off shotgun.

"Popiski?" she yelled. "What are you—Put that thing away!"

He turned to her and pointed the weapon. "Stay back!"

"Mom!"

Misty started for her, until the man turned the gun on her. "Stay there!" Then to Pilar again. "Don't move!"

Pilar slowed to a stop, more angry than concerned. "What are you doing with that thing?"

Lightning flashed above them, followed by a clap of thunder that faded to a rumbling growl.

"It's a trap," Misty shouted. "Bianco's not here. This jerk lured us out here so he could—"

"Shut up!"

"Don't tell my kid to shut up!"

The man tightened his grip on the gun. "You too. Both of you, shut up!"

Only then did Pilar notice how much he was sweating.

"What's going on out here?" She heard Virgil slam the truck door. "Luke? You okay, son?"

The boy nodded, fingering a cut below his left eye and glowering at the fat man.

Pilar noticed shadows from the headlights dancing on either side of her as both preachers approached.

"You're Joey Popiski," Travis said as they arrived. "The comedian. What are you doing out here with the children?"

"He's trying to kill us, that's what he's doing," Misty answered. "Just like he did with the reporter."

Popiski spun the gun back on her. "Shut up, I said!"

Pilar took a tentative step forward. "Misty, do what the man says."

"But—"

"Misty!"

The girl crossed her arms in a huff.

Travis continued past Pilar heading directly toward the man. At first she didn't understand ... until a flash of lightning revealed the gun shoved in the back waistband of his pants. The gun she'd left in the truck.

Popiski trained the shotgun on him. "Stay back!"

Travis slowed but continued forward. "Listen, nobody's going to hurt you."

"Stay back!"

"This isn't all your doing. I'm sure Bianco pressured you into—"

"Travis ...," Virgil warned.

But the young preacher wasn't listening. "I bet you didn't even know he was part of this drug-trafficking thing, did you?"

"Drug trafficking?"

"See." He continued forward. "And as far as we can figure, down there—" he motioned to the canyon just beyond them—"is going to be the center of their operation." He was a dozen feet away and still closing in.

Popiski took a hesitant step backward. Realizing his threats to Travis were doing no good, he turned the shotgun back on the kids. "Stop right there!"

"Do what he says!" Pilar yelled. "Do what he says!"

Travis slowed to a stop, holding out his palms. He was nervous but doing his best to hide it. "So where do we go from here, friend?"

In the lightning, Pilar could see Popiski's face glistening with perspiration. He took a shaky assessment of the situation, then pointed the weapon back on Travis.

Misty started toward her mother, until Popiski swung the shotgun back at her. "Don't—"

That was all the distraction Travis needed to pull the revolver from his pants.

Still holding the shotgun on the kids, the comedian turned, squinting into the headlights, startled to see that he was now looking at the barrel of a handgun.

"What are you doing?" he demanded.

Travis clumsily pulled back the hammer.

"Are you nuts?" Nervously, Popiski nodded to the shotgun he still had on the kids. He turned to Pilar and Virgil. "Is he nuts?"

Travis's voice quivered slightly. "Probably."

"No," Pilar ordered. "Travis, don't."

Virgil couldn't agree more. "Do what she says. That ain't a solution."

Travis shook his head, gun still in hand.

"I'd do like they say." Lightning flickered and Popiski forced a grin. "'Cause if you don't—" he raised the shotgun higher on the kids—"their blood will be on your hands."

"Listen to him, Travis," Pilar urged.

"Seems I've already got one man's blood on my hands." Travis's voice seemed unusually flat. "What do I care about a couple others?"

Popiski's grin faded. Suddenly he wasn't so sure the preacher was bluffing.

"Besides," Travis continued, "they're not my kids."

"Travis!" Pilar shouted.

"This ain't the way, son," Virgil called. "You're a man of God, we've got other weapons."

"Really?" Travis answered without looking back. "Because at the moment I'm not seeing them."

More lightning and thunder.

Virgil shouted, "Those who live by the sword die by the sword!"

"As far as I can tell, I'm not the one who's about to die."

"Travis," Pilar pleaded, "please don't!"

He glanced back to her, and instantly, Popiski spun the gun on him.

That's when Luke made his move. He sprang at the man, hitting him hard in the side and knocking him to the ground.

The shotgun went off and Misty screamed. Travis rushed into the fray. Pilar followed, but the kid and the preacher seemed to be doing enough damage.

"Mom . . ."

She turned and was practically knocked over by her daughter throwing herself into her arms. Only when they separated did she see Travis dragging the unarmed Popiski to his feet, holding the gun on him.

Virgil joined Travis's side. "Nice bluff."

"You sure it was a bluff?" the pastor asked, still breathing hard.

Virgil gave him a look, then chose his words a bit more carefully. "Though not exactly the behavior I'd expect from a servant of the Lord."

"I'll seek His forgiveness later."

"I certainly hope so."

An approaching roar caught their attention. Pilar looked up just in time to see a cargo plane pass overhead—illuminated only a moment by more lightning, before it disappeared into the clouds.

"What was that?" Misty asked.

But Pilar already knew. "You and the boy, I want you to head back to the car. Get home as fast as you can."

"But—"

"Now!"

"Mom!"

"Can you just this once do what I say without arguing? Go! Now!"

Misty turned and sulked toward the car, Luke trailing behind.

"And what about me?" Popiski sneered at Travis. "Still planning on killing me?"

The pastor seemed to hesitate.

"Travis ...," Virgil admonished.

The young man shrugged in resignation.

Virgil turned to Popiski. "You're lucky he's in a *good* mood."

"Misty?" Pilar called.

She came to a stop, dripping in attitude.

"If we tie up Mr. Popiski here good and tight, you think you can take him into town?"

"You don't even have to tie him. We'll get him there."

Pilar turned toward Travis and Virgil. "I've got some rope in the truck."

Virgil started toward the vehicle, giving a nod. "I'll handle it. I almost joined the Navy ... twice."

Pilar looked back up into the sky. She knew the plane was circling. No doubt looking for an opening in the clouds.

Gun still trained on Popiski, Travis asked, "You really think we can stop that?"

She turned to him. "Do we have a choice?"

He looked at her, then back up into the clouds. "Whatever we do, we haven't much time."

"Reverend Swenson." Fiona pushed open the screen door. "Please come in."

"Thank you." The tall, gray-haired man stooped slightly as he stepped through the door and entered the living room.

"I appreciate you coming with it being so late and all."

"Certainly. Particularly, if what you say is—" He came to a stop, seeing the handful of clergy sitting before him.

Fiona joined his side. "I believe you know everyone here. Father Riordan, Reverend Williams, Beth Lawton—Pastor Lawton's wife ..."

They exchanged nods.

"... and Reverend Susan Lewis."

Fiona noticed the briefest hesitation on his part. Apparently, so did Reverend Lewis. She was immediately on her feet, reaching for his hand. "How are you, Reverend?"

"Fine." He smiled politely as he shook her hand. "Just fine. And you?"

"Couldn't be better, thanks."

"Please—" Fiona offered him a spot on the sofa—"have a seat. Can I get you a cup of coffee?"

He smiled. "I'm Lutheran. Coffee is always welcomed—particularly at this late hour."

"You've got that right," Father Riordan chuckled. "Don't know if you're aware, but the church leaders nearly persuaded Pope Clement VIII to outlaw it as the drink of the devil."

Reverend Swenson arched an eyebrow.

"Thank God they failed." Father Riordan grinned as he took a sip from his mug.

"Yes," Reverend Swenson smiled stiffly. "Thank God."

Hoisting her own coffee before the group, Reverend Lewis laughed, "Well, that's at least one theological issue we can all agree upon."

She was greeted by a round of silence and even stiffer smiles.

"Please make yourself at home." Fiona turned toward the kitchen. "We should get started in just a minute." She disappeared, adding under her breath, "... provided we survive that long."

Virgil thought it strange that Pilar refused the shorter route to the canyon floor, the one directly beside Smashing Wall. Of course, he knew all about Cahuilla folklore, but he never suspected Pilar to be the superstitious kind.

So, instead of the quicker route, they followed the road twenty to thirty feet off to its side lest there be cameras along the way. It was a lot longer and far more tiring—a fact that Virgil didn't mind pointing out ... frequently. It wasn't that he was a complainer; he just knew that in order to make a point you sometimes had to repeat it ... frequently.

Then there was the matter of Travis's arsenal. Besides the handgun stuffed in his pants, he was now toting Popiski's shotgun.

"You know how to use those things?" Virgil asked.

"What's to know?"

"You didn't answer my question."

Travis gave no reply.

"Remember, we do have a greater power at our disposal."

Again, no answer.

Finally there was Pilar's insistence that she'd seen a landing strip where none existed. An obvious mistake, but one she refused to admit.

"Maybe you were in a different canyon," Travis suggested.

"I think I can tell the differences in canyons."

"I'm merely suggesting—"

"I don't need any suggestions right now, thank you very much."

"I didn't meant to imply—"

"Guys," Virgil interrupted, "maybe we could all be a bit more—"

"Virgil, please." Travis cut him off.

"I'm just saying—"

"I know what you're saying, but could we hear a little less of it, please?"

"A man oughta be able to express himself."

"And enjoy occasional silence," Pilar muttered under her breath.

And so the happy trio continued until they arrived at the canyon floor and studied the area. There were three buildings. One was no bigger than a ranch house. A second, attached to it, was the size of a large barn. The third was a small outbuilding near the parking area where the generator appeared to be housed. As lightning flashed it was possible to see that all three buildings were painted in camouflage colors with rock and dirt scattered on their roofs.

The parking lot before them had two unmarked vans. Beyond that, directly in front of the doors to the main building, sat another limo. Milling near it were two middle-aged men dressed in dark suits.

Pilar was the first to spot them and motioned for the group to take cover behind a pile of rocks.

As they settled in, Travis whispered, "Do you see any cameras?"

She was already counting, pointing to opposite ends of the main building and the barn. "Two … three … and four."

"Nothing in the parking lot? The other building?"

She gave a hard look at the utility pole near the vans, then over to the generator shed.

"Nothing I can see." Again she scanned the lot. "Long as we keep those two vehicles between us and the cameras we'll be okay. At least for starters."

Travis nodded.

She continued, "Virgil and I will go first. You follow."

"Got it."

Turning to Virgil, she asked, "You ready?"

"Am I ready? Young lady, as a man of God I'm always—"

"Let's go then." She rose to her feet. Virgil followed her lead. They dashed across the parking lot to the nearest van. There was no sound except for the rumble of thunder and the crunch of rocks under their feet. Once they arrived, Virgil crouched near her, catching his breath.

"You okay?" Pilar asked.

He nodded, gasping, "Couldn't ... be ... better ..."

A moment later Travis joined them.

"Ready for the next one?" she asked.

"Of course," Virgil wheezed.

"Let's do it."

They sprinted to the next van, Virgil arriving the worse for wear. He was debating whether to go into cardiac arrest or just pass out when Travis joined them and asked, "Now what?"

W ill you quit fooling around?" Luke fidgeted outside the limo as Misty, who had plopped into the driver's seat, took a quick survey of the controls—the AC seats, the plasma TV, the mood lighting.

"Ever ridden in one of these?" she asked.

"We're supposed to take him back."

Next she tried the moonroof. "Right, but they didn't say which vehicle."

"I'm sure they meant your car, not the casino's."

"Actually, they're both the casino's."

Frustrated, Luke turned back to the truck where Virgil had left Popiski tied up on the ground.

Well, where he *had* been tied up on the ground.

"Oh, no." Luke started toward the vehicle.

"What?" Misty called.

"He's gone."

"What?"

"Popiski. He's disappeared."

O ver there!" The voice was faint and high above them. Virgil turned to look at the mountain. In the flickering light he caught a glimpse of a figure standing above and just to the right of Smashing Wall. He was obviously trying to get the guards' attention, waving, but with his hands clasped together.

"Guys ... over there!"

Virgil rose and glanced through the van's windows to see the two guards searching the rocks.

The voice shouted again, "By the van!"

The first guard spotted the figure and pointed. "Up there!"

"Behind the van! They're behind the—" Thunder drowned out the rest.

The guards peered up into the darkness. "Who are you?" they yelled.

"Behind that van!"

"Who are—"

"Joe Popiski."

"Joey?"

"They're behind the van!"

Although they didn't fully understand, the guards had the good sense to turn their rifles in the direction of the van, just in case.

Immediately Virgil dropped out of sight.

"All right," the first guard shouted, "who's there?"

The other joined in, "If someone's there, you better show yourself, and you better do it now."

"Behind the van!" Popiski repeated.

Virgil, Travis, and Pilar flattened themselves against the vehicle.

"What do we do now?" Virgil whispered. He spotted Travis tightening his grip on the shotgun and groaned, "Oh, brother."

He heard the scrape of footsteps approaching. Unable to resist, he scooted toward the front bumper to take a peek.

"Virgil," Pilar hissed.

He leaned around it ... until he was staring directly into a pant leg.

"Well, hello there."

It was owned and operated by one of the guards ... who had a rifle pointed directly at Virgil's head. Before he could respond, he heard Travis make his move—though he didn't get far before another voice at the opposite end of the van ordered, "Hold it right there."

Travis came to a stop.

"Now hand that over to me ... nice and slow."

Looking over his shoulder, Virgil saw Travis giving up his rifle—as Pilar slowly rose to join them.

"Pilar?" the guard asked. "What are you doing here?"

"Get up, old man," the first voice demanded.

Reluctantly, Virgil rose and joined the crowd.

The second guard motioned his rifle toward Travis. "And the one in your pants."

The pastor reached for the gun in his waistband.

"Real slow."

Carefully he removed it and handed it over to the guard.

Virgil sighed, just loud enough for Travis's benefit. "So much for 'living by the sword.' "

uke spotted him shouting on the edge of a precipice some ten feet below.

"Mr. Popiski!"

The man spun around, so startled that he lost his footing. With hands still tied, it was impossible for him to keep his balance.

"Mr. Pop—"

He fell from sight.

Luke scampered down after him, sliding with the dirt and rocks. He arrived at the edge, barely stopping himself from going over.

Popiski was just below, pressed against the mountainside, standing on a steep incline of loose gravel that was rapidly slipping under his feet. Luke dropped onto his chest and stomach, barely aware of the earth moving around him as he stretched down as far as he could.

"Grab my hands!" he yelled.

The man looked up, eyes wild in the flash of lightning.

"Grab my hands!"

Popiski looked down, searching for another option, feet still slipping.

"Reach up and—"

The earth gave way and Popiski fell. He threw up his arms, but he was too late.

Luke lunged for him, barely grazing his hands before the man slipped away. The thunder drowned out any cry he might have made as he fell into the night, his body slamming into the rocks again, and then again.

But Luke barely noticed as the rocks under his own arms and chest broke free, sending him sliding over the edge.

"Luke!" Misty cried.

He turned, grabbing and clawing at the liquid earth, desperate for any hold, for any way to stop himself. His right hand caught a chunk of rock that didn't give way. He threw his other hand to it as well, slowing himself to a stop, clinging for all he was worth.

"Luke!"

Virgil searched the cliff, seeing nothing in the darkness until the lightning flashed.

"There!" Travis pointed. "Up there!"

He caught sight of someone twisting and squirming, hanging onto an outcropping of rock. And above him ...

"Misty!" Pilar cried. She cupped her hands. "Misty, get back!"

But the girl did not listen.

"It's Luke!" Travis shouted. "He's fallen."

Pilar broke from the group, immediately heading for the cliff. "Misty!"

Travis was on her heels.

"Hold it!" the first guard shouted. "*Hold it!*"

The couple slowed to a stop.

"Nobody's going nowhere."

"What are you talking about?" Virgil argued. "The boy's barely hanging on. If he falls—"

"Then I guess he falls."

"What?" Travis exclaimed.

The second guard agreed. "Can't go around protecting every trespasser who sneaks onto the property."

Pilar and Travis stood, mouths agape. But Virgil had had enough. It was time to show these boys what the Holy Spirit of God could do. Travis had proven what little impact the flesh had with all its worldly weapons. Now it was time to take off the gloves and get down to business.

He started toward the guards. "Listen, fellows ..."

They turned to him.

"He's a kid. He needs our help."

They simply stared.

"All right, fine. You do what you have to do." He turned and started toward Pilar and Travis. "But there are children up there and we're going to help them. So if you'll excuse us." He held out his arms, herding the couple toward the cliff.

"Stop right there, old man."

But Virgil didn't stop. He didn't have to.

"I said stop!"

Finally, gathering himself, he turned and exercised his authority. "In the name of Jesus Christ, I command you to lower your guns."

The two guards glanced at each other, perplexed.

"Virgil?" Travis warned. "What are you—"

He held out his hand for silence. "Watch and learn." Then to the guards he again commanded, "In the name of Jesus Christ, I order you to lay down your arms."

The men shifted their weight—surprised, unsure what to do.

With confidence, Virgil turned back to Pilar and Travis. "Let's go, they can't hurt us now."

The couple hesitated.

He nodded them forward.

After an exchange of nervous looks, they obeyed, Virgil following.

"Stop!"

"Don't worry," Virgil said, "they can't harm us. We're the ones with the authority." Then for Travis's benefit he added, "And you may have noticed it's not through the arm of the flesh. Because the real auth—"

A rifle exploded, kicking up dirt and rock two feet to his left.

More angry than frightened, Virgil turned back on them. "The Lord rebuke you! I rebuke you in the name of—"

Two more shots fired, chipping up rock just inches from his feet. Then a third, directly between them.

"Get back here!" the guards ordered. "All of you!"

Travis and Pilar hesitated.

"Now!"

After another round of glances, all three headed back to the guards.

"Well, that worked nicely," Travis muttered under his breath.

Virgil was too surprised to reply.

The door to the building opened and Bianco appeared. "What's going on? What's all the shoot—" He came to a stop as he saw the group.

"Well, Pilar ... this is a surprise." Then, nodding to Virgil and Travis, he added, "Gentlemen."

There was no need to answer.

"I wish you would have called first. At the moment, we're so unprepared for company."

"Luke!" Misty's voice again shouted from above. "Hang on!"

Bianco cocked his heard toward the mountain. Lightning strobed just enough for him to see portions of the scene.

"My, this is quite a turnout."

"We've got lots of trespassers," the first guard agreed.

"Yes. Well, bring them inside. We'll decide what to do with them in a bit. Right now things are a little too—"

He was interrupted by the sound of three horn blasts that echoed through the canyon.

Virgil spun around. Just beyond the parking lot, the entire length of the canyon floor—rocks, boulders, even the brush—started to glow. He squinted into the night, trying to understand.

No, the rocks and vegetation weren't glowing. The ground under them was. And not uniformly. Instead, there were balls of light, spaced about twenty feet apart. Two lines of them, running parallel with each other all the way to the end of the canyon.

But that wasn't his only surprise.

Suddenly the canyon floor began to rumble—not from thunder, but from the ground's movement. It was sliding to one side! Exposing first one line of the lights, then the other ... until a runway appeared.

"Get inside," Bianco repeated.

The guards motioned the group with their guns. Only then did they notice they were one shy.

"Where's Pilar?"

Virgil turned to look. She was nowhere in sight.

"She's gone after the kids!" The second guard moved into action.

"Relax," Bianco called after him.

"But—"

"Relax. We've closed the gate; there's no way she can get out."

"And the kids?"

"As I said, no one will be leaving."

thirteen

fighting for breath, Pilar continued climbing the steep
bluff. She was 170 feet above the floor of the canyon
when a foothold gave way and she lunged for the nearest
outcropping of rock. She clung tightly as dirt and boulders
slipped away.

"Mom!" Misty shouted from above. "Be careful!"

"Well, all right," she gasped. She found a foothold,
wedged her toes in, and rested a moment. "If you say so."

"I'm serious."

There was no missing her daughter's concern. Had it
been anywhere else, it might have been touching. But not
here. Not directly beside Smashing Wall.

The boy was still thirty feet above—hanging from a
boulder that had broken his fall. Hanging, while kicking
and twisting, his grip slowly slipping.

Misty had scrambled down to another ledge, a dozen
feet above him.

The lightning came quicker, the thunder closer, though
there was still no rain. The wind had also picked up, whipping dirt and sand into Pilar's eyes. But that was the least
of her concerns.

Because as the storm increased, so did her memories ...

"Come on, babe."

"Matthew, stop it!"

She forced herself to resume climbing—though she
could not resist glancing over to Smashing Wall, then down

to its base—the flattened area where they had spread their blanket for a picnic. She'd chosen the location as a dare, to tease him about its ghoulish past. But, for whatever reason, the place seemed to turn him on. And soon their customary make-out session had grown out of control.

"Matthew, you're scaring me ..."

Pilar dug deeper into the cliff, pulling harder with her hands and arms.

But the memories did not stop.

His mouth over hers. Nothing like before. Now it was relentless. Demanding.

Pilar blinked the memories away, but only for a moment.

Thoughtful and caressing hands had turned urgent, insistent, yanking at her cutoffs, ripping her peasant blouse. She tried to slap him, but he pinned her arms. She tried screaming, but his weight made it impossible to breathe.

"Hurry, Mom! He's slipping!"

She looked up.

There was Misty, staring down at her in concern. And between them, on the ledge, the boy in danger. The boy who in many ways looked like—

Lightning flashed.

Matt's long hair hung over his face as he leered down at her.

"Mom!"

More lightning. It was the boy again. And Misty.

She hesitated, took a breath to steady herself, and continued.

More images ... bare arms flailing.

"Yeah, babe, I like it rough too."

Other memories rushed in. Forgotten. Buried. Legs and knees, squirming, kicking. Raw panic. Suffocating weight.

And still Pilar continued climbing, tears filling her eyes.

"Matthew, please ..."

Her heart hammered in her chest, but not from the climb.

"Come on, Mom, you're almost there, come—"

"—on, baby, come on!"

She was gasping now, barely able to breathe.

He yanked back her hair, slamming her head into a rock—she screamed but was unable to scream, moved but unable to move—the impossible weight.

She kneed him in the groin.

He swore and punched her in the face. "Settle down!"

"Mom ..."

Another head slam. Seeing stars. More clothes giving way. Those animal eyes, jeering mouth, and the panic, and pain, relentless, unstoppable ...

"Mom ..."

Tears streamed down her face as Pilar fought for air. But she refused to give in. Not this time. Mustering all of her strength, she continued climbing toward the boy.

Well, I'd say this is getting pretty interestin', wouldn't you?"

Travis didn't bother looking up from the gray metal table. The day had been too long, the defeats too many.

But always a bundle of opinion, Virgil was up on his feet pacing. "Praise God, least they didn't tie us up in back-to-back chairs and gag us."

Travis glanced over to the locked door of their six-by-ten windowless room. "I think they only do that in movies."

"Could be, could be. So ..." Virgil slapped his little belly. "You got any more tricks up your sleeve?"

"Please, I'm not in the mood."

"No, I'm serious. We're missing all the action cooped up in here, and I'm plum out of any ideas."

"What? No more authority to call down from heaven?"

"Nope. And I'm guessin' you've run out of swords for the arm of the flesh."

Touché. There was a moment's pause. But only a moment.

Virgil resumed his pacing. "Tell you the truth, I don't know why it didn't work. The Bible, it says we got authority to trample on vipers and scorpions and such. And them boys, well, I don't see them much farther up the food chain, do you?"

Travis said nothing, which of course didn't stop Virgil. "I can tell you it's a real puzzle. I just don't know what's going on." His voice grew a bit softer. "Not anymore."

Travis looked up, surprised at the old-timer's candor.

"Nothin' seems to work. And not just tonight. Me and Fiona, we've been binding and loosing spirits around this valley over thirty years now ..."

"And ..."

"Same thing. Nothing. Oh, we get a convert or two, and there's always the poor to help and all ... but when it comes to spiritual warfare, we've barely scratched the surface." He slowed to a stop and quietly sighed.

Travis nodded. "No argument here. Our church attendance ..." He hesitated, unsure if he should continue.

Virgil looked to him, waiting for more.

"Well, at best, it's flatline."

"Us too," Virgil agreed. "Us too."

Travis eyed him before continuing. "And we're doing all that Scripture calls us to do—praying, tithing, preaching the Word. We've seen it work in other places, but not here, not in this valley. It's like we're stuck."

Virgil returned to his pacing. "And that's not what the Lord promised, no, it's not." The room shook with another peal of thunder. "We ain't supposed to be stuck. We're supposed to have the power and authority. That's what He promises." He paused, then added with a trace of sadness, "And now ... all of this."

Silence again fell over them as the thunder rippled away.

Virgil gave another sigh and pulled out the chair opposite Travis. "Well, at least we can do some worshiping. They can make us their prisoners, but they can't stop us from doing that, right?"

Travis blinked in surprise. "What? Here?"

"Sure. Not much else we can do." Before Travis could reply, he asked, "So ... you got a favorite hymn we can sing?"

"Now? Locked up like this?"

Virgil shrugged. "Seemed to work for Paul and Silas, back when they was in prison."

Travis started to respond but could find no argument.

Virgil gave his head a scratch. "Let's see, what's a good one. Oh, I got it." He cleared his throat. "This is one of Fiona's and my favorites."

"All hail the pow'r of Jesus' name!"

His voice was thin and wavy, changing keys with nearly every line.

"Let angels prostrate fall."

"Come on." He nodded to Travis. "Sing. Let's you and me at least do some worshipin'."

"Bring forth the royal diadem
And crown Him Lord of all!"

But Travis had no desire to sing. Or to worship. To be honest, it made him feel all the worse. For, as Virgil continued, the all-too-familiar waves of guilt poured in. Guilt over his failures. Guilt over the sin that brought him here in the first place. And, as always, guilt over his hypocrisy.

"Bring forth the royal diadem ..."

Instead, Pastor Travis Lawton lowered his head onto the table and closed his eyes against the burning he felt in them.

"And crown Him Lord of all ..."

Luke's arms were losing feeling. Somehow he had to get a foothold, fast. Somehow he had to pull himself back up on top of the rock. But he kicked his legs uselessly in the air, unable to find a thing. And lowering his head to look under the rock for a spot would be suicide. His arms simply wouldn't hold.

"Mom! Hurry!"

He looked up to Misty. She shouted down at her mother, who was somewhere below him. And behind Misty, up in the sky ... well, it was odd, but from the moment Pilar had started her climb, he had noticed a tiny opening, its edges bordered in light. And the higher Pilar climbed, the larger it seemed to grow.

"Can you reach him?"

The scrape and crumbling of rock told him Pilar was close.

"Mom, can you—"

"No," the woman gasped. "There's no way!"

He looked at his hands. Knuckles white. Fingers starting to bleed.

"Luke!" It was the first time the woman had ever used his name. "Move your foot over to the left."

He turned and shouted, "What?"

"There's a tiny ledge below and to your left."

He kicked, scraping the side of the mountain with his foot, but felt nothing.

"It's below—just a couple feet below."

Again he tried but felt nothing.

"You'll have to let go. Swing yourself to the side and let go. If you slide down you'll catch it."

"That's crazy!" he shouted.

"It's the only way."

He tried again. And again he failed—the movement taxing his arms to their limit.

"You have to let go!"

"Do what she says!" Misty yelled.

He looked up to her. "Do you see it?"

"Not from here, but she does!"

"You have to trust me!" Pilar shouted. "It's to your left and a couple feet below. If you slide down the face you'll hit it."

"What if I miss?"

"You won't miss. Not if you swing hard to the left."

Lightning flashed.

"Do what she says, Luke! Do what she says!"

"To the left and let go!"

He stared at his hands, his arms. They'd nearly lost feeling.

"You have to let go!"

He only had one try left. It was all or nothing. He looked back up to Misty—noticed the hole of light in the clouds had nearly tripled in size.

"Trust her!" she shouted. "You gotta trust her!"

He nodded, more to himself than to her. Then, after a silent prayer, he took a deep breath. Lightning flashed as he kicked to the side as hard as he could. But he felt nothing.

"Let go!" Misty shouted. "You gotta let go!"

His hands gave way, dragging his fingers across the boulder. He was falling, sliding down the cliff, flesh ripping off his hands.

And he felt nothing! No rock, no ledge, no—

His left foot hit a toehold.

"That's it!" Pilar shouted.

He dug in, making it bear all his weight as he brought his right foot to join it, clinging to the face of the mountain for all he was worth.

"All right!" Misty yelled.

"Now inch your way to the left," Pilar ordered. "It widens out to a ledge. Keep going and it's wide enough to sit on."

Still on the very tip of his toes, with legs shaking from exhaustion and fear, he carefully worked his way to the left.

"That's it. Keep going, keep going ..."

Gradually the ledge widened until he was able to drop down onto the balls of his feet and continue working his way across. It kept widening until he eventually collapsed to his knees.

"You okay?" Misty shouted.

"Yeah ..." He turned over and sat. "I'm all right."

"Now you're just above Smashing Wall," Pilar explained. "There's no way I can get to you. Not from down here. And as far as I can see, not from above. We'll have to get ropes, maybe a rescue crew."

He looked up and around. She was right, he was completely cut off, surrounded by the smooth, flat wall.

"Are you going to be okay there?"

He checked again. The ledge continued to widen. Just a few feet away it was broad enough for him to even lie down if he wanted. "Yeah."

"You sure?"

"I could stay here all night if I had to."

Pilar nodded, then looked back up to her daughter. "Misty!"

"I heard."

"Go into town and get somebody."

"Where are you—"

"I'm heading back down there to see if I can help."

"Not by yourself."

"They need—"
"If you're going down there, I'm going with you."
"Misty."
"Sorry."
"What about Luke?"
"You heard him. He can stay all night if he has to."
"Mist—"
"Sorry, Mom, I'm coming." Before the woman could argue any further, her daughter started her descent. Then, realizing she needed both hands, she called down to Luke, "Hey, cowboy!"

He looked up just in time to catch the goggles she threw at him.

all right." Fiona glanced nervously at her watch, then read from the list in her hands. "So far we have: No prayers to Mary, no liturgical prayers of any type, nothing from the rosary, nothing to the saints ..."

"And no tongues," Reverend Lewis added.

Fiona nodded, writing it down, "And no ... tongues."

When she'd finished, she looked up. "Anything else?"

The group took a moment to think as Father Riordan mumbled, "Thank God, we've still got Jesus."

They chuckled uneasily and Fiona repeated, "Thank God, we've still got Jesus."

She waited another moment, then continued, "Well then, let's get started. Reverend Swenson, will you open us up, please. And the rest of you pray as the Spirit leads—" catching herself she amended—"pray as you feel led."

The group nodded.

Reverend Swenson cleared his throat and bowed his head.

Some followed his lead. Others simply closed their eyes. One or two silently slid from the sofa to their knees.

"Heavenly Father ..."

His voice was so theatrical it made Fiona wince. But she kept her eyes shut and forced herself to silently join in.

"We ask for Your presence here amidst us. And, as Christ prayed in Gethsemane, we ask that You do, indeed, make us one, just as You and the Son are one. We ask that You heal our divisions so that we might come together, interceding on behalf of our humble community, so that we might ..."

And so the prayer began. Stiff and formal at first, but over time, as others joined in, it began coming more and more from the heart.

Luke had no desire to put on the goggles. He'd seen enough of the spirit world. He knew it was safer and lot saner just to live in normal, everyday ignorance. Then there was his pride—the way it had taken over without him even knowing it, making him think he was somebody special, that the rules no longer applied, that he was more "worthy" than others.

Something was about to happen. He knew it. He also knew it was something he could no longer be a part of. That was his punishment. He could no longer be a player. It hurt, but he understood the punishment and knew that it was just.

And yet, since he was out of the action, he also understood that, at least for him, it would be safe. He could watch. He could no longer participate, but he could watch.

And he could pray.

That's how the goggles could help. They would show him how to pray.

Not for himself. Not this time.

Now it was for others.

He took a moment to listen to Misty and Pilar's fading voices as they descended to the canyon floor, bickering about how to stop the bad guys ...

"Burn the whole place down," Misty was insisting.

"With what?"

"If it's an airport, it's gotta have fuel."

"We can't assume—"

"Airplane fuel really burns. I saw it in *Raiders of the Lost Ark*."

"Misty ..."

"Did you see the movie?"

"Well, no, but—"

"Then how can you say it doesn't work?"

And so they continued, disappearing into the night.

Luke sat for a long moment staring at the goggles in his hands. Once again he looked up to the opening in the sky. It was still growing bigger, flashes of lightning outlining its edges. Finally, with a quiet prayer for protection, he slipped them on ...

And he caught his breath in astonishment.

The opening was full of light, but it was not empty. It was filled with creatures similar to those he'd seen over the church and more recently standing on the road. There were dozens of them. And as the hole grew, more appeared.

They formed a circle, their backs toward the center as they faced the blackness of the surrounding clouds. But, of course, they were not clouds. They were a thick swarm of amphibian faces, complete with the mandatory fangs, spindly arms, and long, sharp talons.

And the lightning? He saw it clearer now too. Its flashes surrounded the edge of the opening, yes. But it was not lightning. It came from the light creatures as they wielded what appeared to be swords against the darkness. And with each sword's contact against the blackness came the sparks. Brilliant, blinding sparks.

See," Misty whispered, "I told you they'd have the stuff."

Pilar didn't bother to reply. She was too busy checking out the brightly lit hangar twenty yards ahead of them. Inside was a private jet. Not far from it two, no, three men sat in overalls around a table, putting down chips and sodas, obviously waiting to service the next plane when it arrived. It had passed overhead again—as she and Misty crossed the parking lot. Its ominous drone made it clear it was circling, still looking for an opening in the clouds.

Just outside, not far from the men, a small tanker truck was parked. It had no lettering, no logo, but definitely proved Misty's point.

"So what do you think?"

Pilar continued looking around, evaluating. From her last visit she knew it would be impossible to get inside without being detected by the surveillance cameras. Then there were the guards, Tweedle-Dee and Tweedle-Dumb. Who knew where they were.

"Well ...," Misty demanded.

Pilar shook her head. "Too risky."

"What do you mean? We just open up the valves or whatever on that truck, empty the fuel, and light a match."

"And how do you propose we get there with all this light ... and those?" She motioned toward two cameras mounted on opposite sides of the hangar's opening.

"We take them out."

Pilar snorted. "With what?"

"Please ..." Even in the dark Pilar could hear Misty roll her eyes. "What do lights and cameras use for power?"

"Electricity."

"Very good. And how do they get electricity?"

"Misty, what are you—" She came to a stop as her daughter looked up to the wires overhead. The ones leading to the generator building near the parking lot behind them; the ones suspended over the parking lot by a single utility pole.

Pilar shook her head. "No way."

"Mom ..."

"Absolutely not. I'm not going to let you climb up to those wires."

"But—"

"No."

Misty fumed, but only for a moment. "All right, fine. If I can't climb to them, we'll bring them to us."

Pilar scowled.

Misty motioned to the white vans in the parking lot. "I bet the keys are still in them."

Her scowl deepened.

"One good thwack and that pole would be down."

"What—"

"Take out the power, dump the fuel, light a match and ... *k-whoosh!*"

Pilar looked back to the pole, studying it. Once again the drone of the plane approached.

"Well?"

The plane grew louder.

Finally she nodded. "All right ... all right. But you stay here till I get back."

"Mother!"

"Right here!"

Before Misty could argue, Pilar turned to the vans, hesitated—

"Moth—"

Then took off, sprinting toward them as quietly as possible.

She arrived at the closest van, kneeled at the driver's side, then rose up, peering into the glass.

It was too dark to see anything.

She reached for the door handle. It was unlocked. Quietly, she opened it. The *ping-ping, ping-ping* told her the keys were still there. She climbed inside and shut the door. It took a moment for her eyes to adjust before she spotted the key and reached for it.

She turned the ignition and the engine fired up ... along with a blasting Latin station. She fumbled for the radio and turned it off.

Taking a breath, she reached for the gearshift and dropped the van into reverse. She pulled out as quickly as possible and turned the vehicle. Lightning flashed, revealing the pole just fifteen feet ahead.

Thinking a seat belt might come in handy, she reached over and buckled herself in. She pushed the hair from her eyes and shifted into first. She stomped on the gas. The van fishtailed, nearly yanking the wheel from her hands, but she hung on, accelerating.

The pole lay ten feet ahead.

She pressed the pedal to the floor.

Four feet.

She closed her eyes as the van slammed into the pole. The impact threw her forward, the sound of twisting steel and crumpling metal filling her ears. The shoulder strap dug into her chest and the air bag exploded in her face, nylon fabric scraping and burning her nose and chin as she lurched to a stop.

She leaned as far back into the seat as possible and looked over to the building.

The lights were still on.

The van hissed, making all sorts of noise, but the building lights were still on.

Struggling against the air bag, she rolled down the window and stuck out her head.

The pole was tilted but not down.

With an oath, she reached for the gearshift, trying to remember where reverse was. The air bag made it impossible to see. She fought it, trying to push it aside, but it was no use.

Unsure what to do, knowing the guards would be out any second, she unbuckled and reached for the door. She slid out of the seat and stepped onto the pavement, just as she heard the roar of another van.

She turned, saw the backup lights, and barely had time to flatten herself against the door as the second vehicle raced by in reverse.

It hit the pole, finishing it off, then careened sideways to a stop as the complex plunged into darkness.

A car door slammed, a voice shouted, "Mom? Mom, are you all right?"

"Misty!"

Her daughter arrived. "Are you all right?"

She nodded. "You?"

"Hey! *Hey!*"

They looked up to see Tweedle Dee racing toward them from the main building. Other men were coming at them from the hangar.

Instantly, Misty reached out and grabbed her mother's hand. "Come on!"

t he room fell into blackness and Virgil stopped singing. "Whoa ..."

"Power loss?" Travis asked.

"Could be." The old-timer rose and shuffled toward the door, stumbling over a chair. "Ow! Praise God, that smarts!"

"Be careful."

He arrived and tried the light switch, clicking it several times.

The room remained dark.

He rattled the door, than banged on it. "Hello. *Hello!*"

No answer.

He turned back toward Travis. "It's the Accuser of the Brethren."

"I'm sorry, what?"

"Accuser of the Brethren, that's one of the names the Bible gives Satan."

"I know what it is. I don't know what you're talking about."

"That's why you can't sing. You're feeling guilty, like you're not worthy enough."

Travis opened his mouth, unsure how to respond.

"Don't worry, happens to me all the time." Again Virgil banged on the door. "Hey, it's dark in here!" Then back to Travis. "It's one of his oldest tricks. Stops us from worshipin' and pluggin' into our power source." More banging. "Hey!"

Travis swallowed back his irritation. "Maybe I'm just not in the mood, maybe I don't want to."

"Maybe it don't matter what you want. That's why it's called a 'sacrifice of worship.'" More banging. "Hey!"

"And if it makes me feel hypocritical?"

"You can feel like bird droppings for all I care, it's still His due."

The lock rattled as a voice on the other side shouted, "What's all the ruckus?"

Virgil took a step back as the door opened and a flashlight beam shown into his face.

"What happened?" Virgil asked.

"Some worker hit a power pole." The voice belonged to one of the bodyguards. He took a half step inside. "You two okay?"

"Pretty dark in here," Travis replied. "Any way you can leave the door open?"

"Very funny." The guard stepped back out. But before he withdrew his hand holding the flashlight, Virgil slammed the door on it. Hard.

The man swore as the light clattered to the ground.

"What are you doing?" Travis shouted.

Virgil swooped down to pick up the flashlight, but the guard threw open the door, knocking him to the side, and sending the flashlight spinning under the table.

More swearing as the guard stooped over looking for it.

That's when Virgil leaped onto his back, tackling him into the chairs and down to the floor.

"Run!" he shouted to Travis. "Run!"

But Travis wasn't about to run. He tried joining the wrestling match. Not that there was much wrestling. The big man easily pulled Virgil off with one hand while reaching toward the light with the other ... until Travis gave it a quick kick, sending it smashing into the opposite wall.

It sputtered then went out, plunging the room into blackness.

Travis felt his way into the fray, trying to guess the difference in bodies, unsure where to grab or who to hit.

The burly man's oaths gave him a reference. He felt a head, a face, then took aim and swung. Bone cracked—though the pain shooting through his hand made it unclear what exactly he'd broken. He swung again. Again he made contact and again he felt pain ... as the big man crumpled to the floor.

"Nice shot, brother! You got him!"

"Where's the gun?" Travis groped in the darkness.

So did Virgil. "It ain't here, I can't find it."

They heard voices, faint but approaching.

"Let's get!" Virgil whispered. "Come on!"

"The gun?"

"Come on!"

Travis rose to his feet, surprised that Virgil was already on his. They stumbled out into the hallway.

The voices came from the right, so they turned and ran to the left.

The hall quickly ended at a pair of doors opening up to a large room with long tables. There was more light inside, but not much. A handful of skylights allowed the lightning to filter in.

Down the hall and behind them, a flashlight beam appeared.

Travis threw open the doors. Virgil followed.

"This way!" Travis whispered as he darted to the right.

Which, of course, meant Virgil darted to the left.

Travis shook his head in disbelief, then whispered, "Look for an exit!"

If there was an answer, it was drowned out by a voice from the hall, the other guard from the parking lot. "All right, fellows, playtime is over."

Travis flattened against the wall, not five feet from the door.

The beam swept into the room accompanied by two men—the tall, heavyset guard and another, much thinner. Lightning flashed, glinting off a pair of assault rifles in both sets of hands.

Travis pressed flatter, scanning the room for Virgil. But he was nowhere to be seen.

The men stepped farther inside as the smaller one grumbled in a thick accent, "Time to put the animals back into their cage."

The beam danced under and over the tables—following large exhaust hoods up to the rafters.

"You know what you fellas need?" Virgil's voice suddenly asked.

The light swung to where Virgil stood midway in the room.

"You need to get yourselves washed in the Blood of the Lamb!"

Travis glanced to the closest man, the one with the accent. He stood less than two yards away, his body tensing, his hands tightening around his weapon.

"You know what I'm saying? I'm talkin' about confessing your vile and ugly sins, getting saved, and being baptized in the Holy Ghost of God Almighty!"

Travis turned toward Virgil, frowning hard, hoping he would see.

The men moved deeper into the room. Now both stood in front of Travis.

"Church time is over, preacher," the taller one said.

For the briefest second, Virgil caught Travis's eye. And in that instant, Travis understood: The old man was acting as a decoy. He'd pulled them into the room so Travis could slip behind them and escape.

"No, my brothers, church is always in session. Jesus is always here waiting to touch and heal your lost and festering souls."

But he didn't see what Travis saw. He didn't see the effect his words were having upon the small man. He didn't see the way his hands gripped and regripped his weapon.

Virgil continued: " 'Behold, I stand at the door, and knock: if any man hear my voice, and open the door—' "

Travis watched the small man's jaw grinding, getting the workout of its life.

" '—I will come in to him, and will sup with him, and he with me. To him that overcometh will I—' "

The man leveled his weapon at Virgil.

" ' —grant to sit with me in my throne, even as I also overcame, and am set down with my Father in his throne.' "

His finger reached for the trigger. No one saw it. Not Virgil, not the other guard. Only Travis.

Again he tried signaling Virgil, and again he was ignored.

" 'He that hath an ear, let him hear what the Spirit saith unto—' "

Why wouldn't he shut up?

The man's finger tightened.

Travis could stand no more. *"Virgil! No!"*

Startled, both men spun their rifles to Travis.

But it was the small one who focused on Travis's chest, curling his lips, preparing to fire.

"*Nooo ...*" Virgil raced at them. A flash of lightning caught his arms raised and spread out.

Both men twirled around.

But only the closest fired. A burst of five, maybe six rounds, illuminating the room as bright as any lightning.

The impact threw Virgil backward, his feet flying out from under him.

"*Virgil!*" Travis ran for him.

He saw the men turn toward him, expected to be next.

But there were no more shots. No more sounds. Except Virgil's body collapsing onto the floor followed by the pounding of thunder.

amma stood before the dark window in her bare gnarled feet. Before her rose Tahquitz Peak, a storm raging around it.

It had been a strange dream. One that left her unable to sleep. She was a little girl. Nine or ten. Lost in a canyon, crying out to her grandfather through a fierce electrical storm. She'd never met the man—he had died long before she was born—but she knew it was him.

"*Grandfather, Grandfather, what is happening?*"

"*Tematsuwet!*" he had shouted over the wind.

She looked up to see a giant crow circling above their heads.

"*Stealer of souls,*" the man shouted. "*He has come to join forces with his brother, Tahquitz.*"

"*What do we do?*"

"*We must pray, little Iktomi! Pray hard, pray deep!*"

Distant lightning flickered through the window.

But it was more than a dream, Amma knew that.

The time had come. She moved closer, pressing her hand and wrinkled cheek against the glass to watch.

And to pray.

fourteen

dear Jesus!" Fiona doubled over as if hit in the stomach. The group looked up, startled from their prayers.

"Fiona!" Beth moved to her side and kneeled. "What's wrong?"

The old woman closed her eyes as tears filled them. Tears of victory ... and of unbearable loss.

"Fiona ..."

Her throat was so tight she could barely speak. Still, she forced out the words. "Keep ... praying."

"But—"

"It's broken," she gasped. "After all these years ... But it's not over. Keep praying."

the gunfire rang sharper than the thunder. Crisper. Luke recognized the difference immediately. And with it came an explosion of light filling the sky above him.

Not lightning. Somehow brighter ... whiter.

Forcing himself to squint up into it, he saw that the light came from the hole. It seemed to empower the larger, light creatures, allowing them to push back the dark perimeter of arms and fangs and faces more quickly. So quickly that, like ripples, the faces piled upon themselves, forming rings—thicker, darker. So dense that their weight eventually forced them to start falling, the innermost ring first. Falling toward the mountain.

Falling toward Luke.

He scrambled to the rock wall, pressing against it, as the first ring passed. It made no sound, at least not in Luke's ears. But he could feel it. In his gut, he heard the shrieking, the roaring rage.

As it fell, it sucked the wispier, surrounding faces down with it.

The next ring, slightly larger, dropped—pulling down its surrounding shadows.

Then the next. And the next. Each ripple larger than the last—until the final ring fell and the darkness above him had all but disappeared.

He looked up, amazed. The core of light was also gone. So was the storm. Now there was only the star-filled sky.

And the light creatures. But only for a moment.

They too swooped past him, in groups and individuals—some so close he could feel the rush of air from their wings. They had wings! In fact, he actually caught glimpses of what he guessed to be feathers. But as they dropped below the ledge, they disappeared from sight. He could still see their glow in the night, but both the rings and the creatures were no longer visible.

With a curiosity stronger than any fear, Luke inched toward the ledge until he finally peered over it and stared directly into the heart of ... well, there was no other word for it, but ... a battle.

In some ways it was similar to the storm that had been hovering over the mountain. In other ways much different.

For starters, it was below, floating midway between him and the canyon floor. Also, the light creatures were on the outside of the rings, instead of the inside. And they were rapidly closing in. It was as if they were corralling the darkness, forcing the rings to draw closer and closer together.

There was no sound, but he could still feel the screaming and the sense of rage.

From time to time a whipping tentacle of darkness would shoot out from one of the rings. But it no sooner started before it was hacked off by one of the light creature's swords. Shrieking and howling, the blackness would then slither back to its source.

The darkness became so tightly packed that it was no longer possible to see the rings. They had been forced into a single, twisting pillar of blackness. But not a pillar. This was alive. And the denser it became, the more specific its features appeared. It looked like some sort of animal—almost thirty feet tall.

Near the top a head had begun to form. Like a lizard.

The light creatures continued pressing in, forcing the darkness to grow more and more defined. Soon Luke saw appendages. Five of them. Legs.

No, four of them were legs. The fifth was a tail that flipped back and forth.

Two wider growths appeared on its back, moving in unison. Wings! It also had wings!

It raised its head until it looked directly up at Luke, its glistening snout not a dozen feet away. It was covered in black, shimmering scales. Black like the cloud, but shimmering as if made of flames. Black flames.

It lunged at Luke and he jumped. A moment later he was looking directly into an eye the size of a basketball. The pupil was a shiny, vertical slit, like a cat's, but filled with multiple reflections of himself. Some as he appeared today. Others much younger, even as a little boy.

Luke stared, unable to move.

A translucent membrane blinked over the eye.

Slowly, the creature opened its mouth to reveal the fangs of a serpent. But made of fire. White fire—with a flicking tongue and a throat of swirling orange-red flames that stretched forever.

Luke could not breathe.

The mouth opened wider, unhinging its jaws. The fire inside continued to swirl as the creature came closer and closer, preparing to devour him.

Luke tried to scream but could find no air.

It lunged again when suddenly a flashing sword appeared, wielded by one of the light creatures. It slashed deep into the side of the animal's snout, causing it to throw back its head and roar, black plumes of smoke and fire roiling out ... until it lowered its head ... then lunged at Luke again.

The light creature struck again.

The dragon pulled back, glaring at Luke, whipping its tail in frustration, no longer willing to attack—at least for the moment.

Pilar trailed a dozen steps behind Misty as they raced to the tanker. It had taken little effort to lose the men in the darkness and circle around. Of course she'd told the girl to stay put and of course she hadn't listened. What else was new.

She arrived a moment after Misty and immediately searched the dozen valves, hoping to find the right one.

"Try this one!" Pilar pointed.

"I already have!"

"No, this one here?"

"Mother ..."

Grabbing the handle herself, Pilar gave a jerk. It moved ever so slightly. She tried harder, tugging until the valve gave a grudging squeak. Immediately liquid roared out, shooting five, six feet, before splashing onto the concrete and rushing into the hangar.

"I think I found it!"

There was another roar. She turned to see a second pipe gushing. Misty stood beside a control box, having just pushed some buttons. "Me too!"

The fuel swept into the hangar and disappeared into the darkness. They heard it wash against the closest wall, hoping it would find its way into the attached building.

"Okay," Pilar yelled. "Light her up!"

"Right!" Misty agreed. Then, "With what?"

"With what? A match, a lighter ..."

"I don't have one."

"You what?"

"I don't smoke."

"You're a rebellious teen, what do you mean you don't smoke?"

Misty shrugged. "Sorry."

"Great ..." Pilar's mind raced, searching for a solution. But not for long.

"Get away from the truck!"

She turned to see all three mechanics approaching, doing their best to avoid stepping in the fuel. One had a crowbar, another a lug wrench. None of them appeared happy.

the more Luke's eyes grew accustomed to the battle, the more details he was able to see.

Besides the dragon with its scales of shimmering black fire and the winged creatures with their swords of light, he noticed something else. Just as he had earlier seen black tentacles feeding the darkness of the mountain, he now saw two streams of dazzling brightness feeding the winged creatures—pouring light into them. A light which they absorbed and that increased both their size and their power.

The first stream shot up like a fountain from the building Virgil and Travis had entered. It took little effort to imagine that Virgil was responsible, probably doing the same sort of stuff he did when they stood in front of the porn shop.

But there was another stream, equally as bright and thick, and equally as empowering.

He couldn't see its source; the ridge of the canyon blocked it. But it came from the direction of the town.

the bullets had sprayed up and across Virgil—the first three catching his thigh and hip, the last two lodging deep in his abdomen. The gut wounds were Travis's greatest worry. There was so much blood that, even in the darkness, he could see the trail it left on the floor as they carried Virgil back to the holding room.

Of course Travis had begged the men to get a doctor, to do something to stop the bleeding. But of course, they didn't.

And, though he applied pressure where he could, even stripping off his shirt and shoving it against the old man's stomach, Travis knew Virgil's life was quickly fading.

Fading, but not changing.

For even as he held Virgil's head in his lap, trying to make him comfortable, the old-timer chattered away.

"Why didn't you run?"

"Shh ..."

"I gave you the perfect opportunity and you just frittered it away."

"Maybe I didn't feel like letting you be the martyr."

Virgil shook his head. "You Baptists are such a stubborn lot." He began to cough.

"Apparently not as stubborn as you Charismatics."

Virgil stopped coughing long enough to grin. "Yeah ..." He took a gasp of air. "Listen—"

"Shh, rest."

"No, this is important." Virgil swallowed and took another breath. "You know that girl you were making out with?"

Travis closed his eyes. "Please ..."

"No, listen. Be sure to ask Fiona about me and the church organist—" more coughing—"up in Sacramento."

Travis's eyes widened. *"You* had an affair?"

Virgil shook his head. "By the grace of God it never came to that. The grace of God ... *and* the fury of Fiona."

Travis smiled in spite of himself.

"We're all tempted. Enemy's got a bull's-eye painted smack dab in the center of every servant-of-God's chest."

"Tell me about it."

"But we don't give in." He coughed. "We got moments, it comes with the territory, but we don't give in."

Travis nodded.

More coughing.

"Take it easy ..."

Virgil gasped. Breath was coming harder. "Sing with me."

"What?"

"Sing."

Travis hesitated. When it was obvious he wasn't going to start, Virgil began.

"Christ the Lord ... is risen ..."

He broke into another fit of coughing.

"Virgil ..."

Catching his breath, he carried on, as off-key as ever.

"... today. Aaaa ... lle-luu-ia ..."

"Be quiet," Travis admonished, "save your strength."

But the old-timer wasn't about to start taking orders now.

"Sons of ..."

He coughed harder, more violently.

"... men and angels ... say ..."

His body wrenched so fiercely that he gagged.

"Virgil ..."

Weaker, more breathy, he continued.

"*Aaaa … lle-luu …*"

He paused, struggling for air, the silence broken only by his uneven wheezing.

Travis felt him shudder on his lap, knew he was still fighting to sing until finally, with no other choice, the young pastor softly joined in.

"*Raise your joys and triumphs high.
Alleluia.*"

Underneath his singing, he could hear occasional words, wavering notes that came less and less frequently. And, despite the tears filling his eyes and the tightening of his throat, Travis continued.

"*Sing, ye heavens, and earth reply
Alleluia!
Lives again our glorious King …*"

And so he sang, sometimes choking out the words, but singing, nonetheless.

Singing for the old man.

Singing for himself.

Pilar and Misty had no sooner stepped from the tanker than they heard the sound of a gas-powered generator firing up. The lights to the complex and the runway flickered back on, and Pilar's heart sank.

"Oh, well," taunted the largest of the men, his face pitted from acne. "Better luck next time."

"I'd settle for any luck, anytime," she muttered as they were motioned toward the parking lot and the building's main entrance.

A fork of lightning sizzled directly overhead. They looked up to see it explode into a portion of Smashing Wall, throwing chunks of mountain and debris. The larger sections slipped away and fell toward the canyon floor ... directly toward the buildings!

"Look out! Get back!"

No second invitation was necessary. Pilar and Misty turned and ran with the group. She was unsure if the crashing that followed was thunder or the building being struck. She threw a look over her shoulder and had the answer.

A handful of car-sized boulders were slamming into the roof. Some broke through effortlessly. Others bounced off like toy balls. Dirt and dust followed, pouring onto the building, then boiling up and over it.

For the most part, the structure remained intact— though it was again plunged into darkness. Except for the tiny flicker of flame ...

Pilar saw it through the window nearest the hangar. A tiny flicker that rapidly grew. Apparently, electrical wiring had been snapped off and fallen into the aviation fuel.

Fire spread in both directions—through the building and toward the hangar. There was no fireball, no dramatic *whoosh*, just quick and silent spreading ... until the flame danced across the hangar floor and reached the tanker.

The explosion lit the sky.

Pilar turned her face from the heat as it struck her body, then immediately spun toward her daughter. "Misty!"

"I'm okay!" she yelled. "I'm right here!"

They turned back to see half of the structure now in flames.

"What about the preachers?" Misty shouted. "The preachers are in there!"

For the second time in as many minutes, Pilar's heart sank. She whirled to the other men. "We've got to go in there!"

They barely heard, watching the flames.

"There are people in there!"

"Not for long," Acne Face replied.

"We have to get them out!"

"They know where the doors are."

Pilar spun back to the building. If they knew where the doors were, they sure weren't using them. Her concern turned to anger. Somebody had to do something! And with that understanding came the resentment ... as, once again, she realized who the somebody would be.

Reading her mind, Misty shouted, "Mom!"

She turned to her. "You stay here!"

"No way. If you're going, I'm—"

"Stay here!" She turned to the men. "Make sure she stays!"

The closest one nodded and grabbed Misty.

"Let go of me," Misty shouted. "Let go!"

Then with a silent oath, Pilar started for the building.

"Mom! Mom!"

She was twenty paces away when the doors flew open. Bianco, a woman, and a handful of men, including Velasco, stumbled out.

"Where are the preachers?" Pilar shouted.

They continued coughing and catching their breath.

"The preachers!" she repeated.

Bianco only shook his head.

She looked back to the flames, which were growing larger. Then, with another oath, this time louder, she started toward the building.

"Pilar," Bianco coughed behind her. "Don't go in there!"

She continued forward.

"Pilar, that's crazy!"

"Tell me about it," she muttered.

uke stared down at the burning buildings.

Although the winged creatures had confined the darkness and compressed it into a dragon, they could go no farther. It seemed all their energy was spent holding it prisoner. Whenever it tried to escape, they would strike it with their swords.

Its most recent attempt had nearly succeeded. The thing had darted to the right, then changed course to the left, then changed again and shot up the wall. Fortunately one of the winged creatures had anticipated the move and countered. He had arrived and swung his weapon. The dragon barely withdrew in time, leaving the sword to strike the wall. The impact dislodged rocks and boulders, which had fallen onto the building just moments ago, causing the statue to burst into flames.

Luke heard the drone of the cargo plane and looked up. It was lower than before, making what appeared to be a final pass before dropping toward the lit runway.

But it was more than a plane.

At least through the goggles.

It was another source of darkness—complete with the thickest tentacle of all. Like those over the Spirit Dancers, the arm snaked back and forth a half dozen times, the shimmering blackness coming so close to Luke that he pressed himself against the wall ... until it finally found its target.

The dragon's shoulder.

It shot down its chest and attached to the center of its belly.

Once in place, it began pumping in its darkness. And as the darkness flowed through the tentacle, the dragon grew. It began expanding until it pushed back the light, until the winged creatures began losing ground.

How could that be? For them to have come so far, only to lose now? But it was happening. Before Luke's very eyes. And there seemed no way to stop it.

Of course he could pray—add his own bit of light to the brighter stream flowing in from the building below and the one from town. Or he could sing as he had in the casino, or quote some Bible verse.

But his efforts had barely kept the things at bay back when they were tiny puffs of darkness. Now they'd combined into something a thousand times bigger and more powerful. How could he—

Suddenly, he heard it. Virgil's voice. A memory so loud and clear that he glanced about just to make sure the man wasn't there.

"I tell you the truth, whatever you bind on earth will be bound in heaven ..."

Luke scowled. What did that mean? He'd heard Virgil quote it when they were outside the porn shop. But what did it mean?

"Whatever you bind on earth will be bound in heaven ..."

Whatever *who* bound? Him? Hardly. He was just a kid ... some stupid kid who'd got so caught up in his pride that he'd made even stupider mistakes.

No, the power lay in quoting the Bible. Or in singing. It certainly did not lie with him. That's what got him in trouble in the first place, thinking he was somebody special.

"I tell you the truth, whatever you bind on earth will be bound in heaven ..."

No, the verse didn't apply to anybody special. And certainly not to Luke Kauffman, Wannabe Savior of the World. They didn't apply to him any more than they applied to anyone else. As far as he could tell they were for everyone. Everyone, including ...

He came to a stop, the realization slowly sinking in.

Everyone ... including himself.

fifteen

travis continued singing, softly, his voice clogged with emotion.

> *"Love's redeeming work is done,*
> *Alleluia ..."*

He'd heard the explosions, felt them through the wall and floor where he sat. It didn't sound like part of the storm, but it didn't much matter. From time to time he caught the smell of smoke. But it didn't much matter.

Not anymore.

> *"Fought the fight, the battle won ..."*

Occasionally, he felt Virgil stirring in his lap, heard his raspy, uneven breathing.

> *"Alleluia ..."*

He was singing by himself now. Common sense told him that it was over, that he could stop. But something deeper than common sense drove him to continue.

And so, tears streaming down his face, Travis Lawton sang.

> *"Death in vain forbids Him rise,*
> *Allelu—"*

The banging on the door startled him.

"Virgil ... Travis ... you in there?" It was Pilar.

The knob rattled.

"Yes!" Travis shouted. "We're here, we're—"

The door opened and dull orange light flickered in—not from a flashlight and not from lightning. With it came the smoke.

Pilar stepped in, coughing. "Let's go! The whole place is on fire!"

Travis was already rising, carefully holding Virgil's head. "Give me a hand. Take his feet!"

Pilar moved to the old man's legs. "He's soaked," she shouted. "What is—it's blood!"

"Take his feet!"

She grabbed them and lifted as Travis transferred his grip from Virgil's head to his shoulders.

They started toward the door, smoke already burning the back of his throat.

Once in the hallway Pilar motioned with her head, shouting, "To the right!"

He turned and followed.

Luke stepped closer to the edge. The wind from below whipped at his clothes, blew grit into his eyes. He wasn't sure how to start, or even what to say.

"*Whatever you bind on earth will be bound in heaven.*"

That was all he had. But if that was it, it would have to do. With hair flying, he squinted into the wind, looking down at the dragon.

"I bind you!"

He swallowed and watched.

Nothing.

He tried again. "I bind you! I bind you and ... and I command you to—"

The laughter stopped him. He didn't hear it, but *felt* it ... through his body. With it came the taunts.

"We are your choice ... we are your power."

He recognized the voices immediately. They'd returned.

"We belong to you and you belong to us."

He closed his eyes. "No!"

"We are one."

"No!"

"We know the power for which you hunger, for which you have always—"

"That's not true, that's not—"

"And we possess it. That and so much more ..."

Before Luke could respond, desires again surged through him—lust, power, greed—the ones he'd felt in the elevator, the casino, the ones he'd invited inside with the drug.

But how could that be? He'd seen them go! He'd seen them flee from the Man carved in light.

"Did you really think we would leave? That we would never return?"

He stepped back, unsteady.

A bright light flashed into his eyes. The plane had turned on its landing lights. It was approaching the runway, its thick tentacle still attached to the dragon's belly.

But there was another stream Luke spotted. Much smaller. A tiny tributary that rose from the dragon. It had slithered up along the crevice of rocks, then disappeared below the ledge. He looked side to side, trying to find it. Only when he glanced down to his leg did he see that it had approached from behind and attached itself to his ankle!

travis heard the cracking of wood and looked up just in time to see the ceiling give way.

"Look out!"

Still carrying Virgil, he staggered back as a burning rafter broke through the ceiling. He could feel its heat against his face as it crashed to the floor in front of him.

"We've got to go back!" Pilar shouted.

He peered through the smoke and fire. "No!"

Pilar coughed. "There's no way through!"

"There's no way back. I've been there. Just a big room."

"What about windows?"

He shook his head. "Just skylights."

fiona remained on the floor, cheeks wet with tears. But she would not stop praying. Beth held her in her arms, trying to comfort her, urging her back up to the sofa.

But the woman refused.

Touched by her urgency, the group pressed in harder. Something was happening. They all sensed it. They weren't sure what, but Fiona had become a catalyst, the inspiration leading them beyond clerical obligation and into heartfelt passion.

Gradually, one by one, even the most reserved began slipping down to join her on their knees.

What do we do?" Pilar coughed, nearly gagging.

Travis could find no way around the burning beam and its fire. "We have to go through it!" he shouted.

"How?" Pilar yelled.

"Run! As fast as we can!"

She motioned to Virgil's body still in their hands. "We'll have to leave him!"

"No!"

"He's gone. There's nothing we can—"

"We're not leaving him!"

"There's no choice! We have—"

She was interrupted by more creaking ... and groaning.

Travis shot a look up to the ceiling.

But it wasn't the ceiling coming down. It was the wall beside them!

"Go!" Travis shouted.

They retraced their route but had only taken a few steps before the groaning gave way to a loud cracking as the entire wall toppled into the hall before them. Pilar screamed and Travis staggered back as it came down with a deafening *whoosh-thud*, kicking up ash and hot cinders.

But as the smoke cleared an opening appeared. Where a wall had been there was now a hole leading outside. The extra oxygen fueled the flames around them, but it made little difference. There was a way out.

Luke dropped to his knees, trying to rip off the tentacle. But his hands passed through it like mist.

The words running through his mind continued, the desires overwhelming.

But words were only words. And desires were only desires.

He still had his will. And from what he remembered, that was the key.

That, and the Man with the holes in His hands.

He glanced over to the cargo plane. It now taxied toward the burning building, though careful to keep a safe distance.

With resolve, he looked back to the tentacle around his foot. "No!" he shouted. "I refuse you!"

Nothing.

He tried again. "I refuse you! I bind you in the name of Jesus Christ!"

The scream he felt from the tiny arm startled him. So did its sudden withering. Immediately it released his ankle and started to evaporate. What little remained slithered back into the larger stream of darkness.

Watching it retreat, Luke's confidence grew. Not in himself, but in his authority. If he had that type of authority over the smaller stream, than maybe, just maybe ...

He rose and stepped closer to the edge. He focused upon the thick cable of blackness stretching from the plane to the dragon's belly.

"I bind you!" he shouted. "I command you to — "

"You are nothing! You have no power!"

He hesitated, then rephrased the command. "In the name of *Jesus Christ* I bind you! In the name of Christ I order you — "

He felt a vibrating roar as the thick tentacle begin to shudder.

He bore down harder. "I bind your power ... from this mountain ... from this ..." What was the word Virgil had used?

"Territory! In the name of Jesus Christ I bind you from this territory!"

The roar rapidly increased in pitch until it became a shrill scream. A piercing shriek that reverberated through him, stronger and stronger, filling his head, his consciousness ... until he was struck by a blinding white flash — the glint off a blade, a massive scythe, swung through the air and hitting the tentacle.

It effortlessly sliced through the blackness, severing it from the beast's belly.

Still holding Virgil, Pilar and Travis ducked through the burning opening in the wall. They staggered into the storm, gulping in breaths of cooler air, coughing and purging their lungs of the smoke.

Pilar was the first to spot them running toward the cargo plane — two groups illuminated by lightning and the craft's landing lights. In the lead, closest to the plane, were Velasco and his entourage, as well as a handful of workers.

Trailing behind and obviously sucking wind were the older Bianco and his two guards.

Above them, the electrical storm continued.

the dragon writhed and thrashed, its power quickly diminishing as the winged creatures moved closer, compressing and fencing it in.

Luke took a breath and continued. "I bind you and I ..."

But what? He couldn't just leave the thing floating there. It had to be removed. But where? Where could he send it so it wouldn't hurt others? Where could—

He had it! The place he'd seen last year when reality had been torn apart. The fiery place Dad had visited to try and save his sister.

"In the name of Jesus Christ, I throw you into the Lake of Fire!"

The shrieking grew so loud Luke grabbed his head. The entire mountain shook. And still he shouted, "I bind you and throw you into the Lake of Fire!"

A ripping sound filled the air—like cloth being torn, gristle stripped from flesh.

He spotted a blackness in the dragon's chest. Blacker than its fire. A slit. A hole. Like he'd seen over the porn shop, over Misty's car radio.

"Go!" he shouted.

The shriek flooded his mind, gripped his gut with such force that he dropped his head and vomited. And again.

He rose, dizzy, disoriented. The mountain shook so violently that he could not keep his balance. He stumbled, then fell. His face smacked the ground so hard that it knocked off the goggles—but not before he caught a glimpse of the dragon starting to be sucked into the hole.

He scrambled to his hands and knees, looking for the goggles.

There! On the edge!

He reached for them, hands nearly touching, when the mountain lurched with such force that it threw him forward, arms splaying, hand knocking the goggles out into the night.

"No!" he screamed.

He dragged himself to the edge, looking over, but they were out of sight. Gone. As were the dragon, the winged creatures, the battle itself. Now only the violent electrical storm remained.

But that wasn't true. They were still there. The battle still raged; he just couldn't see it. Now, like everyone else, he was blind to it. Like everyone else, he was disadvantaged by not knowing what—

But that wasn't true either. He *did* know. The battle was still before him and he still knew the weapons. He had seen them. Used them. Not only seen and used, but by all appearances, he had been winning with them.

There was no reason to quit. Not now. Being blind was a minor setback compared to what he now knew.

Luke rose to his knees.

It was true. Seeing had very little to do with winning.

He took a deep breath to clear his head, and another for resolution. Then he rose to his feet.

It was time to finish it.

Pilar and Travis laid Virgil down. Travis immediately kneeled to his side when a searing crackle filled the air—so close Pilar felt the hair on her arms rise.

She looked up to see lightning fork into the canyon floor, directly into Bianco's group.

Light and dirt exploded, throwing all three men to the ground.

Only Bianco rose, scrambling to his feet.

Pilar shouted, "Peter! Get out of there!"

But he did not hear. He continued for the plane, yelling at the people boarding it, pleading for them to wait.

Another hiss and crackle. Another explosion of dirt and light, just to Bianco's left.

He veered to the right, running faster, screaming.

The group quickly clambered into the plane, not looking back.

Another sizzle and another explosion, this time to his right.

Bianco darted to the left, then to the right, then to the left again—back and forth, like an animal being hunted.

"Get out of the open!" Pilar yelled.

He tripped and fell.

"Get out of the open!"

He staggered back to his feet and threw a look over his shoulder.

In the strobing light, Pilar saw his mouth open, his eyes widen. He screamed, raising his arms in defense as another shaft of light forked from above. It struck him in the chest, bathing him in light and sparks before his entire body exploded.

Pilar stared, not believing her eyes. Finally, she looked over to the plane.

The rear door had closed and the drone of the props increased as it turned and started down the runway.

"Mom!" Misty's voice came from the burning building.

Pilar barely had time to turn before the girl arrived, throwing her arms around her.

"I was so worried. I didn't know if—" Misty's voice caught as she hugged Pilar fiercely.

Pilar could barely respond. "You ... you went back in for—"

Misty buried her face into Pilar's neck. "I didn't know—" She tried again. "I didn't know if you were ..." But she could no longer speak for the tears.

"It's okay, baby," Pilar whispered, her own eyes filling with moisture as they hugged tighter. "I'm here, it's okay."

How long they held one another, she did not know. But when she finally opened her eyes and glanced up, she saw Luke standing above them on Smashing Wall—tall and erect in the flashing light ... his arm stretched out over the canyon.

go!" Luke shouted.

The wind was gale force. But instead of blowing against him, it was pulling at him. He understood perfectly. If the dragon was being sucked into the hole that had appeared in its chest, it only stood to reason that the storm was being sucked in as well.

With absolute confidence and authority, he shouted, "In the name of Jesus Christ, I bind you and I cast you into the Lake of Fire!"

The end had come.

"Now!" He shouted a final time, "I ORDER YOU TO GO NOW!"

The air filled with light—so powerful that it threw him back against the mountain.

the plane was thirty feet off the runway when lightning struck its left engine. It exploded into sparks and fire, immediately dipping to the left, then to the right, the remaining engine straining to keep it level.

But it did little good.

Once again the craft dropped its left wing, turning it sharply, toward the canyon wall. The engine whined harder but it could not pull up.

The plane smashed into the rocky face and immediately burst into flames.

Instinctively, Pilar shielded her eyes as two more explosions followed, their yellow and orange fireballs rising into the night.

She heard Travis approach, joining her and Misty. Together, they watched the flames in silence.

At last, it was over.

Several moments passed before Travis cleared his throat. "The storm ... it's stopped."

She glanced about. It was true: the lightning had quit, the thunder had faded. Now there was only the glow and crackle of the burning building behind them.

She turned back to the tarmac where the remains of Bianco and his bodyguards lay somewhere in the darkness.

"Do you think ...," Travis asked, "could they still ..."

She shook her head. "Nobody could survive that."

He nodded.

"Check it out," Misty said, motioning to the sky.

Pilar looked up. The clouds were already breaking apart. Bright stars began to appear.

"Hey! ... Hey guys!"

They turned around to Smashing Wall.

Luke stood on the ledge shouting, "Is everybody all right down there?"

"We're fine!" Misty yelled. "What about you?"

"Oh, I'm okay."

"You have a nice rest up there?" she shouted.

"What?"

"While we were working our butts off down here, did you have a nice little rest?"

Ignoring her comment, he shouted, "Any chance of getting me down?"

"You getting bored?"

"A little."

"Poor baby."

Pilar looked at her daughter, marveling. The resiliency of youth. She cupped her hands and shouted, "Hang on, Luke! We'll get some rope and be up there in a few minutes!"

"Thanks."

"Do you—" Travis coughed. "Do you think you'll be needing me?"

She turned to see that he had kneeled back down at Virgil's side. "You want to stay with him?" she asked.

"For a little bit . . . if you don't mind."

She looked on a moment, then softly replied, "If we need your help, we'll give a shout."

"Thanks."

"Guys," Luke hollered. "*Guys!*"

She looked back up to the cliff.

"What now?" Misty called.

"If you could bring some water too, that would be great. I'm kinda thirsty."

Misty shook her head, snorting in contempt.

Pilar smiled and motioned her forward. "Let's give the boy a hand, shall we?"

Misty shrugged. "Whatever."

Together, they started off as Pilar shouted up to the cliff, "Hang on, cowboy, we're on our way!"

epilogue

"This is really weird." Luke stared down at his bare feet in the plastic wash basin.

Travis was kneeling beside him. "I know what you mean." He lifted water in his cupped hand and poured it over Luke's left foot. "Interesting, though, that some churches do this every time they have communion."

"*Awkward.*"

Travis nodded. "And humbling." He began to rub the balls of Luke's foot, then his toes, as the boy tried not to squirm.

"Still, to do it at a memorial service." Travis shook his head. "This is a first for me."

Luke glanced across the tiny storefront church to Fiona. The old lady was on her knees washing the feet of the woman minister who had been at her house the night of the encounter. "Didn't anybody tell her when she dreamed this up that it might be, you know, a little … odd?"

Travis looked up and grinned. "Do you want to?"

Luke shook his head.

"Me neither." He began working on Luke's other foot. "No, I think she knows exactly what she's doing."

Luke nodded. Folks were giving the grieving widow a lot of leeway … and by the looks of things, she was taking advantage of every inch. Rumor had it that all the religious leaders in the valley were here. Many looked as uncomfortable as he felt, but they were here—sitting in folding metal chairs having their feet washed by one leader, then turning around and kneeling to wash that leader's feet.

"To symbolize our community coming together," she had said.

And from what Luke could see, it just might be working.

Three days had passed since Virgil's death. And in those three days more had been done to turn the city against the casino than in years. People who barely spoke to each other had met and begun making decisions. No one was entirely sure why. It was like some door had suddenly been opened, some dam finally broken.

Of course the Tribal Council was still resistant, but not like before. If Peter Bianco had seen how vulnerable Casino Rancheria was to drugs and other vices, there would certainly be others with similar or even worse plans. And that was something neither Pilar nor the Cahuilla people would tolerate. If there was a way to generate revenue without the gambling and accompanying vices, the community would find it. Maybe an amusement park, a health spa, a place for headline performers and Broadway shows, or some combination of all of them. Who knew. It would be a difficult task, but Pilar, Travis, and other leaders had already agreed to begin exploring the possibilities. Together.

Luke glanced over to the far corner where Pilar and Misty were having their own private foot washing. As representative of her tribe and as a symbol of cooperation, Pilar thought she should be here. And she probably figured the ceremony would be a lot easier with someone she knew.

Well, guess again. The poor woman looked anything but relaxed as Misty kneeled before her, washing her feet.

And next up, waiting in her wheelchair, sat Amma.

Luke watched, a little amused and a little sad. Things between him and Misty were already falling apart. She was still the drop-dead gorgeous, shoot-off-her-mouth self—but her patience toward his so-called "immaturities" was growing thin ... especially since he'd lost the goggles.

Still, he wasn't so sure that life without the goggles was such a bad thing. After all that he'd been through, he'd begun to suspect that maybe some things were best *not* seen. Maybe, in some cases, ignorance really was bliss. Besides, hadn't the very last of the battle been fought without him even wearing them?

"So are you boys about finished?"

He looked up to see Beth smiling down at them.

"Yes, ma'am," Travis said. He lifted Luke's feet out of the water and patted them dry with a towel. "Good to go."

Gratefully, Luke grabbed his socks and slipped them on.

"So did you tell him about the baby?" Beth asked.

Travis shook his head.

"What about it?" Luke asked.

Travis answered, "What do you think of the name Virgil?"

Luke looked up, trying not to snicker. "For a baby?"

"That's usually how they start off."

Slipping into his boots, he answered, "I don't know. I mean, that's really thoughtful and all, but 'Virgil,' that's a pretty funny name for a kid these days."

"True," Travis agreed, "but we're hoping he'll grow into it."

Beth nodded. "In more ways than one."

"What does Fiona think?"

"We haven't told her yet."

"I think she'd really be honored," Luke said.

Travis nodded. "I know we would."

Luke grinned and rose to his feet just in time to catch a glimpse of a Jeep Cherokee pulling up outside. *Dad's* Jeep Cherokee!

Without a word he slipped on his sunglasses and moved across the room, weaving in and around the various clergy until he reached the door and burst into the bright sunlight.

"Dad!"

He rounded the front of the vehicle as his father climbed out and hit him with a bear hug. He'd cut short his New York trip and they'd talked by cell phone a dozen times. But to be able to hold him, to be held by him—well, right now, it meant a lot.

They'd barely embraced before an old, gravelly voice muttered from the passenger side, "Don't mind us none. We're just 'long for the ride."

Luke glanced over to see a barrel-chested old-timer open the door on the other side of the vehicle. "Preacher Man!"

"Not jest me." He motioned to the backseat where their mentally and physically impaired friend sat.

"Nubee!"

The young man broke into a lopsided grin.

Preacher Man continued climbing out and explained, "He gave the nursing home no rest till they agreed to call your father and me. Said you was in a war and needed all the prayer we could muster."

Luke nodded to his friend, once again impressed at how he seemed to know things that others didn't. "Thanks, Nubs."

With his twisted hand, Nubee gave a thumbs-up.

"But everything's okay now?" his father asked for the hundredth time since he'd gotten the news.

"Yes, Dad."

"And your eyes? You're still wearing your glasses?"

"Yes, Dad."

"All the time?"

"Yes, yes, *yes* ..." Luke had almost forgotten how smothering the man could be.

He decided not to mention the goggles. No need to give the guy more fire for the inquisition.

"How's Fiona?"

Luke glanced down and shrugged. "They were married forever."

Dad nodded sadly. A moment later he threw his arms around him again. "I'm so glad you're okay."

"Me too," Luke said, patiently enduring it as he tried to breathe. "Me too."

When they finally separated, Dad looked over to the church. "Well, I better go on in there. Pay my respects. You want to help Nubee out?"

"Sure."

He gave Luke a squeeze on the shoulder then started around the truck. Preacher Man joined him as they headed for the church.

"Hey, Nubs?" Luke opened the back door. "How you been?"

Nubee's grin broadened. But he wasn't grinning at Luke. He was grinning beyond him.

Luke turned and saw the homeless man approaching, the one in the gloves and Hawaiian shirt.

"So was it everything you expected?" the man asked.

Not wanting to talk, but not wanting to appear rude, Luke answered, "Yeah, you could say that."

"Good ... good."

Luke crossed to the back and opened the tailgate to drag out the wheelchair. He was hoping the man would leave.

He did not.

"How's Fiona?"

Luke glanced up in surprise. "You know her?"

The man nodded. "I was the one who suggested the foot washing."

He came to a stop. "You?"

The man didn't reply but turned to Nubee. "I think you'll enjoy it."

Luke stood speechless.

"Provided Luke, here, gets the lead out."

"How did—" Luke swallowed—"how do you know my name?"

"I'd be hurrying if I were you." He motioned to the church. "They're getting ready to wrap up."

More than a little suspicious, Luke unfolded the wheelchair and rolled it to Nubee's open door. He reached in and slid one of the young man's legs out, and then the other. As he did, Nubee finally decided to talk. As always his speech was cryptic and slurred. "You come too?"

The man grinned. "Thanks, Nubs, but I'm afraid my feet are a little gross for that."

"Gross?" Luke asked.

"Got some pretty ugly wounds."

Luke glanced down at the man's high-top tennis shoes. "What happened?"

"From the war."

"War ... wounds?"

He nodded. "Long time ago."

The hairs on the back of Luke's neck slowly rose. "And your hands? They also have ... wounds?"

The man looked over to the church. "You need to get a move on."

Speechless, Luke could only stare.

The man smiled and nodded for him to hurry.

Luke turned, clumsily fumbling to get Nubee into the chair. Somehow, he succeeded. He looked back to the man, who was still smiling.

"I, uh ..." Luke's voice clogged and he tried again, not entirely sure what to say. "I guess you'll be around then?"

"You bet."

Still unsure what to do, head still spinning, he focused on the chair before him. At last he started pushing Nubee toward the church.

"Oh, and Luke?"

He slowed and turned.

"You're right about the goggles. They'd just get in the way. It's better not to look at the storm when you're walking on water."

"I'm ... sorry?"

"Better just to keep your eyes on God."

Luke blinked, then looked down, trying to comprehend it all. And when he looked back up ... the man was gone.

He searched up and down the street, but he was nowhere to be found.

Not entirely surprised, but entirely unnerved, Luke turned back to the church. Then slowly, thoughtfully, he resumed pushing Nubee.

"Better not to look at the storm when you're walking on water."

It made sense and he began to nod. He had no idea what adventures waited for him in the future. But he did know one thing. Whatever they may be, whatever storms he had to face, he'd found a way to get through them. And it didn't include fancy goggles, or supernatural visions, or encounters with spirit creatures. In fact, it was so simple that a child could do it.

They arrived at the church and he wheeled Nubee inside.

"When you're walking on water ... better just to keep your eyes on God."

That was it. And that was all he needed.

Three ways to keep up on your favorite Zondervan books and authors

Sign up for our *Fiction E-Newsletter*. Every month you'll receive sample excerpts from our books, sneak peeks at upcoming books, and chances to win free books autographed by the author.

You can also sign up for our *Breakfast Club*. Every morning in your email, you'll receive a five-minute snippet from a fiction or nonfiction book. A new book will be featured each week, and by the end of the week you will have sampled two to three chapters of the book.

Zondervan *Author Tracker* is the best way to be notified whenever your favorite Zondervan authors write new books, go on tour, or want to tell you about what's happening in their lives.

Visit *www.zondervan.com* and sign up today!

ZONDERVAN®

ZONDERVAN.com/
AUTHORTRACKER
follow your favorite authors